THE DARK SIDE
OF GRACE

Also by Ronald Chapman

Progressive Recovery Through the Twelve Steps: Emotionally Sober for Life (2019)
A Killer's Grace (2016)
My Name is Wonder (2016)
Seeing True:™ Ninety Contemplations in Ninety Days (2008)
What a Wonderful World: Seeing Through New Eyes (2004)

Audio Sets
Seeing True:™ The Way of Spirit (2016)
Breathing, Releasing and Breaking Through: A Practice for Seeing Seeing True:™ (2015)

THE DARK SIDE OF GRACE

Ronald Chapman

Terra Nova Books
SANTA FE, NEW MEXICO

Library of Congress Control Number 2022949740

Distributed by SCB Distributors, (800) 729-6423

Terra Nova Books

Published by Terra Nova Books, Santa Fe, New Mexico.
www.TerraNovaBooks.com

ISBN 978-1-948749-87-9

*Finding beauty in a broken world is
creating beauty in the world you find.*

—Terry Tempest Williams

If you bring forth what is within you,
what you bring forth will save you.
If you do not bring forth what is within you,
what you do not bring forth will destroy you.

—Gospel of St. Thomas

Trauma that is not transformed will be transmitted.
—Richard Rohr

LIGHT FALLS THROUGH TURQUOISE SKIES. A BLANKET OF SNOW carpets the valley, reflecting the light and amplifying its effect to an ethereal quality. For artists and wanderers who find their way to New Mexico, it is the expansiveness of the light that holds and embraces them.

To the east, the light glints off snow-mantled mountains, their shadowed pinkish hue a near-perfect contrast to the sky. High desert stretches endlessly westward as the Rio Grande threads its way through the city of Albuquerque. Beneath the river lies a former canyon created when the plates of the earth wrenched apart. Over millennia it filled with layers of boulders, gravel, soil, and detritus that is now miles deep.

Atop this makeshift foundation of earth the world is nearly motionless, seemingly poised for the unexpectedness of the day at hand.

▸1◂

JUST SOUTH OF LA BAJADA, THE LONG, STEEP UPSLOPE TO Santa Fe that takes Interstate 25 away from the valley of the Rio Grande, the Jeep moved steadily atop asphalt threading darkly through endless reaches of white. The cold front that passed through and deposited a layer of ice and snow had left early enough the previous day to let bright sunshine do its work. Then temperatures had plummeted overnight. It was all part of the high desert winter in New Mexico.

Now as the morning broke, Kevin Pitcairn drove carefully, wary of black ice, as the long-time love of his life, Maria Elena Maldonado, slept curled in the passenger seat. It was the Monday holiday for Martin Luther King Jr., a perfect day for an escape to the City Different, as the state's capital fancied itself.

Just before La Bajada, the first sign appeared that their plans for the day would not unfold as expected. Pitcairn sensed movement in the back seat and looked in the rearview mirror. Lincoln rose to rapt attention facing northeast, his head cocked to listen since eyes made opaque by congenital defects could not see distance clearly.

Seconds later, a dull thud vibrated up through the ground, and the Jeep trembled. Then, muffled by distance, the sound of an explosion concussed through the air. Beside Lincoln, Lucy, whom they affectionately referred to as the Clown Boxer, also lifted to attention.

"What the hell?" he muttered as the Jeep downshifted on the hill. Pitcairn felt a slight tension creep into the day. Maria Elena stirred beside him.

"What happened, Cito?" she asked groggily. As a child he had been Little Kevin, which she had converted to the Spanish, Kevincito, Cito for short. It was ironic given his tall, rangy and powerful build.

"An explosion of some kind. Lincoln sensed it before I heard it."

Maria Elena stretched and yawned as she sat up, rubbing her eyes with her palms. They were both quiet for a few minutes until reaching the top of the hill let them see to the east. What they saw stunned them.

A huge, gray cloud cascaded up directly ahead of them, towering against the idyllic blue skies, endless carpet of snow-covered land, and brilliantly backlit mountains. It seemed surreal—a perfect landscape scarred by what was clearly a plume of destruction.

Pitcairn pulled quickly to the shoulder as Maria Elena gasped.

"What the fuck!" she exclaimed. "What the fuck, Cito?"

"Turn on the radio please, Emmy," he urged. It was his term of endearment for her, a playful take on her initials.

Pulling off the pavement into the grass, he snapped open the door and stepped out. Suddenly, Lucy responded to his owner's distraction and bolted into the brush.

Pitcairn cursed and darted after her. Then he stopped as he realized catching her was hopeless. He took a deep breath, looked around, and began thinking of a plan to keep her from running into the road.

An instant later, Lucy burst from behind a clump of scrub and raced toward him, only to find her breakneck speed impossible on the ice hiding under the snow. Madly scrambling her legs, tongue lolling from the side of her mouth, she tumbled out of control into a chamisa just beside him. A powdery coating of snow exploded. Lucy yelped, spun around like a crab, and emerged dappled in white and panting. Looking up at Pitcairn, she shook herself, then leaped toward him with great exuberance.

He braced himself on the slippery surface and caught her before she knocked him down, then grabbed her collar firmly. Knowing her frolic was over, Lucy settled quickly and gazed at him lovingly.

Pitcairn could not help but laugh. It was an insane moment which brought with it a release.

"When you've seen the humor, you've seen the truth," he reminded himself as he turned to watch the billowing cloud. Already its fringes were beginning to dissipate and feather off into the morning light.

As he walked back to the Jeep, Maria Elena came out with a look of deep concern.

"I just heard a first report on the radio, Cito. The explosion was at a Sufi compound near Glorieta. No details, but it sounds really bad."

"There's a Sufi place up there?"

"South of the Christian retreat center."

Pitcairn thought for a moment. "Could be a gas line, but I have that sixth sense it's some kind of violence."

Maria Elena pressed herself reassuringly against him. Sliding her hand gently across his shoulder, she kneaded his neck muscles lightly.

"Want to drive up there and check it out?" he asked.

Maria Elena looked up at him. The deep, dark pools of her eyes studied his face. "Given how this stuff seems to find you, do we have a choice?"

He kissed the top of her head. "Always a choice. Except when there isn't a choice."

"Okay," she shrugged. "Let's see what happens, but I want to try to get some of the plans for our day back on track."

Captivated by the sight of the looming, dark cloud, they continued to watch for long, silent moments.

▸2◂

STEADY UPDATES ON THE RADIO PAINTED THE EMERGING story. It had been a massive blast, with a number of deaths and injuries. Local emergency responders were arriving, followed by FBI and ATF investigators who were en route. Pitcairn turned off the radio when the broadcaster said the Department of Homeland Security had mobilized personnel and raised the terror alert level.

The noise of the tires masked the quiet in the Jeep until Maria Elena spoke: "That's some serious shit."

Deep in thought, Pitcairn nodded and glanced toward her. Looking back at the road, he noticed his near-death grip on the steering wheel. He could always feel the tension grow with his first steps into a place of violence or destruction. It was a visceral response, a kind of psychological hangover from his childhood.

He noticed Maria Elena's light touch on his forearm, and remembered to breathe. Pulling his shoulders back and rolling his head from side to side, Pitcairn drew in a long, measured inhalation, then exhaled quickly. After several repeats, the release felt dramatic.

"Thank you," he said, reaching over to squeeze Maria Elena's thigh.

"*De nada*. Sometimes a troubled man needs a good woman to remind him who he really is."

"And . . . ," he cued.

She danced her hands in the air. "And . . . you are an exceptionally good man who is occasionally lost in a history that no longer applies."

Pitcairn laughed.

"Were you in Traumaland?" she asked, using their whimsical take on a theme park filled with false realities and twisted characters.

"No, I was there for a moment, but as soon as I started breathing, it released and Kari came to mind." He smiled wistfully, thinking about Kari Claussen, the trauma counselor who'd taught him the technique. "Who could imagine that a guy like me would have the good witch of the high desert for spiritual advice?"

The question hung in the air as they heard the first of many sirens. Traffic was light, but even though the radio said the interstate was unaffected by the explosion, emergency vehicles blocked off the next several exits. As they climbed steeply to Glorieta Pass, they could see the blast cloud continue to dissipate, leaving behind a haze of smoke and dust.

"Guess we're going to have to be creative," Pitcairn said as he took the first exit that wasn't closed. Turning south, the road narrowed as it wound up into the mountains. At a hairpin curve, he quickly shifted into four-wheel drive and veered right onto a snow-covered forest road.

At first, the white blanket under overhanging rocks and fir trees wasn't especially deep, but drifts began to appear as they gained elevation. The tires crunched steadily forward. The dogs had roused as soon as they'd left the pavement. Pitcairn cranked up the heater. Slowly, they navigated the narrowing track through the trees.

After a few stops where openings and possible vantage points proved illusory, they crept through a tight, rocky niche at a broad curve and saw an overlook where the tree cover fell away. Pitcairn stopped in the middle of the road and turned off the ignition. Reaching into the back seat, he grabbed his winter driving duffle and pulled out a wool scarf for Maria Elena and leather gloves for both of them.

The doors of the Jeep whined as they opened in the cold. Lucy was vibrating with energy that needed release again, while Lincoln just stood quietly. Pitcairn let them out and walked up a slope with Maria Elena. Their lungs worked harder with the elevation, while their breath formed into small clouds of vapor.

After about forty feet, they came to a view that would have delighted them any other day. But now, the scene below was only debris and destruction. In a large flat space in the southern lee of a mountain, the Sufi compound's wreckage radiated out. Trees were flattened for several hundred yards. The buildings and walls that remained looked from afar like the Anasazi ruins Pitcairn and Maria Elena had seen in canyons across the Southwest. Crumpled vehicles still smoked, and he even thought he could smell the carnage. Tiny black figures moved in the distance as a helicopter rose in the air.

Maria Elena pressed her head into his chest and began to cry. He wrapped her in his arms and continued looking below. Pitcairn felt the sorrow rise, a bittersweet ache just above his heart, and began another kind of breathwork Kari had shown him to help blunt the effects of retraumatization.

Maria Elena pulled away to rub her eyes and blow her nose. She shook her head. "I don't know how you can be with this as often as you are."

Pitcairn brushed her cheek. "Kari says I have a very high threshold for discomfort. She tells me it's the basis for a high degree of empathy that's growing in me." He shrugged. "All I know is to stand in the presence of it and breathe. To bear witness . . ." His voice fell away.

Pitcairn scanned the horizon again. "Emmy, this is what I seem to have been called to do. And somehow, I can simultaneously see a great beauty amid the ugly." He smiled tenderly as she looked at him.

"You know," Maria Elena said, "I always thought it was the violence that lurked in you that was so alluring. But right at this moment, I realize it's the compassion that I love so much."

Pitcairn quickly raised a hand. "I still can't see what you and others see in me." He chuckled. "Most people can't see their own inner darkness. Me . . . I can't fathom anything other than that."

Maria Elena nodded. "Me, I cry. Then I start trying to figure out how to catch the bastards and make them pay." A wry smile crept to her face.

Pitcairn had a last look at the blast site, then took her hand and led her to the Jeep. Lincoln and Lucy clambered in. The ride into Santa Fe was quiet, with emergency vehicles and black SUVs passing them in both directions.

"It's quite a response," Maria Elena said.

"Yeah. Seems like the recent years of high alerts have made them all really efficient." He paused. "That's a sad commentary, isn't it?"

In town, they first dropped Lucy and Lincoln at a doggy daycare whose twenty-four-hour "concierge" service was the choice of the wealthy when visiting their second homes in Santa Fe. Then they drove to the Teahouse on Canyon Road, a funky, new-age-meets-Tibet restaurant that they both loved. After getting a very strong latte for himself and a large hot chocolate for Maria Elena, Pitcairn pulled out his notepad and started writing. Some of it was the on-going written inventory he kept to process and reflect as part of his recovery from alcoholism. The rest were notes for his work as a commentator and journalist with the *Albuquerque Chronicle*.

Pitcairn sipped from the mug and realized he needed to call his editor, Sean Mortensen. Finding a spot outside in the morning sun, he tapped the speed dial.

"Sean, I'm up here in Santa Fe."

"How come? What are you doing there?"

"It wasn't planned. Maria Elena and I were coming up for the day, and the explosion happened while we were driving. Coincidence but timely."

"Sean, it's really bad. I can't imagine how big the bomb must have been. There must be a whole lot of dead." He told Mortensen what he'd seen.

The editor knew that violence often brought out the best in Pitcairn's writing, and told him he wanted a reflective piece built around his on-the-scene observations and feelings.

Pitcairn disconnected and jotted down a few more thoughts, then went back inside to Maria Elena. "What's up?" he asked.

She smiled as she looked up from a newspaper borrowed from a nearby rack. "After the compound, I'm just happy to be sitting here reading in quiet comfort."

"What time are we due at Ten Thousand Waves?" he asked, knowing she'd had a tough time getting a reservation at the chic spa in the mountains north of Santa Fe.

"The only time they had is five o'clock. Guess I'm not the only one who wants to sit in hot water underneath the stars with my honey."

Pitcairn laughed. "I like the light at the end of day better anyway. Come on, let's go gallery hopping and see if some beauty can dispel the ugly we've seen."

▸3◂

PITCAIRN WOKE WITH A START, JOLTED FROM SLEEP BY A vivid dream. In it he and Maria Elena were in the Jeep as it did an elegant, slow-motion pirouette over the edge of a cliff toward a chaotic storm of swirling debris. The dream was strangely devoid of feelings except for an overwhelming sense of inevitability.

He slid quietly from the bed so as not to wake her. The dogs arose as he took his journal off the nightstand and went to the kitchen. Pitcairn's counseling work with Kari had evolved to include recording his dreams. After a nearly lifelong problem with nightmares—a consequence of his history of trauma and violence—his current dream life, though still often disturbing or distorted, was vastly improved from the terror that used to wake him nearly every night.

He wrote as the coffee maker gurgled. This dream was easy enough to categorize. It was clearly influenced by the previous day's experiences, and it was no stretch to see that he was being drawn into something. But he was extremely curious about Maria Elena's involvement.

After noting all he could recall from the dream, Pitcairn segued to his morning ritual. Sipping coffee, he read a short piece from a book of meditations, a standard Alcoholics Anonymous collection. Then he sat quietly, as much without thought as possible. A few moments later, ideas began flowing onto paper.

His writing drifted to the previous evening. After wandering through several Canyon Road galleries, and delicious afternoon tapas at El Farol, they had spent a lovely time soaking in a hot tub amid the piñon and juniper that studded the hillsides north of Santa Fe. Before their time ended, Maria Elena had lured him into the private sauna and seduced him. It was one more addition to

11

their lengthy list of adventures in love-making in curious places, something that had a strange appeal to her.

Pitcairn stood up to get more coffee, felt a pang of hunger, and pivoted to the refrigerator. A bowl of leftover charro beans with red chile seemed perfect. A staple of Maria Elena's cooking, she admitted they were a bastard dish stolen from West Texas and not authentic New Mexican fare. He couldn't have cared less. They were a solid start to the day.

As he turned to the microwave to heat them, Lucy whined to be fed.

"Dogs and chile are a really bad idea!" He reached into the refrigerator again for two bones Maria Elena had used to make a stock base, then led the dogs to a corner where they settled down to gnaw contentedly.

As he ate, Pitcairn continued writing and pausing for reflection. As usual, his thoughts were a mashup of past and present, recovery and spirituality, together with the passion for writing that fueled his profession and his journaling.

While a foundation of his recovery from alcoholism, this meditation and journaling work had rocketed forward during the time of the Crucifix Protests fifteen months earlier. His life had been transformed by the nationwide demonstrations that had co-opted the Christian crucifix as an upside-down expression of distress for the church, and for the world beyond it.

Before the Protests, he had become deeply involved in the world of serial killer Daniel Davidson and his graphic murder on the tarmac at the Albuquerque Sunport. It had thrust him unwillingly into a national dialogue on violence, innocence, and forgiveness. With the Crucifix Protests still occurring sporadically, he was often invited to offer commentary, and also was continuing a series of articles on violence and its effects for the *North Country Reader,* a progressive publication that mostly catered to provocative thought.

The more important change for Pitcairn was the inner one that had given him a kind of reconciliation with himself over his lifelong history with violence. Regardless of his comfort with the subject and gratitude for the ways he'd changed, he had more than a little reluctance each time violent events seemed to conspire to engage him. He had made peace with the fact that his life was not his own in these matters. And as a result, he was willing to go wherever he was drawn, though not always happily. Despite his reconciliation with himself, the effects of violence on others remained a source of heartache.

Pitcairn was certain those events had been the catharsis for a great deal of inner healing, and equally sure that his morning journaling, contemplation, and meditation helped cement the healing into place. While anxiety still often dogged him, he had no doubt the practices were very useful.

In yet another surprising experience during the Crucifix Protests, Pitcairn had met Father Anthony de Franco, leader of the Center for Enlightened Spirituality, which instigated the first demonstration using the inverted crucifix. Tony had become a trusted confidante and spiritual mentor, though it remained curious that the priest was advising a man like Pitcairn whose beliefs wavered on any given day from atheism to agnosticism and back again.

It was Tony who had referred him to Kari despite Pitcairn's skepticism. "She knows and walks on holy ground," he'd said. "Now would be a good time to be open-minded."

Pitcairn smiled at the memory and recalled his response: "Tony, I can only be as open-minded as my closed mind permits."

The priest had persisted, and to good end. Kari was now a steady presence in Pitcairn's program of recovery. Where once he had focused exclusively on his alcoholism, she had broadened his perspective into a number of arenas. Trauma recovery was but one of them.

Moments later, he was aware of Lucy staring at him. He stared back. The stub of her tail began to wag.

"Walk?" Pitcairn asked.

She began a dance of anticipation.

"Off we go," he announced as he pressed himself up from the seat. Almost immediately, Lincoln came forward.

A few minutes later, they were moving through the darkness up Twelfth Street toward an early morning AA meeting at a chapel near the old Indian school. The Morning Has Broken group had been founded by a bunch of aging hippies, then added a collection of bikers. Its proximity to downtown also made it attractive to office workers, all of which added up to a very interesting mixture of recovering drunks. A number of members enjoyed it when he showed up with the boxers, which Pitcairn now thought of as a useful contribution to their sobriety. It was especially helpful to a young guy known as Lost Jimmy who had some kind of deep organic damage from sniffing and snorting substances not intended for such use.

Twenty minutes later, they were hailed with a chorus of hellos as they entered the chapel's back room. As expected, both dogs made a beeline for Jimmy who was huddled on a couch. Lucy hopped up beside him and stuck her head in his face to lick him, while Lincoln curled up on the floor at his feet.

There was a lot of chatter about the bombing, as well as the usual bullshit that crept into conversation between alcoholics. Promptly at seven, the meeting began and quickly moved to a reading on acceptance, which was stock material for recovering alcoholics despite the inevitable groans from some members who hated the subject with a passion.

Doris, the discussion leader, a former nun who'd been expelled from her order for drunkenness and debauchery, read from AA's *Big Book*: "Acceptance is the answer to all of my problems today. When I am disturbed, it is because I find some person, place, thing, or situation—some fact of my life—unacceptable to me, and I can find no serenity until I accept that person, place, thing, or situation as being exactly the way it is supposed to be at this moment. Nothing, absolutely nothing, happens in God's world by mistake. Until I could accept my alcoholism, I could not stay sober; unless I accept my life completely on life's terms, I cannot be happy. I need to concentrate not so much on what needs to be changed in the world as on what needs to be changed in me and in my attitudes."

Then, despite an excellent explanation from Doris, who had very good long-term sobriety, the next three speakers went into a variety of riffs about why the notion of acceptance didn't apply to them. It was the usual routine. AA vigorously defended everyone's right to their own opinion as long as their reason for being at the meeting was a desire to stop drinking. Pitcairn viewed it as minimally controlled anarchy.

A few more members spoke before old Abe did. He was a Buddhist and a bastion of wisdom, as well as a bit contrary. "Damn," he announced before pausing for a long, careful scratch of his ear. "Seems to me we've forgotten why we're here. It doesn't say you gotta like it. Shit . . . you can hate it till you die . . . which we're going to do if we don't stay sober. But until I'm willing to play with life exactly the way it is, I'm a fool. And what Doris said about lack of acceptance is likely to make me a drunk fool . . . which is not an improvement!" Laughter burst forth as Abe looked around the room. "If there's one thing I know from more than thirty years in these rooms, it's that I gotta make peace with what is."

Duly chastened, the speakers who shared their thoughts after Abe took his words as gospel. As they spoke, Pitcairn thought about how very hard it is to accept the unacceptable, like the bombing or any of the other countless forms of violence and tragedy in the world. After the meeting, he and Doris talked about it. Her final words stayed with him on the walk home: "Accepting the unacceptable is real work, Pitcairn. It's why Jesus told us it didn't count for much to forgive our friends."

As he came in the door, the odor of cigarettes was unmistakable. Though he didn't smell it often, it always meant that Maria Elena was disturbed. As someone with an alcoholic personality, Pitcairn could never understand anyone's moderate use of an addictive substance.

Beneath the haze at the kitchen table, the mask on her face showed only how significantly she was disturbed.

"What's up?" he asked.

"Pat called."

"Pat?"

Her face showed her exasperation. "Pattie . . . my friend from Oklahoma!"

Realizing the depth of her distress, Pitcairn settled into a chair and placed a hand on her knee as he leaned toward her. "And . . ."

"Lucas was on retreat at the Sufi compound."

"Crap. . . ." his voice trailed away. Lucas had grown up in southeastern Oklahoma under the tutelage of a very wise old man who'd asked Pattie to assume the role of godmother when he died. With all that loving attention plus really good parents, he had grown into one of the most exceptional young men Pitcairn ever met.

"He was airlifted to the university trauma center. Pattie says he's in a medically induced coma." Maria Elena looked at him as she took a breath. "It's bad, Cito."

Nodding, he leaned in closer and pressed his lips to her forehead. She shuddered and pulled away so she could see him.

"Pattie had some minor surgery and can't get here. She wants us to check on him. She said his dad will take a few days to get here from the job he's on in Bulgaria."

"What about his mom?"

Maria Elena rolled her eyes. "Don't you remember? She passed away from cancer a few years ago."

"Oh yeah," he nodded, "that's what sent Lucas on his search."

"Right. And what sent his dad to work so far from their place in Oklahoma."

Pitcairn shook his head empathetically. "Sometimes, the shit just multiplies."

"Pattie gave them our names at the hospital. We need to get over there. I called in for a personal day already."

"Let's do it."

She smiled at him in a distracted way.

"What. . . ?" he asked.

Tears glistened in her eyes. "You."

"Me?"

"How you show up for me."

He grinned at her. "Emmy, how could I not?"

▶4◀

LUCAS HAD BEEN ADMITTED TO THE CRITICAL CARE UNIT AFTER emergency surgery. In addition to removing several pieces of shrapnel, doctors amputated his left leg mid-thigh. He was torn and tattered, placed in a coma principally because his skull fracture had led to swelling of the brain. Officially, Lucas's condition was considered guarded, but Bonnie, one of his nurses, assured them the EKG gave reasonable cause for optimism.

Pitcairn struck up a conversation with her in the hallway to thank her for being so considerate, but, as often happened with him, they soon discovered a connection: Her father had been an AA member whom Pitcairn vaguely remembered.

Bonnie told him how her dad had gotten sober. She had come home one night to find him drinking despite serious liver and pancreas dysfunction. "My mom was sobbing, and I just snapped," she said, looking down in embarrassment.

"I was so angry. I went to the closet in his bedroom and took out his pistol. Then I stood there like some crazy woman staring at him. He asked me twice what I was doing before I could say anything.

"'Dad,' I told him. 'I am so damned tired of this. Let's just go out to the West Mesa. I'll leave you there and you can just blow your brains out.' "

"Dad looked really shocked," she laughed at herself. "Of course, that would be a reasonable reaction."

"Anyway, I just glared at him. And I told him it would be merciful to me and the entire family if he put an end to his slow, alcoholic suicide with a real one."

Pitcairn smiled at her sympathetically. "That's quite an intervention."

Bonnie looked him in the eye. "The only virtue I can find in it is that he got sober after that."

"No shit?"

She nodded firmly. "No shit."

Clarity came to Pitcairn. "That's where your kindness came from, isn't it? It broke your heart open."

Bonnie looked away again, perhaps out of discomfort from being seen so clearly.

Pitcairn placed his hand on her shoulder and squeezed lightly. "Thank you for telling me your story. And for your kindness. It makes a real difference."

She nodded and placed her hand on his forearm in appreciation. "It's nice when something good can come from something that awful."

"Boy, do I understand how true that is," he reflected.

She went on down the hall, and he told Maria Elena about his conversation with her, then turned his attention to Lucas.

"Looks pretty peaceful, doesn't he?"

"Well, yeah," she said with an edge of sarcasm, "there's no one home to be stressed."

She told Pitcairn about visits with Pattie that had left her deeply affected by the young man. "He's an old soul," she said, "wisdom beyond his years." The last time she'd seen Lucas, he had just been kicked out of the University of Tulsa for selling peyote on campus. Maria Elena had met Pattie in Tulsa for a weekend of the arts, and found Lucas entirely unrepentant. She thought it was probably not coincidental that his mother had died only a few months before. Regardless, Maria Elena remembered him saying that "ultimately every path has to end because it cannot take us where we next need to go."

Soon after that, Pattie began to report his searching and travels. She told Maria Elena he was a great deal like his godfather and mentor, Etido, also a wanderer and searcher. Pattie had also been profoundly affected by the old man. She had worked with him for a number of years on his memoir, which was close to publication.

"Emmy," Pitcairn asked, "why is this deal with Lucas affecting you so much? I mean, you didn't know him that well. Not really."

She raised a hand and lightly spread her fingers over her lips as she thought. "I don't know, Cito. Maybe it was the horror of the bomb site, or maybe Lucas and I are kindred souls." She gazed into the distance as her eyes moved back and forth. "I don't know."

The corners of Pitcairn's lips rose in a hint of affection. "To quote Tony, 'Then stay in not knowingness.'"

Maria Elena stayed in her reverie for long moments, then looked him in the eyes. "Actually, I do know."

"Do tell, Emmy."

"You converted me, Cito. You have showed me how important it is to care."

His raised eyebrows and rapt attention encouraged her to continue.

"I hated that you advocated for Davidson." She shook her head as she recalled the feeling. "A serial killer for God's sake. And your crazy ideas about inherent innocence. Then I saw it change you in the most amazing ways, and how it changed those who engaged you on it. Even Daddy."

Her face softened dramatically. "When you confronted him about incesting me, and somehow still extended innocence even to him, I would never have imagined it could get him to reconcile with me before he died."

"I still didn't like him. Still wish he hadn't done it." She laughed and shrugged as she looked away. "Still wish I didn't have to work so goddamned hard to keep my own inner peace despite how badly he hurt me."

Turning back to him, Maria Elena lifted her hands and opened them. "The whole experience changed my mind." She tilted her head. "Changed me."

Pitcairn wrapped her in a hug. "And what's that got to do with your affinity for Lucas?"

She leaned away to look into his eyes without breaking the embrace.

"It's not just Lucas, Cito. I give a damn in ways I never did before. There is something about trying to find innocence in others that just opens me up."

"Wow, Emmy."

"It's the craziest thing. But I'm convinced. And I'm all in. I'll support your crazy pursuits with my crazy feelings."

He pulled her very close again.

For several days, they kept vigil at the hospital as Maria Elena also kept up with her work as an assistant for Albuquerque Mayor Carlinda Dixon. She was fortunate that her success in guiding Dixon's re-election campaign had led the mayor to give her a great deal of autonomy.

The campaign had also gained her a moniker from a local conservative Spanish-language newspaper: La Diabla de Albuquerque. Dixon really liked the devilish nickname, and said often she'd been elected to play "smashmouth" politics after years of leadership neglect had undermined the community's vitality. In private, she gave huge credit for that success to Maria Elena.

When she was first labeled *La Diabla*, Maria Elena had confided to Pitcairn that, "I haven't decided how I feel about my new title. On the one hand, I'm pleased by the impression it creates . . ."— she smiled mischievously—". . . but on the other, it just doesn't seem to fit my self-concept. Then again, nothing wrong with a chica like myself commanding a little respect."

During the days they waited with Lucas, Maria Elena called Pattie regularly, though there was little to report. Zack, Lucas's father, was due in on Saturday.

On Thursday morning, Pitcairn sat alone beside Lucas with a pad of paper and pen in hand. His column was due the next day, but he'd been waiting for his impressions and experiences to sink in. Now he began to write.

IS THE STORY ENDING OR BEGINNING?

His name is Lucas. He lies in a bed in a medically induced coma at the University of New Mexico's Regional Trauma Center.

He is one of thirty-two victims of the bomb blast at the Sufi Center of Mercy near Santa Fe. Seventeen of those victims perished, their bodies torn apart by shrapnel from what is now known to be a bomb detonated by a suicide-bomber from Upstate South Carolina.

While the bomber's background and reasons are slowly becoming clearer, Lucas is lucky to have survived despite the amputation of his left leg and severe brain hemorrhaging.

It is not yet clear how the damage will affect him. He could lose a great deal of mental functioning. At a minimum, he is likely to suffer from post-traumatic stress disorder, which impairs lives dramatically. Time alone will tell.

For several days, my companion and I have been holding a bedside vigil at the request of those who love Lucas. It is a fruitful time for contemplation. How is it that a young man from Oklahoma could come to harm at an otherwise-peaceful spiritual enclave in New Mexico, the victim of hate presumably inspired elsewhere?

More than a year ago, I made a commitment to tell the stories of those affected by violence. It was a result of a complicated experience involving the Crucifix Protests that began in downtown Albuquerque.

I will not dwell on those events; rather let me tell you about Lucas.

Lucas is a spiritual seeker. After his mother died from cancer, he was expelled from the University of Tulsa under a cloud of accusations related to the use and distribution of peyote. While his wandering is not especially clear afterward, we know he spent time at a Fourth Way Retreat Center in central Idaho working to build a sanctuary, explored the Self-Realization Fellowship in Encinitas, California, went on a year-long silent retreat at Christ in the Desert Monastery in Abiquiu, New Mexico, and is reported to have dropped in on a number of churches, mosques and synagogues for services of all kinds.

There is a certain irony that he and others were attacked at a center named for mercy, and that they had just completed a long weekend celebration that included prayer, chanting, meditation and dance.

For those not familiar with Sufism, it is a mystical branch of Islam. Sufis focus on love, tolerance, worship of God, community development, and personal development through self-discipline and responsibility.

We now know that Lucas had been a part of that religious community for some time, and that he'd attained quite a degree of regard from the Sufis and also a number of residents of Santa Fe who had benefited from his involvement in community projects. What we do not know is the effect this bombing will have on him or others.

Each time I explore a human being who is affected by violence, I am struck with heartache that it takes such an act for us to truly notice that person. It's as if their victimization brings them into focus. And it is then that we truly see them . . . and marvel at their stories.

Perhaps it is in those moments that our self-absorption falls away. I'd like to think compassion is the result. It is a tragic pattern.

After reading over what he'd written, Pitcairn set it aside. There was more to be added but he'd do it later and send it to Mortensen.

Then he settled into the quiet and studied the young man's face. Beneath the bandages that swaddled his head, Lucas's features were soft and relaxed. Pitcairn began to breathe, imagining the breath easing over and through the pain he felt in his heart. The noises of the hospital ebbed away as he descended into silence.

Pitcairn never knew if the breathwork for trauma simply soothed his own injuries or somehow projected beyond him to others. But after some time had passed and he gazed again at Lucas, the face he saw seemed younger than before. Pitcairn felt a wisp of a smile come to his face.

▶5◀

E<small>ARLY</small> S<small>ATURDAY</small> <small>MORNING</small> <small>FOUND</small> P<small>ITCAIRN</small> <small>WITH</small> <small>A</small> <small>MUG</small> of coffee in an easy chair across from Father Anthony in the sitting room of the Center for Enlightened Spirituality. Lincoln and Lucy were curled on a large, colorful rag rug that covered the saltillo tiles in front of an old kiva fireplace. Several piñon logs crackled softly amid bluish flames.

The two men often sat together before they chatted. The priest said it was a time of meditation and communion. Pitcairn had simply come to trust the quiet. For someone who formerly could not sit still in his own presence, a man who was constantly fueled by and through action, this was no small matter.

His eyes scanned the room, noting the shelves filled with books of all spiritual persuasions. While the building and compound were old, as the scarred, adobe walls made clear, the center's members believed in beauty, and had covered much of the wall space with art.

Pitcairn's attention was drawn to a vivid oil painting by a local, internationally renowned realist. It was a garden scene in a lush tropical setting. Off center to the right stood a wizened old man draped in a soft linen robe. His hand was raised in an open gesture, and his light-filled eyes looked past his hand at something beyond the frame. It was so easy to see the joy in the man, but as always, Pitcairn found himself contemplating the missing object.

His reverie was broken as Tony cleared his throat. "Wondering again?" asked the priest.

"Ha!" Pitcairn replied with a snort. "Tony, I'm not sure I will ever stop wondering."

"Isn't it interesting how that word actually spins in two directions? On the one hand, it implies curiosity. On the other hand, it can be a condition of appreciation or awe. And somehow, the two coexist like hand in glove."

"That's what I love about you, Tony. You're always demonstrating how to live in the question."

With a nod of acknowledgment, a pensive look came to the older man's face. "I read your piece yesterday. Very sympathetic."

"Yeah . . . though I'm not sure where this is going."

"Kevin, none of us have ever known where things lead; we only think we do, which is a comfort but also a significant delusion."

"Right. Got that. Especially the delusion part, for which I have a rich history."

The priest smiled broadly. "Don't we all." He took a sip of coffee. "I thought it noteworthy the same newspaper had the background on the bomber. Did you know anything about that group?"

"Honestly, Tony, it doesn't sound like it qualifies as a group. Just a collection of hate mongers from the hollers of Appalachia. Probably the descendants of Scottish Celtic berserkers. I'm thinking *Deliverance* meets *Braveheart* with a strange spin of unfinished business from the war of northern aggression."

De Franco laughed heartily. "It sounds to me like you are already into another story of violence, aren't you?"

"Tony, this stuff follows me like a starving, stray mongrel. It knows I've got something to say and won't leave me alone until it pulls it out of me."

"And. . . ," the priest said.

"Damn, you're as good at seeing into me as Maria Elena, who by the way has a dog in this fight too apparently, though I'll get to that in a minute."

Pitcairn felt a sudden urge to move. He stood and stretched.

"Tony, here's where I'm hooked. That kid who blew up the Sufi place, Grady Donovan, was the son of a decorated, Vietnam war veteran." He shook his head as he pulled his shoulders back and stretched his neck. "There's a story there. From what I've been able to find so far, his daddy probably had some serious shit going down. You don't collect multiple medals in jungle warfare without it."

The priest nodded behind his hands, which were drawn together over his lips.

"I haven't decided, but I'm thinking I'll head out there and see what I can learn." Pitcairn shrugged. "Never been in that part of the country, so it will be interesting. Donovan lived in a little wide spot in the road along the border between North and South Carolina, but it seems he spent a bunch of time up in some really wild county around the Nantahala River."

"What are you thinking, Kevin?"

"I don't know, Tony. I'm just going to follow where I'm led."

"And so it shall be."

"And so it shall be what?"

"You will be led, Kevin. I am always surprised when you are unable to see how deeply you trust."

"Ahhh . . . I have no idea about that. It's more like I'm compelled." He laughed. "Okay, just to stay with dog metaphors. I'm like a bloodhound. Totally incapable of ignoring a scent. The tantalizing pull will have its way with me whether I like it or not."

The priest nodded again. "And you will have to trust me, Kevin, that you have an exceptional capacity for what we here at the Center would call faith."

A silence crept into the room. Both men eased into it for long moments.

Pitcairn felt a breath rise up inside. "Tony, I'm concerned about Maria Elena." He described the dream of the Jeep in pirouette over the bomb site as well as her obvious connectedness to Lucas.

Father Tony nodded slowly as he thought. "Kevin, this may be the place where your trust is to be tested."

"What do you mean?"

"Honestly . . . I don't know. It's an intuition that has passed into my thoughts several times this morning."

"Is Emmy in danger?" Pitcairn asked.

The priest's face became more somber. "Kevin, I don't know her well enough to be able to answer that question. However, my sense of you has become considerable." He paused to consider his words. "Your faith is strong as it applies to yourself, though you do not see it. But it does not extend beyond yourself. I think you are not sure the guidance in your gut can be trusted with regard to Maria Elena."

Pitcairn contemplated the words. "Tony, I think I just heard you say that she has her own Higher Power . . . and it's not me."

A laugh barked from the priest. "My goodness, Kevin. Someday I hope you can understand why your insight is such a delight to me. You see with a kind of clarity that is quite uncommon."

Raising his hands in an expansive gesture to show his lack of understanding, Pitcairn shook his head. "Tony, I just say what comes to me."

"Jesus uttered comparable words."

"Whoa . . . whoa . . . whoa. . . ."

"Not to worry, Kevin. I am not comparing you to Jesus, only to his words. 'Why callest thou me good, only my Father in heaven is good.'"

"Oh! You mean he wouldn't take on the attributes others tried to place on him."

"Precisely."

"So what the hell does that all mean, Tony?"

The priest gestured with open hands. "You forget that our agreement is to simply play with things, Kevin. And to do so, we try to avoid fixed conclusions. I would suggest you just allow those thoughts to find an appropriate place within you."

"Said one of the wise men from the original Akron AA group, 'Let's keep this thing simple.'" Pitcairn moved forward and embraced De Franco. "Thanks, Tony."

"Truly, it is my pleasure."

▸6◂

LUCAS'S FATHER ARRIVED AT THE HOSPITAL LATE IN THE AFTER-noon as Pitcairn and Maria Elena were getting ready to leave for the day. Zack Johnston had the unmistakable appearance of a devastated man. Barrenness showed in his eyes, and Pitcairn imagined he could feel the emptiness inside him. The death of his wife, Dianna, and now the critical injuries to his son had clearly traumatized the man.

Unerringly, Maria Elena moved to embrace him. Pitcairn couldn't hear what she whispered, but any awkwardness vanished. Zack turned to him, and the two men shook hands somberly. Pitcairn quickly moved aside as the father's eyes swung toward his son. He and Maria Elena stood for a few moments, then slipped into the hallway.

"Damn," she muttered as they moved slowly and quietly.

"What'd you say to him, Emmy?"

With an achingly soft voice she replied, "That we loved Lucas and would do anything to help."

He smiled at her tenderness. "I'm going to see if I can find Bonnie, the nurse. Her heart is so open, I can't imagine anything but good coming from that."

She nodded. "I'm thinking we need some green chile chicken enchiladas at the Back Door."

Pitcairn looked at his watch. "How about I meet you there after the Serenity meeting? After all that has gone down, I could use a dose of good AA."

"Perfect! Six-thirty?"

He bent to kiss the top of her head and eased her toward the door. "I've got to run if I'm going to find Bonnie and get to the meeting."

A short search found the nurse emerging from another room. Pitcairn quickly briefed her. He knew it was the right thing to do when he saw a hint of tears creeping into her soft, hazel eyes.

Her head moved in a quick nod as she turned to go find Zack. Pitcairn touched her shoulder, which caused her to pause and look back.

"Thank you for being who you are."

Bonnie shrugged.

"No," he said firmly. "Don't shrug it off. It's empathy and compassion that heals brokenness. And you have a remarkable amount of it. So, thank you."

Her eyes studied him, and he could see the validation registering inside her. They parted without another word. Zack would be in good hands.

The Serenity Group had chosen to meet at five on a Saturday to attract those who either really needed a meeting or really took the recovery program seriously. Its meeting format—small breakout groups using literature not approved by AA—tended to drive away the closed-minded types. The result was rich conversation that met the ultimate AA standard of weight and depth sufficient to spur recovery.

A young woman nicknamed Skeevy led the meeting. She was a beautiful, slender, doe-eyed graduate student, an appearance totally at odds with the ten-minute story she told of her path to AA. Her bottom had come not from alcohol alone but from crack cocaine as well as the wild orgies that followed. As she shared, Pitcairn saw a vacant look in her eyes, a sign of disassociation that is a common consequence of unresolved trauma.

Regardless of her history or condition, what she said made clear the good recovery work she had done. Then she proposed a topic from a new source, *The Way of Powerlessness*. Skeevy began by humorously assuring the group that the author's name really was Wayne Liquorman, which produced a good laugh from the eleven members present. Then she quoted from the book, "We don't always get what we want, or what we ask or pray for, or what we think we need or deserve. We get what we get."

"The issue," she added, "seems to be what we do with what we get."

Skeevy smiled sweetly, "I'm not going to add another word to that to distract you from the subject. But since we're such a small group, I'm going to suggest we just stay together tonight." An open-handed gesture followed as she added, "It's your meeting."

What ensued was unusual, more like a meditation meeting or a meeting of Friends at the local Quaker House. Long periods of quiet were punctuated infrequently by brief comments.

After a particularly long silence, a transgender guy named Phillip offered a somewhat lengthy comment on the difficulties of making peace with what you get when it is something so challenging as gender orientation. But in the end, he landed squarely in the program of recovery by talking about how important the Seventh Step had become to him.

"Humbly asked Him to remove our shortcomings." Phillip paused after reciting it. "Somehow I had to get right with myself. Otherwise, drinking myself into oblivion was the only option. And getting right meant to stop thinking of my problems as shortcomings."

As if on cue, Pitcairn felt words rising from him as he nodded to the young man. "Thanks, Phillip. Never heard it said that way, but right on."

Pitcairn closed his eyes and recalled the retreat at which Kari had said the words he was about to share. She had just asked him and another man to lightly lay their hands on the forearms and thighs of an older woman who lay trembling on a cushion on the floor surrounded by a small circle of spiritual students. Terrie was a survivor of horrible sexual violence, and Kari was attending to the throes of trauma cascading through Terrie's body and soul.

He would never forget the searing heat rising from the woman's body as they sat with her while she slowly and steadily used breathing techniques Kari taught. It was almost like waves flowing and ebbing through the woman, though waves that were clearly storm-tossed.

At the end, after what seemed far longer than the twenty minutes it proved to be, Terrie emerged from the tremors and tears more at peace with herself than she could ever recall being.

Pitcairn came back to the present moment and opened his eyes. "I've got this spiritual teacher I call the good witch of the high desert." He chuckled as others laughed with appreciation. "I remember her saying that the secret is not in getting what you want but in wanting what you get."

His eyes were drawn to Skeevy, who was watching him in rapt attention. Then he scanned the others, deliberately making eye contact with Phillip.

"I think that's the point. In the end, getting right with yourself means wanting what you get." He shook his head wistfully as a wave of gratitude rose in him. "What a great deal."

The tenor of the meeting shifted then as the conversation gained energy and the quiet subsided. Pitcairn just listened. After the meeting had run its course, Phillip and Skeevy both cornered him to talk further. Finally, he excused himself to meet Maria Elena.

She waved as he found her tucked in a dark corner booth of the tavern, a cup of hot tea steaming in front of her. Before he could utter a word, she slid over on the cushion for him to sit beside her, then boldly kissed him and laid her head on his shoulder.

"What was that about?" he inquired.

In response, she reached up with her hand and placed it over his heart, patting him lightly. When the waiter arrived a moment later, she pulled away and sipped her tea.

After ordering the Back Door's signature enchiladas, Pitcairn told her about his meeting with the priest that morning, including his impression about how these matters were affecting her. She leaned against him as she distractedly nodded her head.

"I just don't know, Cito. But I have an inclination to hike the West Mesa with you tomorrow."

"Really!" he replied in surprise. "Not sure I can remember the last time you went tromping around with me."

"I am not a tramp," she giggled.

He chuckled and played along as he realized she was toying with him: "Nope. Only and always high class."

"You can bet your ass . . . or mine. . . ."

"How in the world has the conversation taken a turn like this?"

She sighed. "Because I didn't want to get any more serious about the situation with Lucas and what implications it may have for me. And I was trying to steer the conversation to sex." She looked at him coyly.

"Got it. Bomb blasts to psychology to hiking to sex. That makes perfect sense to me, and sets up the arrival of our enchiladas."

The waiter swept in with their plates, and they ate quietly for a few minutes until Maria Elena picked up the point she'd begun with: "Seriously, I feel an urge to go to the West Mesa with you tomorrow."

"I'm sure Lucy and Lincoln will enjoy your company. Me too!" He gave her a serious look. "Now, about that sex. . . ."

▸7◂

A GRAY DAY PRESENTED A THREAT OF SNOW SQUALLS ON THE West Mesa. Although sunshine could be expected almost every day on the high desert of New Mexico, there was still no exemption from winter. Only a few years before, Pitcairn had taken advantage of a snowstorm to traverse this terrain on cross-country skis that emerged from storage only infrequently.

Today however, he and Maria Elena hiked steadily on bare ground toward Ja, the volcanic cone on the ridge of the mesa that had always held a powerful attraction for him. Lucy wandered far afield while Lincoln protectively trailed Maria Elena. Both she and Pitcairn were caught up in their own thoughts, and few words were exchanged.

They entered a good-sized arroyo more than fifteen feet deep carved by the runoff that drained a large portion of the West Mesa. Rather than climb up the slope onto Ja, Maria Elena was drawn to the striated bands of soil making up the earthen walls. Following the arroyo to the west, she was mesmerized by the composition of the layers, pointing here and there as she muttered to herself.

Pitcairn had turned his gaze to a darkening cloud cover and didn't see her stop. Her words brought his attention back to the arroyo wall: "Cito, is that a ring?"

Moving forward, he reached up well above her head and gently pried something from the compressed sediment. Brushing the soil away, he dropped a segment of broken, tarnished brass loop into her open hand. Her forehead creased as she looked up at him. "Can you dig into the dirt some more? Maybe the rest of the ring is there."

Pitcairn picked up a stick and worked away the soil around where the loop had been. A few minutes later, another piece dropped at her feet. They both kneeled as she lifted it carefully.

The broken section was one of three around a central hub with an ornate, raised fleur-de-lis. It was less than three inches across, with no identifying marks. She turned it over several times before handing it to Pitcairn. "What is it?"

"Saddle hardware?" he suggested before giving it back. "I don't know, Emmy."

Suddenly, a blast of wind whipped down the arroyo followed by a cascade of large snowflakes. They both looked up. The gale's swift intensity felt like the onset of a blizzard. It had crept up on them as they explored the wall of the arroyo.

Moving swiftly to a cut and upslope through the bank, he spoke urgently. "There's a small cave on the south side of Ja. Follow me."

The wind was filled with blowing snow that tore at them as they ducked their heads and pressed into it toward the only available shelter. Ten minutes later, plastered with white, they stumbled into the deep recess in the basalt. The cave turned left and tapered to an end. It was deep enough to keep out the wind but still let the light penetrate the shadows. As the dogs shook the snow away, Pitcairn reached into his daypack and pulled out two ponchos that he spread on the blown silt cushioning the rock at their feet. It was surprisingly comfortable when they settled down on crossed legs.

"Wow!" she announced. "That's a storm."

He laughed as he rummaged in the pack for energy bars and water which Maria Elena accepted gratefully. Digging deeper, he found the dog biscuits and slowly fed them to Lincoln and Lucy. Maria Elena pulled the brass object from her pocket and slowly rotated it as she chewed small bites of her snack.

"Cool find, no?" she asked as she settled on her back and lifted the piece of brass into the light. "Do you suppose we can have it repaired?"

Pitcairn nodded. "Someone who knows how to weld can braze it. Why?"

"Don't you think it's curious that the one time I come to the West Mesa with you, I find this? And that it's got a fleur-de-lis on it? You know how much I love lilies. It's a talisman."

Pitcairn smiled but didn't speak. He sprawled on his side facing her as Lincoln curled behind his legs. Lucy dropped to the floor at the bend in the cave. The swirling wind was the only sound. He extended his arm and let his fingers play lightly across Maria Elena's stomach. She sighed softly, dropped her hand and closed her eyes. Before long, he could tell she was dozing. With his head propped up on his hand, he studied her as she slept.

It was only ten minutes or so before Lincoln suddenly stood and looked at Maria Elena. An instant later, Pitcairn felt a tremor shoot through her as an obviously painful and guttural sound escaped her lips and she was startled awake. Despite the shadows, he could see bewilderment on her face as she tried to locate herself in the strange cave, then turned toward him.

"What is it, Emmy?"

She took several deep breaths. Pitcairn moved closer and put an arm around her. He felt her tense, and pulled his head a bit farther away to look into her eyes.

"Emmy?"

"You're not going to believe this, Cito."

"Try me."

"Okay. . . ." she began haltingly, then stopped as she lifted the brass piece to study it for a moment before clasping it firmly and returning her eyes to his. "This cave is one of those magical places. It's like. . . ." Maria Elena shook her head as she sought the words. "Cito, it was like a dream, and I could hear the voice whispering so quietly. . . ."

Since the Crucifix Protests, Pitcairn had occasionally heard what they now referred to as "the still small voice." Once it had spoken to them both, but only that one time. It had whispered "*preciosa*," an endearment Maria Elena had received as a child from a dear aunt. The reverence they felt about the episode had led them to speak of it with great care, as if anything else would be improper.

"What did the voice say, Emmy?"

She shook her head again, looking puzzled. "I don't know. It's just . . . it felt like the Holy Spirit resides here, Cito. And there were dozens of souls of seekers who have retreated to this cave . . . of course they're not really bound to this place, which would make no sense . . . but Cito, this is holy ground. . . ." A softness crept across her face. "And baby, we belong here with them."

Quiet rose. He held her close. Lucy and Lincoln slipped in beside her.

After a time, she took another deep breath and pushed herself into a seated position. He leaned back and watched her as she swept her hair upward and allowed it to fall loosely. She breathed deeply and looked at him with a lopsided smile.

"Shit, Cito."

Pitcairn reached out and caressed her face.

"I don't know how I know it, but Lucas has journals you need to read."

"Okay," he replied, with a hint of skepticism.

Maria Elena's look bored into him. He raised and waved a hand in self-defense. "Emmy, I don't have any idea what just happened. But I believe that you believe. And you can count me in. Just don't expect me to act like I get it."

"Fair enough," she replied as her face softened.

He rolled into a seated posture as well. "What else?"

"Arghhh. . . ." she laughed. "How did you know I didn't tell you everything?"

"No idea. I may not see beyond the boundaries of the world like you just did, but I do see."

"It sounds like the wind stopped blowing. Can we talk as we walk?"

He peered out the mouth of the cave. "Yep, the squall is gone but still some flurries."

They quickly packed up and stepped out into a world transformed. Layers of clouds stretched low over the mesa, and beneath it a thin carpet of snow stretched as far as they could see. The cloud cover hovered over the river valley and city like a bank of marine fog. It looked nothing like the New Mexico they knew and loved. The light had lost its crystalline quality, softening the landscape into an impressionistic work of art they trudged through.

"Cito. . . ." she began after a few minutes. "You've got to go learn about the bomber too. I know you already mentioned it as a possibility, but it was so clear to me in the vision I had."

"Vision?"

She stopped in the track to whack him on the arm. "Yes, the vision!"

He laughed. "Okay, okay."

She stared at him with obvious appreciation. "And I'm going with you."

"You are?"

"Yes."

It was stated so simply and with such clarity of purpose that he simply smiled.

"Did the Holy Spirit tell you when we were supposed to go?"

"Argh . . . you are so maddening!"

He stepped toward her swiftly and swept her up in his arms.

"Stop it, you buffoon! There's more."

Pitcairn couldn't keep from laughing as he kissed her on the cheek and eased her down to the ground. "More?"

"I was given a phrase. A mantra for the trip."

He lifted his hands in mock surrender.

"True our souls," Maria Elena said somberly.

She watched him as he contemplated it. He looked down and scratched his head, then kneeled to pet Lincoln thoughtfully.

"Looks like we have a plan," Pitcairn said as he peered up at her. "Not quite sure how a trip to the Carolinas in search of the backstory on a suicide bomber is going to affect our souls, but some things simply have to get done."

She smiled.

"And . . . you've been one on one with the Holy Spirit, with an old broken talisman and a mantra. How could we possibly fail?"

▶8◀

IT TOOK THE FULL WEEK TO MAKE THEIR ARRANGEMENTS. **O**N the first Sunday in February, they were airborne to Atlanta, the start of their drive north to Upstate South Carolina. Zack had gratefully accepted the offer to stay at their house with Lucy and Lincoln. There was still no indication when Lucas might emerge from the coma.

Despite Pitcairn's unvoiced questions about how the young man's journals could have survived the bombing, Maria Elena's intuition proved correct. He had been bartering his time as a gardener to an older woman in exchange for using a small outbuilding as a space to study and write. He may have been living a spartan lifestyle with the Sufis, but he owned an extensive collection of spiritual and philosophical books. Maria Elena drove up to see the woman with Zack at the end of the week and returned with nearly a dozen matching Moleskine journals filled with careful script.

Zack had not been surprised. Etido, the young man's godfather, had left a great legacy of study and journaling, one that Lucas obviously appreciated and emulated.

"You know," Maria Elena had said to Pitcairn as they lay in bed on Friday night, "It was interesting how touched Zack was by the whole deal. Not just that we were interested but that Etido had made such an impression on Lucas. The old man died when Lucas was still a boy."

"What did you pick up on, Emmy?"

"That Zack thought really well of the old man. And something Pattie said seems to fit. Remember, she is just about ready to publish Etido's memoir, which is somehow part of the legacy to Lucas. I don't know that I understand it all, but Pattie is more like a spiritual adviser to Lucas than a godmother."

"Do you know if Lucas knew about Pattie's plan?"

"No, no idea. But things do seem to get curiouser and curiouser."

Now, on the flight, Pitcairn began to study the first journal as Maria Elena slept. It was mostly the factual backstory to Lucas's arrival at the Sufi Center of Mercy. It was obvious he had been disenchanted by his previous spiritual explorations but was quite optimistic about this new setting.

A short time before landing, on the last page of the first journal, Pitcairn read an entry that said:

New Mexico feels like a homecoming. Teo is with me.

He closed his eyes and searched his memory looking for a deity named Teo. It seemed he had heard some reference in relationship to the Hawaiian healing practice ho'oponopono. He made a mental note to call Kate Delmonico, his resource for all things obscure, though her specialty was brain and cognition research.

Pitcairn settled into the white noise of the descending aircraft, quieted his thoughts, and began once again to breathe as Kari had taught him. He scanned his body for feelings as he brought to mind a mental image of Maria Elena and Lucas. He breathed and watched himself, scanning over and over again. The world around him faded as a place of spaciousness opened within him. Tony called it coming into the Presence. Pitcairn refrained from any opinion. All he knew was that it soothed him, and on occasion, a sense of clarity or direction might emerge.

After a few moments that felt like it could have been hours, he felt the light touch of Maria Elena's fingers on his cheek. Taking one more deep breath, he opened his eyes.

"Almost there, Cito."

"Yep," he replied as he sat up to stretch and yawn.

"Are you okay?"

He looked past her out the window at the city quickly rising up beneath them. "Never better."

"Really?"

"Emmy, we could not possibly be more on track." He grinned hugely. "Of course, we have no idea where it leads, but it wouldn't be worth it if we did."

After securing their luggage and a rental car, they were soon driving into the Piedmont, the rolling foothills of the Appalachians. Three hours later, they arrived at the Westin Poinsett in downtown Greenville, South Carolina. It was the namesake, lobby information told them, of Joel Poinsett, the South Carolinian who introduced the poinsettia to the United States.

Almost immediately, they knew they were in an unfamiliar culture. When Maria Elena mentioned to the bellman that they had come over from New Mexico, he replied, offhandedly but with obvious sincerity, "No ma'am, you came down South." She grinned and winked at Pitcairn.

Before dinner they walked the downtown area, which proved to be quite vibrant and alive for a winter's day. No doubt it helped that the sun was out and the temperature was in the fifties. Still, as they stood on Liberty Bridge, the beautiful, curving suspension bridge above the waterfalls of the Reedy River, they admitted being surprised by the lovely little city. South Carolina's reputation had not prepared them. In fact, Pitcairn recalled a much-dated political comment about the state: "Too small to be a republic, too large for an insane asylum."

Dinner surprised them too: nouveau southern fare at Soby's New South, on the advice of a man they'd met on the street. They found the meal exceptional and comforting, and the cider-braised collards especially hit the spot.

With Maria Elena curled up in their plush bed, Pitcairn studied the second journal at a small table. He wished he could simply read in bed, but his training as a journalist required him to study the material, jotting down notes as he read Lucas's thoughts.

"Emmy, this is really interesting. Lucas deliberately chose the Sufi place to delve into unconditional love. Apparently, his stay in Idaho at the Fourth Way Retreat Center taught him about the importance of making his intentions into what they call a school."

"What? What's the Fourth Way?" she asked.

"A Russian guy named Gurdjieff was kind of the founder. As best I can tell, they say you make an aim, not a goal. A goal is too specific. If I understand Lucas's thoughts, you tie the hands of the Divine when you get too specific. He calls God "X" here."

"X?"

Pitcairn laughed. "Yeah, like the unknown in algebra. You create an aim that is to solve for X . . . I guess. Then you establish a school to practice your aim."

"And I thought the Catholic Church was complicated."

"Sure, but here's the part that makes sense to me. I get it that Higher Power can't be known. Believe me I get that. So I'm good with X. And it makes sense that you'd set this aim, which is probably about as unknown as X itself. Seems like Lucas was aware he had a lot to learn about unconditional love, so all he did was admit that to be the case. Then he decided to use the Center for Mercy as his outer school to learn what he needed."

He turned to Maria Elena. "Make sense?"

"I think you think too much."

"Fair enough, but let me read you this passage." He turned back and paused. "Hey, in his first journal, he referred to some deity named Teo. Does that ring any bells with you? Maybe something to do with Hawaiian healing?"

"No idea. So is it Teo or X?"

"Good question. And I don't know. But I'll call Kate in the morning and ask her about Teo.

"Here's the passage, Emmy."

There has always been hate. Always will be. X, the secret has to be above my human self. How do I see no evil? How do I rise above myself to love even in the face of hate? How do I turn the other cheek? Break my heart open.

"Cito, that is just not right!" Maria Elena exclaimed. "Here's a kid looking to love, going so far as to retreat from the world to learn, and some bastard blows him up!"

He looked up at her.

"W! T! F!"

"Are you trying to clean up your language now?"

"No, you ass. I'm trying to make a point. There is something so so wrong about what happened to Lucas."

He could not disagree

▸9◂

AGITATION WOKE PITCAIRN EARLY, EVEN BY EAST COAST standards. At four o'clock, he was walking steadily through the park along the river. The source of his disturbance wasn't clear, but he was not unfamiliar with the routine. It was one that had repeated itself countless times in his sobriety. When something was working his insides, once the minimal sleep requirements were met, he would awaken with nervous energy that demanded movement. Learning about trauma had helped him find that the alternate-side motion of walking soothed the old wounds he bore. It was the same way that rocking calmed babies and their mothers, and perhaps those who were grieving or had mental health issues as well. An added benefit for him was the clarity of thought that often emerged.

For a time, he increased his pace and simply concentrated on his breath. It was cold enough to see each exhalation. Before long, he could feel the agitation slipping away, replaced by a grounded feeling in the pit of his belly.

Suddenly as he came around a curve in the path, Pitcairn faced a grassy area filled with hundreds of motionless silver and red pinwheels glinting in the streetlight. On a banner, he read: "For all the women who have suffered from needless violence."

In an instant, he realized it was the questions Lucas had posed that had been gnawing at him. *"How do I see no evil? How do I rise above myself to love even in the face of hate? How do I turn the other cheek?"*

In front of him stood a testament to the importance of these questions. And from within rose the need to sit in this place. He went over to a bench and settled into a meditation pose.

But before he could quiet himself, a memory surfaced. It was the heart-aching words of Aaron Everett, a young man who had been in love with Maggie Andrews, a woman raped and murdered by serial killer Daniel Davidson for whom Pitcairn had advocated and launched the Crucifix Protests.

"I've never stopped missing Maggie," Aaron said. "I think about her all the time. She may be all I think about."

Pitcairn had asked the young man if he was going to be all right, to which he replied, "No. I'm not all right. I'm not sure I ever will be."

In a flash, Pitcairn realized that the saga that had begun with Davidson and the Crucifix Protests was not at an end. The exploration of forgiveness and inherent innocence that had started there would be continued through Lucas and his inquiry into unconditional love.

The thought drew a chuckle from him. Those who believed in Higher Power often maintained there were forces at work to which we were oblivious. While Pitcairn could acknowledge the possibility of the Tao, a consistent way of things that included universal laws, the idea of a deity that was rearranging the pieces on the chessboard of life was a stretch.

He sighed, reminded himself to stay in "not-knowingness," then settled into what Tony would call the Silence. After a time, he stood and stretched, then meandered through the pinwheels before heading toward the hotel. Every now and again, he would reach down and spin one. As he did, he saw the names of women written on the vanes of the pinwheels, and felt joy at the unexpected memorial.

After looping through the park, Pitcairn arrived at a coffee shop on Main Street when it opened at six. Over a large cup of steaming dark roast, he pulled Lucas's second journal out of his backpack and slowly began leafing through it. What he saw amazed him. The entire volume was filled with a detailed inventory—an accounting—of the many ways and occasions when Lucas saw himself as failing to love without condition.

Quickly Pitcairn flipped back to the first page.

Where to begin, X? . . . Perhaps honestly taking stock.

It was moments such as these when Pitcairn was convinced that the founders of AA had been in conversation with many others in the emergent spirituality of the early twentieth century. It was simply too much of a parallel that a kid studying the Fourth Way and New Thought from that period would arrive at the same jumping off point as AA's program of recovery. The heart of AA's twelve steps looked toward an inventory of shortcomings, blockages, or impediments rather than seeking pleasant and comfortable reassurances from religion or philosophy. It's much easier, he knew, to exhort others to love than to delve into the limitations on one's own capacity for loving.

He riffled through the journal, pausing here and again to study Lucas's thoughts. Certain words and phrases recurred often: hatred, judgment, punishment, condemnation.

Today I bit a hand that feeds me. Mrs. Carthage has been so kind in letting me use her studio at any hour of the day. But I took it for granted. How could I forget her kindness and snap at her when she told me the weekend events would require me to stay away? It is obvious she appreciates me. I wasn't able to reciprocate when I wasn't getting what I wanted.

Pitcairn paused to make notes in his own journal. Then he checked the time. He knew Tony always wrapped up his morning practice by five o'clock, so he decided to call to chat.

"Hi Tony, it's Pitcairn. Are you available for some counsel?"

"Of course," he replied.

Pitcairn described his unfolding understanding of Lucas's exploration of unconditional love, then asked: "So Tony, what do you make of this kid and his quest?"

The priest considered his response for a long time. "Kevin, I think you are right that this is a continuation of the innocence work you began. In some ways, we might suggest unconditional love as the appropriate response to seeing others through the eyes of innocence." There was quiet again before Father Anthony went on. "I'm hesitant to suggest anything further for fear it will impair your own exploration. As you know from our discussions, one of the worst things we can do is pre-empt someone's search for understanding."

"You mean I've got to hammer it out on the anvil of my own experience."

"Precisely. And I do love that phrase each time you use it."

"Tony, I've been using it so long I can't remember where it came from. But it's probably not original."

The priest laughed. "Is anything?"

"Every now and again it seems like something new and real emerges."

"That urges me to offer you a thought that has occurred several times as we've been talking." Pitcairn heard him take a sip of coffee or tea. "Kevin, I have long contemplated the turning of the cheek to which Lucas alludes. The exact scripture is 'Do not resist one who is evil. But if anyone strikes you on the right cheek, turn to him the other also.' And goodness knows there are more interpretations than we could imagine since on the face of it, it's a pretty radical proposition."

"Exactly my thoughts, Tony. But I have a feeling you interpret it differently."

Father Anthony laughed again, this time much more happily. "Kevin, you know how much I enjoy looking for what many would call the esoteric meaning of the scriptures. So much of what was written should never be interpreted literally. That's definitely true in this case, and I think you'll appreciate it given the ground you have already covered."

"Okay," Pitcairn said, "you have definitely got my attention."

"Good. You see the only possible way to offer up the other cheek with any degree of consciousness is to perceive no wrong in the first blow. That means you must understand that the person who strikes you is innocent, that for whatever reason, they are behaving in a violent fashion that is consistent with their reality. . . that they are not in fact evil but in some way deluded or irrational."

"No shit!" The words fell from his mouth too quickly. "Sorry, Tony."

"Kevin, it's fine. God is not deterred by any word. I believe he hears and responds to the passion and awe within the word."

"You are so not Catholic."

They both laughed as Pitcairn segued to what seemed like another subject. "Before I come back to that, I gotta tell you something. Do you know the song *Hallelujah* by Leonard Cohen?"

"Of course. A beautiful song."

"Yeah, but isn't he saying exactly the same thing when he says, 'the holy or the broken hallelujah?'"

"That is a beautiful observation, Kevin. Yes. It is not the word that matters but that which imbues the word."

"Tony, I can never get my head around the fact that we can talk about bombings, Jesus, resist not evil, and Leonard Cohen in the same conversation."

"It is a delight, but I must ask what you think of this esoteric interpretation of turning the other cheek."

"Perfect, Tony. Perfect. It is exactly what I can see about innocence. And it's the only way to avoid the ripple effects of violence . . . to see no evil. But how do you connect that to unconditional love?"

"Easy enough, Kevin. In order to love without condition, mustn't we be free of the perception of any evil, any wrongdoing, anything being amiss?"

"Oh . . . ." Pitcairn said as words trailed away. A lengthy pause followed.

"Kevin?"

"Yep."

"One more thing. Do not forget the tiger."

This was a central idea that had been provided to Pitcairn during the Crucifix Protests, that the conscious mind is like a monkey perched on the shoulders of the tiger of the unconscious that is hurtling through the jungle of reality at breakneck speed. The monkey creates an unending series of stories to explain things in a desperate attempt to feel in control.

"You mean I'm not in charge."

"Exactly. And it will be helpful for you to remember that, since the monkey tends to forget."

"Got it. Thanks for the reminder. There's a lot of value in that idea."

"Please keep me apprised, Kevin. I've got to go."

After getting his coffee refilled, Pitcairn returned to Lucas's journal. Much of what he'd written showed his exposure to many inventories through AA, a boilerplate of human failings: Anger, resentment, and retaliation permeated the young man's observations, along with the flip side of personality: ingratiation, conformity, and all manner of people-pleasing. While the bulk of it may have been garden-variety humanity, it was still a remarkably honest and expansive self-appraisal.

The book's final page had a mixed bag of observations and comments. The final note caught Pitcairn's attention:

X, I fear my blindness will not allow Your Light to enter.

It reminded him that originally, it was his late sponsor, Clint, who had coined the phrase: "I can only be as open-minded as my closed-mindedness will permit." Clint had always laughed after he said it, but that never diminished the importance the idea held for him.

After a few moments deep in thought, he called Kate Delmonico. She was a long-time connection who had written several books on the brain and its development, possessed a near-photographic memory, and could readily recall obscure information. He was afraid it was too early, but she picked up after several rings. "Kate . . . your brain engaged yet?"

"Pitcairn, I'm guessing you were up early, thinking too much before dawn, and could not wait until a decent hour to call."

"Right on all counts, Kate. And the only reason I would call is because I knew you would appreciate the chance to play with an idea or two just to get your day started. Believe me, if I knew anyone smarter, I'd call them."

"Bullshit," she said as she laughed. "Just plain bullshit. But you're right about playing with ideas. What have you got?"

"Do you know of any spiritual reference to Teo, some kind of deity, maybe from Hawaiian or Polynesian culture?"

There was a long silence. "Well, you're probably pointed to the right culture. With an apostrophe in it, it's a Samoan surname, but I can't recall anything in the religious realm. Let me do a quick online search."

He could hear her keystrokes, glad she'd been awake and at the computer when he called.

A short time later, she replied. "Nope, nothing I can find."

"Damn."

"Why? What strange world are you in now?"

He laughed. "I'm out in South Carolina doing some research on the bombing up near Santa Fe. One of the people who was injured, a guy named Lucas, made reference to it in some of his writings."

"Ah, you wrote about him in your last commentary. Nice. But I'm always amazed how you find your way to these stories."

"Me too, Kate. Me too." Pitcairn stretched. "Anything else you've come across you think I might find useful?"

"As a matter of fact, let me email you some material on some new work on post-traumatic growth. I think you'll find it useful with all your interest in trauma."

"Growth?" he asked.

"Yes sir, PTG, post-traumatic growth. Interesting idea, isn't it?"

"I can't wait. Thanks so much, Kate. You're a peach"

"*De nada*," she responded as she disconnected.

Pitcairn thought for a few moments. He had never in his life called someone a peach. Yet here he was in the middle of the broad swath of peach-growing country, and the phrase had somehow crept into his words. It was moments like this that made it easy to believe there was a lot going on in the unconscious mind.

With that, he could sense a path unfolding before him. It was premature to think he could understand it. Yet experience told him a way was emerging.

▶10◀

THE HOTEL ROOM WAS STILL DARK, BUT MARIA ELENA SPOKE as soon as the door closed. "You were up early."

"Yep, some of the material from the journal was working me. I took a walk, then talked to Tony and Kate." He briefly described the morning's experiences as he settled onto the bed beside her.

"A busy guy," she replied. "Do you have time to take a girl to breakfast? I'm hungry."

"There's a place two blocks from here that includes a grits bar with any breakfast."

"A grits bar?"

"Sure enough. Grits with all the fixin's you can imagine."

"We really are down South," she added with amusement as she slipped out of bed.

After a leisurely breakfast which included multiple trips to the grits bar, he told her he planned to drive north and west of the city to see what he could find about the bomber. He had also located a noontime AA meeting in the town of Easley that he planned to attend. Clint had always said that when you traveled, it might just be so you could hear something you needed to know that you couldn't or wouldn't hear in your usual realm. A good possibility for deepening your recovery, and your spiritual awakening.

"Emmy, do you want to come with me? Or is this going to be a self-care day for you?"

"I found a well-known psychic and made an appointment for a sitting with her."

"A psychic? Here in the most conservative community in the most conservative state in America?"

She laughed. "Greenville is not what it seems, Cito."

"Is anything?" he countered.

"Seriously, Cito. After the time on the West Mesa, I've got my own inner callings along with the curiosity to follow them."

"Fair enough. This should make for an interesting conversation tonight. I'm chasing bombers while you're in the ethereal realm."

She laughed and shrugged.

After ensuring that Maria Elena could easily walk to the psychic's office on North Main Street, Pitcairn drove away to get a feel for the area where Grady Donovan had lived, which began in the small town of Travelers Rest. Meandering west, he followed rural highways past out-of-season fruit and vegetable stands, and through the second- and third-growth forests that ranged along the mountains. The occasional tiny town center appeared, each with its requisite tavern and barbeque joint. He crossed several reservoirs in a country that felt quite remote and underdeveloped. At Walhalla, a rustic little burg, he looped back toward Pickens in route to the AA meeting he sought.

The skanky blonde who stood smoking furiously at the entry to the storefront that housed AA should have been a signal. She barely glanced at him as he walked by, unlike the group's common friendliness. The chilliness continued inside. A few worn men circled the coffeepot, barely nodding when he greeted them.

Pitcairn sat in a chair in a corner near the door to wait for the meeting to begin. He noted that the unwelcoming atmosphere had caused him to revert to an old, self-protective behavior: a wall behind him to protect his back, a corner spot which no one could approach without his knowing, and proximity to the door for ease of exit. He nodded to himself in recognition of the old pattern from his drinking and drugging days.

The room began to slowly fill as alcoholics filtered in. Most glanced his way and nodded, but no one extended a hand or made any real effort to greet him. As the minutes ticked toward noon, he replayed a long-ago conversation with Clint. He had learned, he told Pitcairn, over many years in sobriety, that AA meetings varied widely, and some were just not very healthy places to be.

With that memory a thought arose, a scripture of all things: "And whoever shall not receive you, nor hear your words, when you leave, shake the dust from your feet." He pondered where he might have heard the words but could find no clear answer. Just before the meeting began, he trusted his instincts and left. Though it might keep these folks sober, he had no use for bad AA.

Pitcairn retraced his route into town to stop at a diner for lunch. His interest was twofold. First, to experience local food, which was just plain fun. Second, to see what he could learn about Donovan. Diners tended to be ideal for picking up information from the locals.

After ordering pork chops with mashed potatoes, collards, and cornbread, he pulled out his pad and scanned his notes. He was deep in thought about what to do when the waitress delivered a basket heaped with slices of cornbread.

Pitcairn looked up with some surprise, quickly checked her name badge and asked, "Tillie, I'm researching a local fellow by the name of Grady Donovan and wondered if you might have any suggestions about who or where would be a good place to start."

He watched her face carefully to see if her emotions would betray anything. All he saw was pursed lips as she considered his question. There was no apparent concern or guile, which probably meant she did not know of Donovan's significance.

In a drawl that was smooth as syrup, Tillie replied, "Don't know that I do, honey. But let me go ask Roy up at the counter."

A moment later, as she spoke to an older man wearing an orange Clemson Tigers ball cap, Pitcairn could see that the question had struck a chord. Roy turned toward him with a hardened gaze and muscles that clenched and released in his jaw. Pitcairn nodded politely but the man's countenance didn't change.

The stare-down ended when the man muttered something to himself and walked over and exited.

When Tillie returned with his lunch a few minutes later, she remained quite pleasant. "Guess Roy had to go. Did he say anything to you before he left?"

"No ma'am," Pitcairn replied.

"Well, isn't that the funniest thing. Roy is just the nicest man." She shrugged. "Can I get you anything else, darlin'?"

"No, Tillie, but thank you. I appreciate you."

She smiled brightly and moved on to another table.

The food was only fair, but filling. He scanned the email on his phone and saw that Kate had sent him the promised materials on post-traumatic growth. Unfortunately, it was too hard to read the attachments on the small screen, so it would have to wait.

After lunch, he stopped for gas and asked a woman behind the counter about Donovan. It was obvious from her reaction that she knew he was the bomber, but she didn't seem to have an opinion about him. Just as he turned to leave, she volunteered a suggestion: "Ya know, the boys up at the Country Store know everyone. You might try them."

"Country Store?"

"Yep. Just up Highway 8 outside of Pickens."

"Thanks."

"Sure, hon."

A short while later, Pitcairn pulled into the lot of a tidy but weathered wooden building. In front stood a line of poles flying what seemed to be every flag in the history of the Confederacy, each with a small plaque describing its timing and purpose. A large sign welcomed you to the Country Store, then listed its wares: Southern and Historical Memorabilia. Pitcairn could see a rifle rack in each of the several well-kept, older trucks in the lot, and the Stars and Bars insignia on two bumpers as well.

As he contemplated a scene notably at odds with what "Country Store" had led him to expect, he felt a tightening in his gut. Then he recalled the harmlessness of the clerk at the gas station and, re-assured, opened the car door and stepped out.

As soon as he crossed the threshold, still holding the door handle, he saw that five men had stopped their conversation and were scrutinizing him. He nodded and stepped forward, suddenly aware that he was slightly extending his hand with the notepad in it as if in a non-threatening gesture.

"Woman at a gas station in Easley suggested you guys know a lot about the area, and I should come see you with a few questions I've got."

The men studied him, and he could see they had noticed his notepad. He held it up. "Trying to learn a bit about Grady Donovan. You know him?"

He saw them tense. The man behind the counter slowly stroked his stubbled chin. Pitcairn watched his eyes and could see unspoken communication between the men. When the lean, rugged fellow on the left pivoted slightly toward his right, Pitcairn knew to begin his retreat. With his own history in violent settings, he had that crucial sixth sense for such things.

Raising his hands to gesture openly, he spoke carefully, "Sorry. Didn't mean to pry. No harm intended." Without turning to look away, he stepped back to the door. With a quick glance, he turned the handle, nodded to the men and exited. Moving swiftly to the car, he saw the store's door open and two of the men walk purposefully onto the porch to watch him leave. One of them lifted a cell phone to his ear. Pitcairn felt more than saw a hardened glint on the man's face.

While no stranger to such settings, it had been many years since he'd felt that kind of energy. "Shit," he said to himself as he glanced in the rearview mirror and accelerated so quickly the tires spun lightly. "Shit."

▸11◂

PITCAIRN SPENT THE REST OF THE AFTERNOON DRIVING AND thinking. While his commitment to telling the backstory about violence and its effects on people was unswerving, he also knew better than to stir up the locals in a way that itself could produce violent reactions. No point in becoming part of the ripple effect. How to proceed would require careful consideration.

On multiple occasions, he found himself watching his rearview mirror and scanning his surroundings. The encounter with the men at the Country Store had left him with a nagging feeling of unsettledness. While there was no apparent cause, he'd learned to pay attention to that sixth sense his former life in addiction had cultivated.

His meandering brought him back to Greenville in time for a five o'clock AA meeting at a beautiful brick church overlooking the Reedy River. He'd thought carefully about the slight emotional hangover he felt from his experiences at the Country Store and the earlier AA meeting. It seemed to warrant some good AA if he could find it. After leaving Maria Elena a message about his plans, he sauntered into the basement meeting room.

In contrast to the earlier gathering, he was greeted immediately by a vibrant redhead who introduced herself as Rosemary. After briefly exchanging personal information, she introduced him to Clarence and Elmer, the requisite old guys sitting in a corner, then promptly shuttled him to the kitchen and coffee where two other women were chatting.

"Pitcairn, this is Nicky and this is Betty."

Before he could even say hello, the three of them launched into lightning-fast banter—until Rosemary interjected, "Sorry, Pitcairn. They call us the Harpies, and we're just a little bit crazy. Cocaine will do that." All three laughed.

Nicky jumped in. "But we're good people. Betty honey, will you get this man a cup of coffee."

"Okay," she replied. "First, though, what kind of a name is Pitcairn?"

"Betty, you gossip whore, get the man some coffee," Rosemary ordered.

Betty rolled her eyes. "Fuck you. It's a fair question."

Pitcairn laughed. "It is fair, and I get asked it often enough."

As Betty turned to get the coffee, Pitcairn continued. "It's an old Scottish surname. My dad was known as Scotty, a drunk I might add. Somewhere between being Little Kevvie growing up, and the rooms of recovery, it's just how everyone came to know me."

All three women nodded. Then Rosemary asked, "What brings you here, Pitcairn? Looking for your old Scottish bloodlines here in the Highlands of the Carolinas?"

Briefly he explained as they listened carefully. The women may have identified as being slightly crazy, but he could see they were rock solid sober.

Nicky's lips were pursed as she shook her head. "You're not going to believe this, but I know who you need to talk to." The other women turned to her. "I know the bomber's half-sister."

Betty gasped. "No fuckin' way!" She quickly raised her hand to her mouth, "Sorry! I'm trying not to cuss. But can you believe it? Another AA miracle!"

"Oh, for Christ's sake, Betty. Is there anything you don't see as a miracle?" Rosemary scoffed.

The two went at for a few moments before Nicky stopped them. "Damn it, girls! Can I tell the man what I know?"

She proceeded to explain how she regularly attended retreats and meditations at the Bodhi Mandala Zen Buddhist Center outside of Asheville. During that time, she had come to use the resident teacher at the center as her spiritual mentor. That teacher went by only a first name, Elise, and even that was pseudonym. She had deliberately estranged herself from her family and community, and sought refuge as what was known as a teacher in hiding. She and Nicky had become quite close over several years.

Now Pitcairn interjected. "Nicky, first I have to second Betty. This would be a pretty amazing connection." He winked at Betty, then turned back. "Are you sure, though?" Her explanation quickly slipped into nearly untraceable logic, but it did seem to be the case. She would have continued if Rosemary hadn't reminded them the meeting was starting.

A short while later the meeting rolled into what Pitcairn thought would be the typical behavior improvement realm. Many alcoholics, he knew, believed they just needed to behave better, but after a few people spoke along those lines, a worn-looking man in the back of the room leaped in.

"God damn it! This program is not about gettin' good. It's about gettin' useful. If gettin' good worked, we'd all be in church doin' what they tell us we ought to do." He paused for a breath and laughed at himself. "Sorry. Name's Bob, and I'm an alcoholic, and sometimes a real asshole."

"Hi Bob!" rang the response amid laughter from the attendees.

"Really am sorry to cuss since I know that offends you church goin' folk. But I tried my whole life to improve my conduct. Booze didn't allow it. And AA didn't teach me to get good." He paused to breathe again, limited by his obvious lung disease.

"You remember old Lucky? He said over and over again, 'God's what's left when the bullshit's gone.' What he meant was that AA cleans up the bullshit. When it gets cleaned up, we don't get a better behavin' drunk, but a new man . . . or woman. And what's new is we stop bein' so self-absorbed and start becoming useful."

"That's why just tryin' to help others is a fool's game in the end. I know, that offends you people who think helpin' others is the whole point, but that's just more church behavin'. You know it as well as I do. You can't give away what you don't have. So it starts with cleanin' house . . . gettin' rid of the bullshit. Then somethin' new can emerge, and that somethin' new can work with others. Hell, that somethin' new is a miracle, and I sure as hell can't produce it myself. If I could, I'd never have been a drunk and I sure wouldn't need these meetings and you people."

Bob came to an awkward halt. He frowned for a moment, then went on. "What you just saw is why Thomas Merton went into silent retreat. I'm so shot through with self I can't open my damn mouth without bullshit happenin'. So I'll stop right there. Sorry to those who don't want to hear cussin' in God's house."

With that, the meeting went in a new direction—cleaning one's own house. Rosemary leaned over to whisper in his ear. "Bob does that all the time. And it sets the meeting on track when he does." Pitcairn turned to smile and nod.

When the meeting ended, the Harpies pulled him close again, first chatting at length about Bob and the meeting, then veering back to Grady Donovan's half-sister. Nicky agreed to contact Elise and call Pitcairn with details about meeting her. Then Rosemary announced, "We're going with you!"

He laughed. "Okay. Gotta trust the river knows where it's bound."

With that they parted company. It was only a short drive to the hotel. When he opened the door to the room, he was hit with the scent of lavender and the flickering of candlelight. Maria Elena beckoned to him from the bed. He dropped his jacket and stepped toward her.

"Talking about the river. . . ." he muttered.

"What?" she replied.

"Oh, Emmy, it is so clear that the tiger is having its way with me. But I think that story had best wait."

"You are so perceptive," she purred. "I just spent the better part of the day in a most interesting conversation with the psychic. It stirred me up. I'll tell you more about that, but first, if I was the tiger, Cito, you'd be in great danger of getting mauled right now."

He laughed, cast his arms wide, and toppled onto the bed.

Maria Elena kissed him, then slowly began to peel away his clothes. Pitcairn was instantly aware of her warmth and softness. "You are very pliable."

"Shut up! Don't ruin the moment," she ordered as she slipped close, blanketing him with tiny kisses.

He closed his eyes and surrendered.

Sometime later, he awoke from their play feeling driven by hunger. Emmy was dozing lightly with her head on his chest. She stirred as he leaned forward and kissed the top of her head.

As he gently cupped her neck in his hand, he felt a solid metal form hidden by the braided hair at base of her skull.

"What's this?"

"It's the brass piece from the West Mesa. The psychic told me it would protect me better if I wore it as a charm. She said if I kept it close, and hidden, it would be prayer."

"Sounds like a story to me. First, though, are you hungry?"

"Ravenous," she replied. "Ravenous."

"I'm told there's food for the soul just down the street. A place that overlooks the river."

She looked up and grinned. "I have got to be the luckiest woman alive."

"Say more. . . ."

"Nope. If you don't know why, I'm certainly not going to dispel your ignorance."

As they dressed, Pitcairn listened to a voice message while Maria Elena was in the bathroom. "We're headed to Asheville tomorrow," he told her, "with a bunch of Harpies."

"Harpies?"

"Over dinner, beautiful. I've got stories to tell too."

As they walked, Pitcairn listened as Maria Elena described the sitting with the psychic. She admitted it all seemed rather textbook, but her sense about the wearing of the charm felt strangely prescient.

"Sometimes you just have to trust the feelings," he observed.

"Oh, I do, Cito."

▸12◂

THE NEXT DAY BEGAN IN A TORRENT WHEN MARIA ELENA RE-turned from retrieving items from the car. "Cito, some son-of-a-bitch slit our tires!"

"What?"

"Some bastard slit the tires on our rental car," she repeated emphatically.

"Really?"

"Do I look like I'm anything other than dead serious?"

He chuffed in response. "Punctures?"

"Who the hell knows, Cito? But four flat tires is not a coincidence."

He moved thoughtfully toward the door. "Okay. Let me go check it out. Be right back." He considered the possibilities. Maybe it was random, but Maria Elena was probably right that coincidence was unlikely. His sixth sense again radiated from his gut. Remembering the man on his cell phone, he intuited that he had stirred things up with his visit to the Country Store.

The sidewall punctures, obviously made by a sharp object, gave him pause. "The bastards followed me," he whispered out loud. He could feel his resolve to push forward, and the hint of a grin as he recognized that the tiger had entered new terrain. "Let's do it," he muttered as he made note to himself to exercise more caution.

The rental car company replaced the car in less than an hour, upgraded to a mid-size SUV. Pitcairn tipped the driver generously, then walked around the corner with Maria Elena to the coffee shop where the Harpies soon appeared.

Rosemary, Betty, and Nicky welcomed her like a long-lost sister. Pitcairn could recognize the feeling of kinship typical of recovering communities as he listened to them engage with Maria Elena.

There was a moment when the Harpies broke into their ritualistic banter debating the merits of increasing the number of espresso shots in their drinks. Maria Elena shook her head in amusement. And she laughed when Nicky used her hand like a dowsing wand that began to tremble when she upped her order with the barista to a fourth shot.

"Ha, ha, ha!" exclaimed Rosemary. "That's the buzz-o-meter that tells her when she's almost over the edge!"

Soon both vehicles were easing across the Piedmont into the mountains. It was wonderful to see this new landscape. Pitcairn and Maria Elena chatted as she searched her phone for information about the area.

"Cito, while you meet with Elise, I'd like to drive into Asheville and wander around the River Arts District. You just never know what there is to be found."

He laughed easily. "No doubt you'll find it, Emmy. Tenacity becomes you."

She cocked her head as she thought. "Did you ever realize how perfect is the idea of becoming? We think of it as beauty, when in fact it is to be-come. I be-come tenacious." She paused. "Or maybe it is the reverse, tenacity be-comes me."

Pitcairn sensed something in her words. "Where'd that come from?"

She turned to stare at him. "That's interesting. The psychic. Well, she didn't say that exactly, but when she told me I should braid the charm into my hair, she said it would keep me stronger than I imagined I would need to be."

He glanced at Maria Elena. She was deep in contemplation. He reminded himself to proceed with caution in his pursuit of the bomber's backstory.

They drove in silence following the Harpies and exited from the freeway with them, pulling into a massive farmers' market five minutes later. Even before they opened the doors, they could hear the women bantering. "Fruit stop!" Betty explained. They toured the rows of fresh produce, artisan cheeses and meats, and local arts, returning to their cars fortified with bags of fruit and cheese.

When Pitcairn explained Maria Elena's plan, Rosemary quickly suggested, "Pitcairn, why don't you ride with us. Maria Elena, if you just follow this road a few miles, you'll be in the Arts District. How about if we all meet at the Goldenrod Cafe at five?"

Everyone exchanged cell phone numbers, Pitcairn kissed Emmy, and they went their separate ways. The Harpies planned to traipse around the countryside while he met with Elise.

▸13◂

DURING THE THIRTY-MINUTE DRIVE TO THE ZEN CENTER, Nicky told him a number of details about Elise. Pitcairn realized that her obvious adoration meant what he was hearing might not be entirely reliable but still found it useful.

The last few miles of paved road crept up a steep ascent through tangled undergrowth. Had it not been a south-facing slope, the increasing elevation likely would have made it impossible to clear the ice and snow that lay in shadows and crevices. When the road leveled again, he saw the sign for the center. It was beautifully painted with a turquoise theme that immediately reminded him of New Mexico. A sharp right turn took them onto a gravel road which they followed to the entrance.

Emerging from a massive thicket of what Betty said was wild rhododendron, the forest suddenly gave way to an opening. Rosemary brought the car to a stop and snorted. "Artsy-fartsy, aren't they?"

Nicky promptly took offense. "Damn it, Rosemary, why do you have to be such an asshole whenever you see something artistic? You'd think your sobriety would be better than that. . . ."

"Look you bitch," Rosemary began with a screech as Pitcairn opened the door, grabbed his backpack and stepped out to escape what was quickly becoming a nasty exchange. He surveyed his surroundings as his long stride took him forward.

An expansive meadow had been wrested from the tangled growth. Small splotches of snow were scattered over the dormant grasses. At the end of the long, open space stood a trio of large yurts that appeared to be connected by covered passages. Beyond them was a smaller yurt with a thin stream of smoke rising from a roof vent, which, along with the scent of burning wood, made for an idyllic scene. In the middle of the meadow, carefully tended topiaries and plantings surrounding a labyrinth for walking meditation. Sculptures could be seen sprinkled around the opening.

Pitcairn surveying the scene. It was a beautiful place, though he could hear the muted voices of the Harpies in a heated conversation as the car crept down the road winding through the forest to his left. He saw a dark blue Toyota Prius tucked into a parking area sheltered in the trees, and two sheds beyond it that were probably for equipment. He drank in the serenity, breathing deeply as he walked toward the yurts.

The fragile atmosphere was broken as Nicky's scream of "Fuck you!" carried through the still air. A car door slammed shut, and tires spun on the gravel as Rosemary reversed course. He could see Nicky walking furiously toward the smaller yurt, both arms splayed above her head, each displaying a defiant middle finger.

Pitcairn laughed at the contrast and shook his head a little. The AA community was filled with strange relationships, often punctuated with dysfunctional behavior that marked people in recovery as fully human.

He slowed down and watched as Nicky sat down cross-legged in an oversized, brilliant turquoise Adirondack chair. As he got closer, he could see her breathing deliberately and trying to settle herself, tears glistening on her cheeks.

In that moment, the door of the yurt opened and a very slender and graceful woman appeared. Surely it was Elise. She went toward Nicky, then glanced at him and nodded an acknowledgment before kneeling with her hands on each of Nicky's knees and speaking very softly. Nicky's head moved in apparent agreement as she sobbed. Slowly Elise's presence and words seemed to penetrate, and after a few minutes, Nicky took a deep breath as she pulled her shoulders back and lifted her chin. With her exhalation, she visibly relaxed and began to breathe more gently.

Pitcairn recognized immediately the same kind of calm, gentle attention Kari offered him when working with trauma. In fact, it was so similar that he imagined they might come from the same school of practice.

Elise knelt beside Nicky for a few more moments, carefully watching as she breathed. As she rose, Pitcairn again observed an uncanny grace in her movements. He overheard her speaking more loudly as she turned toward him. "Just be still. Hold the space. Breathe. Just breathe."

An almost-shy smile appeared as Elise bowed her head slightly with closed eyes while she raised her hands to her chest with palms together. Then she lifted her gaze to him with a startling depth and clarity. "Namaste."

Pitcairn smiled in response and replied with a nod of his head as well. "Namaste. Elise, I presume?"

"Yes. You have found me, Mr. Pitcairn, as I knew someone eventually would."

"Please, no need for formality. Most people just call me Pitcairn."

A look of curiosity crossed her face. "Even your friends?"

"Especially my friends, even my girlfriend for that matter. There's a story there of course, but I won't tire you with it."

She laughed. "I'd like to hear it, Pitcairn. Let's have some tea and you can tell me what I need to know about you including that story. I find it good to get a sense of someone before I share much about myself."

"Fair enough. And probably wise all things considered. A little protection."

"Oh, I have nothing to fear, Pitcairn. I'm simply very aware of the value of well-considered comments," she said as she turned and gestured toward the yurt.

"What about Nicky?" he asked.

"She knows what to do with herself. Not to worry."

▶14◀

STEPPING THROUGH THE DOOR, PITCAIRN SCANNED THE CIR-cular, sparsely furnished room. To the left was a small pallet for sleeping and a bookcase filled to overflowing, and to the right an obviously hand-built counter and cabinets that made for a small kitchenette. Toward the back stood the wood stove and a door he guessed to be a bathroom. Scattered around the carpeted floor were a variety of cushions, while several folding chairs leaned against a rib of the yurt.

He noted a faint perfumed smell, and looked to see a small diffuser for essential oils on a table near the stove. Then he realized that the space was all very well-lit with a slightly reddish atmosphere. He looked up to see a large almost-translucent skylight that included a very beautiful stained glass ring. Several metal mobiles hung from the ribs near the skylight.

"Very comfortable," he said as he stepped across the space toward where she stood at the counter. "A bit spartan."

Her laughter was almost musical. "It suits me well. And the larger yurts have much more to offer."

"Why three yurts?"

She concentrated as she poured tea into two ornate cups. "One is the communal space we use for teaching and workshops. The second has bunk beds for those who stay with us. And the one in back is a kitchen and dining hall."

Elise pulled a low, rectangular table from beneath the counter and placed it in the middle of the room directly under the skylight. She cast her arm with an open-palmed gesture, "Choose any cushions you like." Then she turned to bring the tea.

When they had settled, Elise made an easy movement to touch above her heart with her slightly cupped right hand. Then she nodded to him with a very welcoming look.

"So Pitcairn," she began, "Tell me about yourself. Who is it I'm getting ready to encounter?"

An amused look came to his face. "Now that is a most curious question, Elise." He thought for a few moments as her eyes watched him.

"Well, you know I'm a journalist. But I guess I'm more of an observer and a translator. A storyteller."

She sipped her tea as she continued to study him. "That is what you do, and I do wonder about what you've just said. But first, who are you? What do you bring into this world through your being?"

A guffaw shot from him before he could control it, after which he laughed at himself. "Elise, I wish I had an answer to that question. It seems like I was born to inquiry, and everywhere I go, I find more about which to inquire." He paused. "And every now and again something comes clear, and it's beautiful to behold."

Her eyes were wide now. "What do you find, Pitcairn?"

"I guess I see relationships between things . . . and understanding." Now his voice quickened. "It's just remarkable when things become evident, and something falls into place, and it's possible to provide an explanation that seems to defy what we hold to be true."

A comfortable quiet held them for long seconds.

"That's where observation and translation come in. Once you can see something in a new light, then you can describe it so others can see it."

"So you see through new eyes?"

He snorted. "Elise, that seems like way too much credit to give me. It's more like stumbling to be really honest. Like I have a sense of some kind of a scent that I can follow. And I'm told I am damned persistent."

She giggled. "That was my impression from what I learned of you online."

"Oh?" he countered.

"Yes. Based on the work you have done beginning with the Crucifix Protests, I am not surprised we should come to meet."

"And why is that?" Pitcairn asked.

She shook her head. "There is so much to say on that subject, more than we can cover today certainly, but first let me tell you about me. It seems only fair."

"Go to it!"

An easy smile crossed her lips. "I am a student, Pitcairn. A full-time, all-time student of what some call the Work. Aside from that, I am an artist. And often others come to me to learn from both."

"The Work?" he asked with great interest.

"Yes. The Work. And that's with a capital 'W.' Have you heard that idea before?"

"Not that I can recall." He reached up to rub his neck. "I have a feeling this is going to be a long conversation, Elise. Where do you suggest we begin?"

"With the earlier comment I made about the Crucifix Protests, and our meeting under such unusual circumstances. It seems to me that your efforts there would naturally bring you to Grady, and through him to me."

"I think you made a leap I'm not following, Elise."

"Of course. Of course." She paused. "The writing you have done on violence and its perpetuation would eventually have to bring you to Grady, or someone like him who did something horrible. And with that inquisitive streak of yours, you would just as naturally have to seek out the underlying causes. That necessarily would bring you to the conditions that produced such violence to learn all you could about it in order to explain it. Which brings you to me. I am a strange and perhaps inexplicable contrast to my brother. And somewhere amid it all would be this quest of yours for finding inherent inno-cence, even in something so destructive and tragic as a bombing."

"Damn," he replied. "How do you connect the dots so readily?"

She closed her eyes for a moment and took a breath as she col-lected herself. "It is the result of many years in the Work."

"Okay. You have to explain that to me. What is this Work?"

She smiled thoughtfully. "Many years ago, there was a Armen-ian named Gurdjieff."

In a startled moment he interrupted her. "Wait . . . Gurdjieff, the Fourth Way, Teo?"

She looked puzzled. "Yes. The Fourth Way is a variant of the Work, but I am not familiar with Teo."

"Well, shit!" he rolled his head in awkward acknowledgement. "Sorry, but you will not believe this. I'm not sure I do."

"Please go ahead, Pitcairn. I'm very curious about your reaction."

He proceeded to explain the backstory of Lucas and its relevance to the bombing and Grady Donovan. When he finished, she was smiling broadly.

"It would seem our coming together is far more than serendipitous, don't you think?" she asked.

"Elise, I have no idea what to think. And I'm a skeptic for the most part. But my spiritual mentor tells me I'm a man of faith, so I believe that you believe."

"Wonderful!" she replied with enthusiasm. "I can't wait to see what good will come of this otherwise-strange connection we have begun."

She closed her eyes again and breathed for a few moments.

"There is so much to discuss. Let me start with a brief overview of the Work and how it fits into my world here. Then we can talk about Grady. By the way, I was terribly saddened when I heard of what he'd done, and that he is dead. In some ways, I was not surprised; then again, how can I not be stunned how he acted out with such violence." She paused. "We have been estranged for many years. He was just too hard to be with."

Elise shrugged. "More about that later. Shall we talk about the Work?"

"By all means."

In the next ninety minutes, Pitcairn had many questions, and Elise proved to be an excellent teacher. In short, the Work was a process of self-observation and practices that she called psychologically based spirituality. The underlying premise was that the True Self, which Christians would likely call the soul, was waiting to be revealed. But much effort was needed to peel away layers of conditioning that stood between oneself and this inner realization.

At one point, Pitcairn used the recovery metaphor of peeling the layers of an onion, to which Elise quickly agreed as a good teaching analogy. She had even heard of the reference to X, the unknown, which she said was from an obscure group of students of the Work.

It was in her description of her own path that he found the greatest appreciation for Elise. She was solidly Zen Buddhist, though her foundation was more from the vantage point of the

Work. While the community had tried on multiple occasions to christen her with various titles, she had refused them all, preferring simply to be known as Elise. It was consistent with her notion of taking refuge, which she readily admitted was not a mainstream Buddhist perspective.

When Pitcairn compared it with the recovery community's orientation to anonymity, she readily embraced it, saying simply, "I want no distinction." A curious look crossed her face. "I deserve no distinction. As none of us do."

Elise stood and stretched. "Let me get you some fruit and crackers. And I want to go check on Nicky. If I'm not mistaken, I think I heard your friends return."

Pitcairn snacked as he relaxed into the silence of the yurt. It was the same kind of easiness he'd experienced when he visited Tony. He made a conscious note of that. It spoke volumes about the character of Elise.

When she returned, she said Nicky, Rosemary, and Betty were best of friends again, and expected to leave to meet Maria Elena in forty-five minutes.

"Do you mind if we continue this conversation tomorrow, Elise? I feel like we've barely scratched the surface."

"Certainly, that seems appropriate."

"But before we wrap up, can you give me the basics on Grady?"

Elise closed her eyes. Pitcairn sensed she was grounding herself in her practices. When she opened her eyes, there was a notable softness in them.

"So of course, we had the same dad. The main difference is that I was born before Daddy served in Vietnam in 1968 and 1969. Mom divorced him in 1970. She said it was like the man she married never came home. Grady's mom had a lot of emotional problems. I've often wondered about that."

"Wondered what?" Pitcairn interjected.

"Well, Daddy never talked much about what happened in Vietnam. There's no doubt though he was pretty damaged by it. It seems like Grady's mom was just disturbed enough to fit the man my father had become."

He nodded with appreciation for the point.

"At any rate, his mom vanished a few years later. Grady said she just got up from the couch one day and walked away. I don't know if that's exactly true, but it at least explains how he felt abandoned by her."

"Daddy killed himself when I was seventeen. Grady would have been about fourteen then." She paused as a look of sadness crossed her face. "There's so much I'd like to ask my dad, even though he might not have been willing or able to answer." She paused again. "He was not a bad man in any way. He was just not very available. I think it was just too difficult for him to be present."

"What happened to Grady?" Pitcairn asked.

"His Aunt Molly finished raising him, his mother's sister. Who knows how well that went, though it probably doesn't matter since Grady was already quite a mess."

Pitcairn listened expectantly.

"Nothing terrible really, just like he was lost. On the fringes, I guess. I imagine that's how he found his way to some of the more-troubled folk."

He described his experience at the Country Store to her.

"Yes. That fits. Grady couldn't really give voice to what he needed, but it's easy to see how he could be attracted to them."

The conversation waned. It was obvious they were finished for the day.

▸15◂

RIDING WITH THE HARPIES WAS ONCE AGAIN PLEASANT. THERE was no point in asking them about their reconciliation, so Pitcairn answered their questions about his conversation with Elise. They were somewhat disappointed that he had no great revelations to disclose, and, except for Nicky, were only mildly interested in his return the next day. Nicky asked if she could accompany him, to which he readily agreed.

When they arrived at the Goldenrod Cafe in Asheville's River Arts District, Maria Elena was nowhere to be found. They settled in with hot drinks and a few appetizers for which the cafe was well-known: garlic hummus and grilled eggplant spears. As the women continued to chat, Pitcairn studied the paintings on the walls. While not at the level he might find in Santa Fe, he found the artistic talent impressive.

By 5:20, Pitcairn began to wonder about Maria Elena, who tended to be punctual. He called her cell phone and was routed immediately to her voicemail. He assumed she was on a business or other important call. But after another twenty minutes and another call to her voicemail, his inner alarm began to sound, and he told the women he was becoming concerned. Rosemary immediately suggested that Betty and Nicky stay put, while she drove him around the arts district to search for her or the SUV.

While not terribly large, the River Arts District sprawled along the valley, so they agreed it would make sense to drive around first in the hope of finding the vehicle. Since it was Tuesday evening and the galleries and stores all closed by six o'clock, there were not many vehicles. As soon as they turned a corner near the Curve Galleries, he saw the SUV parked on the side of the road in the growing darkness.

Jumping from Rosemary's car even before she stopped, Pitcairn leaped toward the vehicle and quickly looked inside. Seeing nothing obviously amiss, he quickly scanned the shops and noted that only two were still open. Striding into the nearest, he startled the woman who had been moving to lock the door and close up. He quickly raised open hands to reassure her.

"I'm sorry I frightened you. My girlfriend is missing, but our car is out front. Perhaps you might remember her?" Pitcairn described Maria Elena, and the shop owner did recall her. There had not been many customers, and even fewer Hispanic women. Maria Elena had stopped in a few hours earlier.

Pitcairn thanked her and quickly left. He could see Rosemary talking on her phone, presumably updating the other Harpies. In the other open shop, the last customer, an older man, was discussing an abstract terra cotta sculpture with a woman who was obviously the artist. Pitcairn clearly telegraphed his anxiety. The artist graciously excused herself and turned to him.

"How may I help you?" she asked with a kind and gentle drawl somewhat at odds with the formality of her words.

Pitcairn explained the situation.

"Oh yes," the woman replied. "I'm certain it was your girlfriend. She purchased two stoneware mugs that were the last of my China Red Series. She was crazy for them."

"What time was that?"

The artist looked away to think, then refocused to look him in the eyes. "About three o'clock . . . I guess."

"Did she say anything about her plans?" Pitcairn asked urgently.

"Only that she was going to walk around the corner to the glass foundry. It's just down the hill."

Pitcairn remembered passing it as Rosemary drove up the hill. He thanked the woman and moved quickly to the door. As he stepped over the threshold, he heard her say, "I hope nothing is wrong."

Rosemary was standing outside her car, looking worried in the shadows of the approaching night. He gestured for her to follow and told her what he'd learned as they walked quickly toward the foundry. As they moved, his eyes scanned the roadside and vacant lots filled with brush. His senses were fully engaged, and while he wanted to believe all would be well, a fear grew within him.

The foundry was closed. Pitcairn felt a tension rising within him, and knew instinctively that he needed to be in motion.

"Rosemary, I don't think I can stand around. I need to move."

"Oh, honey, I understand. Crazy energy. You go look for her and I'll get the girls to come wait with me. We can call you if she gets here first."

Pitcairn felt a surge of gratitude and gave her a quick hug and a kiss on the cheek. "Whenever anyone, anywhere, reaches out for help, I want the hand of AA always to be there," he said.

"And for that, I am responsible," Rosemary countered, completing AA's responsibility statement. "Now go."

With no further urging, he moved swiftly into the pace he had learned so completely in his many treks across the West Mesa. The strides burned off nervous energy, and the alternate side brain stimulation of walking soothed the jangled neurons in his brain. He felt the edge of a panic. No good would come from losing his shit, Pitcairn reminded himself.

As his steps lengthened, he began to breathe very deliberately, slowing his racing thoughts. Reasoning began to take hold, though he continued to scan the surroundings, hoping to see Maria Elena appear. He knew there would likely be a logical explanation. Yet as a reporter who had spent much of his time in the dark underbelly of the world, he was quite aware of the possibility of something unexpected. Given the experience at the Country Store, and the punctures to their tires, it was clear that his inner urge to caution had been on the mark. "And inadequate," he told himself.

Suddenly he felt the urge to stop. He turned toward the French Broad River, though he could only see it dimly in the growing darkness. He stopped, pulled his shoulders back, and breathed very deeply. Once. Twice. Three times. A settling sorrow swept over him. Tears rose ever so slightly in the corners of his eyes as he stood in silence.

It's okay, and you're okay.

The voice was still and gentle. Left in its wake was a calm that defied understanding. In response, he felt himself settle deeply. Another breath rose from somewhere deep inside. In its wake was nothing but a sense of ease. He shook his head in disbelief, then realized he had no idea what to do next.

Clint had often said that in the middle of the practice of the Twelve Steps, right in the heart of spiritual recovery, one could find serenity amid calamity. It was a comforting memory followed by the phrase Clint added so often: *First things first, and next things next.*

Inexplicably, the next thought was to return to Bodhi Mandala and sit with Elise. He knew it was what was often referred to in the rooms of AA as "the next indicated thing." Even if it seemed strange. After all, he knew he ought to be freaking out.

That gave him pause. Actually, he had been on the verge of a freak-out. Then the still small voice had whispered. From that arose the thought of sitting with Elise.

For several long moments, he considered how this could all have unfolded as it did. Recalling the principles of AA's ideas about emotional sobriety, that being centered and grounded is the result of letting go, he marveled at yet one more gift of sobriety.

Then he was catapulted back to the present. Realizing again that he needed to move, he turned and began his return to the Harpies.

▸16◂

INTERESTINGLY ENOUGH, THE IDEA MADE PERFECT SENSE TO the Harpies. And with the efficiency of people who had learned to keep their lives in order amid the maelstrom of drugs and alcohol, they quickly worked out logistics. Rosemary ordered Pitcairn to call the police immediately. Nicky offered to check in with Elise and also to stay, an offer Pitcairn gratefully accepted. Rosemary and Betty began writing down all the contact information on paper from a pad in the glove compartment so that everyone could have the same information.

While Pitcairn described the situation to the police, he saw Betty placing a note under the SUV's windshield wiper. He realized he would have to call the rental company to get another set of keys. After he'd hung up, Rosemary raced through the details of their plans. They would drive to the police station to file a formal report. Elise immediately and graciously welcomed them to come and sit with her once other matters were settled. By the time they arrived to file the police report, the rental car company had offered another vehicle rather than wait for keys to be driven up from Greenville.

Pitcairn then had to sit through the expected and tedious interview with Officer Stephen Graham. Over and over, Graham crosschecked the details as well as alternate explanations. He was only being thorough, but it annoyed Pitcairn. When he tried to connect Maria Elena's disappearance to the Country Store incident, Graham made notes but did not seem to take it seriously.

By ten o'clock, everything that could be done had been done. The whirlwind of activity pushed Pitcairn's fears into the background, though they emerged over and over again. At each moment, however, there was another question to be answered or another task to be addressed. It reminded him of early recovery when the number of concerns threatens to be overwhelming, and yet a person returns to the moment at hand time after time. One moment, one breath, one step, one day at a time.

Finally, Rosemary and Betty gave him big hugs and told him multiple times to call when he heard something. Nicky joined him in an almost-new SUV to drive once again to Bodhi Mandala.

"Nicky," he said as he focused on the road, "that was fucking nuts." He sighed.

"You okay, Pitcairn?"

He thought for a moment. "I'm probably exhausted but don't know it yet. And all the questions that keep popping up in my thoughts are just too much. I'm worried. And grateful for all the help." He paused. "If I indulged my fears, I suspect I'd lose my shit, but somehow I'm managing to stay in the present."

"I'm sorry for all this," Nicky said. "And I'm glad to be with you."

"Thanks, Nicky. It's not the first morass I've had to find my way through. At some moment, I'm probably going to realize I'm more stretched and stressed than I know."

When they arrived at the center, Elise greeted him with a long and comforting embrace, then leaned away to study his eyes with concern. She nodded with assurance. "I can see you are balanced well enough, though the underlying anxiety is clearly present as well. That's good, all things considered."

He shook his head sheepishly, then told her and Nicky about his experience with the voice only a short while earlier.

"No shit!" Nicky cut in, before immediately wincing and apologizing. "I've just never heard anything like that."

Elise chuckled gently. "It's okay, Nicky. Let's get some tea, something calming. It will be a long night."

"It's okay, and you're okay." Pitcairn uttered the words. "Somehow it must be true, but I really can't get my head around it. Though I have to admit it does seem to ground me and keep my brain from blowing up with thinking."

They talked while the water heated for tea, mostly about what had transpired. When they finally settled down, Pitcairn was aware of his weariness. He'd been running on adrenaline but now felt the powerful emergence of worry and sorrow. When he admitted it,

Elise offered to chant to both soothe them and distract the mind and emotions. Before long, as they sat in the dimly lit space, her soft voice speaking words he did not understand worked on his worry in the same way deep tissue massage eases muscular tension. While he was too hyper-aware to nod off, it was as if he was engulfed in the experience, and quiet rose up around them.

A while later—almost forty minutes when he looked at the time—he became aware Elise had stopped chanting. He took a deep breath and looked first to her and then at Nicky. Their eyes were carefully watching him.

"Wow," he announced simply.

"Yeah," seconded Nicky.

"Let me warm our tea, and then we can talk," Elise offered.

"Okay," Pitcairn agreed, "But I need some fresh air to clear my head. I'm going to step outside. And movement is always useful for me."

The night was clear and cold, with stars hanging brightly in the moonless sky. He began to walk around the open area, stretching his neck and arms. He didn't know where he vanished to during what could only be described as a meditation, though he recalled once that Kari had said such occasions meant he was "being worked on from within." She had resisted saying more about it, preferring to leave it as part of the many unknowns that Pitcairn had grown to appreciate even if he did not understand them.

When he returned to the yurt, Nicky and Elise were chatting in barely audible voices. Pitcairn waited quietly by the door, sensing that their conversation was private. An instant later, Elise waved him forward.

As he settled onto the cushion, he realized he needed to disclose his suspicions about the Country Store, the slit tires, and Maria Elena's disappearance. He admitting that his investigator's brain seemed to have re-engaged.

"Still, if it really is the guys from the Country Store, and whoever they run with, I don't know what they would hope to gain from grabbing Maria Elena. That makes no sense at all—or at least no sense I can discern. Right?"

Elise nodded briefly. "Pitcairn," she said, "one of the things I've come to appreciate is just how desperately our egos and reason will try to explain the unexplainable. Or at least that for which we have insufficient information to understand. We might just call it addictive thinking, hooked to the idea that if we think about it long enough and hard enough, or if we fall into a cycle of worry, that somehow, we will gain that understanding."

Before Pitcairn could reply, Nicky added her thoughts: "I like that. Addictive thinking. It makes so much sense we'd go into overdrive." She looked at Pitcairn. "Honey, explaining those kinds of guys to ourselves is probably as hopeless as trying to explain why an alcoholic drinks despite the consequences. Maybe trying to make sense of a senseless act is itself senseless?"

She caught herself and laughed. "That was really good, wasn't it?"

Pitcairn smiled, then realized he was becoming too inwardly focused, something that AA had taught him was ultimately problematic given its self-centeredness—even under such unusual and disturbing circumstances as Maria Elena's disappearance.

"Elise," he asked, "if you don't mind, could we talk about your brother and your experience. I've learned in recovery that self-absorption is not healthy or useful, and that when we become aware of our preoccupation with ourselves, we ought to turn our attention to someone else. Classic AA strategy. Maybe it's a really good time to stop focusing on myself, even if it does seem like I ought to do something, or at least fret and worry."

Elise laughed as Pitcairn sighed at his awareness of himself and his self-centeredness. Nicky nodded approvingly.

"Where would you like me to begin?" Elise asked.

"I'm not sure it matters. All I know is that while I'm thinking about you and Grady, I won't be thinking about me and my troubles."

Nicky jumped in. "I love that, Pitcairn. It's what AA has been trying to guide us to all along. Stay in the now. Let go, let go, let go."

He smiled at her. "It's not a natural act for me, Nicky. I've had a lot of practice though. Years of trying to fend off every kind of fear. I guess I've made some progress."

He turned back to Elise. "Is it okay if I keep notes? That will keep my brain even more occupied."

▸17◂

ELISE RETOLD THE BACKSTORY SHE HAD GIVEN PITCAIRN PRE-viously so that Nicky would have some context.

"Let me tell you more about Daddy," she began. "He came from a solid, middle-America kind of background and was drafted to serve in the Vietnam war. He was a good man for the most part, nothing particularly exceptional. Military service and patriotism run throughout the family history, not unlike many southern families. I really don't know how he felt about the war, but I'm certain he believed he had to do his part."

"There were a few times Daddy would let something slip that made it clear his time in Vietnam was awful. The only things I know for sure though are in the documentation for his commendations. He was seen as a hero, albeit a minor one, except in his hometown in the Upstate. There was only one time he talked about that, and it was clear he could not reconcile that recognition with what he'd seen and done."

"What did he say?"

"Oh, I don't even know how certain I am about what he said. I was so young. And I've replayed the stories so many times, I'm not sure I can be sure." She shrugged.

"But it seems to me that one night when he'd had too much to drink, or maybe he was high, he said something about how no one who was a part of that mess should have been awarded any medals."

A long pause followed, and Elise sipped from her tea as if to collect herself.

"At any rate, there was no doubt Daddy had PTSD, though at that time it was barely a thought on anyone's mind. He was reliable enough, and with his war hero reputation, people cut him a lot of slack. Down South, war heroes and anyone who serves in law enforcement are a big deal. Frankly, I think it's a bit ridiculous, but I've been taught to honor the ground upon which others walk.

"I'm not sure what I can say about Grady. In so many ways, he is a mystery. It's clear something was always simmering unresolved inside him, but he was so opaque. Most of what you've heard and what you'll hear will be just like every mystifying, violent story we've been forced to examine. He seemed like an okay guy. There was no indication of this kind of trouble. A quiet guy. As a reporter, I'm sure you know such commentary better than me."

Pitcairn nodded, as much to encourage her as to acknowledge the point.

Elise looked away as if gazing across a great distance. A softening came to her face. Pitcairn imagined grief rustling through her like a wind through reeds.

"I told you I'm quite a student of most everything." She shrugged in a self-deprecating way. "I've spent a lot of time exploring how trauma transfers across generations. I'm not sure how much we actually understand about the mechanisms, but the data is very strong that children immersed in what is being labeled "toxic stress" experience the effects, which produce very unfortunate outcomes for many. If we take a child and expose them to someone with PTSD, there is some likelihood that it will transfer to them. It's a lot like how addiction is generationally transferred, though as I'm sure you know, it's a bit of a mystery how that happens."

Pitcairn nodded and Nicky added, "We hear that story all the time in the AA rooms. Sometimes it even skips a generation."

Elise smiled. "Yes, and that transfer is what happened to both me and Grady. Of course, your first thought would be why our lives could have taken such different paths. Here I sit as a teacher in refuge, while Grady has killed others and is now dead too."

She paused to breathe as tears crept down her cheeks.

"These tears are as much about my gratitude as they are about Grady. I understand there is no good reason why my life bent to the seemingly good and virtuous while his turned out awful."

Long moments passed before Pitcairn asked, "Why do you say that, Elise?"

She gazed upward as Pitcairn imagined the wheels of her thoughts slowly, inexorably turning. Or perhaps it was silent prayer.

"Simple enough, I guess. I can find no good reason why my life moved toward growth and Grady's moved toward destruction. It's as if somehow similar conditions moved us in diametrically opposed directions."

"Elise," Pitcairn asked, "have you heard of post-traumatic growth?"

"No, why?"

He puzzled for a moment. "One of my contacts, a brain researcher, sent me some information that sounds a lot like what you're describing. I've not had a chance to read it yet, but now I'm really curious." He turned his attention to Nicky. "It reminds me of what we hear so often in the rooms of recovery—that the same alcohol or drug stories that transform some of us are permanently devastating to others."

Nicky had become quite animated. "Oh! The founders of AA never could quite reconcile it. Even in the Big Book, it says some people are constitutionally incapable of being honest with themselves. And the old-timers always talk about some of those who just never could get it."

Pitcairn nodded pensively.

Elise spoke softly. "Pitcairn, I'm pretty tired. It's late. I'll sit with you for as long as you like, but I'm going to need to stop talking now."

He stood and stretched. "I won't be able to sleep, Elise. I'll go walk for a while."

Nicky leaped up and wrapped her arms around his shoulders to kiss him on the cheek. "Honey, I've got to sleep, but I'll pray for you and Maria Elena before I do."

He smiled at the kindness offered, returned the kiss to her cheek, and turned to nod to Elise. To his surprise, he watched himself raise his hands with palms facing together and offer a slight bow to her.

She returned the gesture and whispered gently, "Namaste."

A feeling of wistfulness rose from within. He turned slowly and exited the yurt.

▸18◂

THE NIGHT WAS EVEN COLDER, AND STILL CLEAR AND QUIET. As Pitcairn stepped into it, he was aware that it offered a kind of refuge for him. He started a loop around the open, grassy area, then realized he would feel too confined, so he strode down the entryway and turned up the road heading deeper into the mountains.

Once he was on the road, his mind began to freewheel. Actually, it was more like squirrels racing round and round as thoughts. Over and over, he had to come back to counting his steps and breathing. His concerns about Maria Elena simply would not cease, and yet worrying about her was the antithesis of a solution. It would only drive him crazy. So, he stepped up his pace, deepened his breathing, and tried to pay attention only to the feeling of each step as it struck beneath him.

After thirty minutes or so of steady movement and refocusing efforts, the craziness within dropped away. He was present again, and remembered this was the wisdom of the author and mystic Eckhart Tolle, though he called it the pain body. After it ran its course, there would be only the power of now.

It was then he realized he'd reached a vantage point that looked across a valley. Even without moonlight, the sky was so clear he could see the Blue Ridge Mountains rolling into the distant west. He noticed that the light sweat he had broken in his upward march was causing chills in the cold mountain air. He would not linger, though he stood for long moments.

A ping from his phone signaling a text brought him from his silent reverie.

"Pitcairn. Unbelievable. You and your charmed life. Kate."

"What's up?" he replied immediately as his attention focused toward this unexpected shot through the dark.

"Late night poking around on this post-traumatic growth. Check out Dr. Antoinette Piron here. She's just up the road from where you are now."

Pitcairn clicked on the link and was taken to a summary of an academic abstract. There beneath the photo of a stunningly attractive woman was a single paragraph that he scanned quickly. He was immediately drawn into the material, which he knew he'd need to study as soon as he found his way back out of the cold. Already his mind was grasping at tendrils of ideas that he knew intuitively were forming something valuable. The sense of being led was yet one more feeling he had come to trust.

A shiver brought him back to the text.

"Brilliant, Kate!"

"Check out the white squirrels while you're there."

"WTF?" he replied.

"Just follow your heat-seeking-missile thing."

"WTF x 2?"

"Your brain and instincts, Pitcairn. Let loose the hounds, dude."

To his surprise he laughed out loud, a sound that echoed in the stillness of the night. When he heard it, he realized that somehow amid the darkness of Emmy's disappearance, there was still what Tony called unbounded grace. A feeling of delight rose from deep within him, and he shook his head in amazement. "Damn, Tony. Nothing is lost, and everything belongs." He muttered to himself the phrase that always seemed impossibly optimistic, no matter how much the priest tried to explain it to him.

"Don't tell my beloved, but I love you, Kate."

"Not a problem. She loves you times infinity."

Suddenly he experienced a raw surge of emotions. Bittersweet feelings crashed into the delight and formed a mash-up of emotions that simply overwhelmed him in the moment. He needed to move in order to process it all, so he pivoted to walk down to Bodhi Mandala. Moving even more briskly because of the chill, he focused on the swirl of conflicting emotions, breathing in and out to stay grounded, long strides and swinging arms propelling him along the road.

It proved to be the perfect tonic, the walking and breathing pressing the feelings outward, then bringing him back to himself.

By the time he opened the door to the yurt, reality, his sorrows and all the seemingly miraculous things that interspersed them held together in the present moment.

All was quiet. Deep in reflection he brewed more tea, then sat comfortably to delve into the information about Dr. Piron.

Dr. Antoinette Lucille Piron had been born in rural Louisiana to parents from Martinique. She was very talented, perhaps a child prodigy, who was derailed by a series of violent, racist experiences while still a young woman. Deeply traumatized, she overcompensated with educational pursuits during which she endured two extended in-patient treatments for those traumas. Fortunately, she was in the care of very good psychologists who tapped a well within her that became her life's work.

He looked back to her photos. He imagined a depth of light in her gaze, and somehow sensed she was an avatar for this whole idea of post-traumatic growth.

Reading on, he noted she was co-chair of the Brevard College Institute for Women in Leadership, and held dual doctorates in criminal justice and psychology. There was a robust body of work around trauma and recovery. It surprised him that he knew nothing of the ideas. Then he read a short commentary she'd written in which she acknowledged that the predominance of attention in her field was on trauma itself and strategies for mitigation. Few seemed interested in how trauma could be a positive force. Yet it had become her life's work precisely because she was intimately familiar with trauma as well as both the downside and upside. She was a product of both.

Pitcairn noted that sometimes life circumstances aligned in the most elegant ways, ways that seemed impossible to explain. Piron seemed to be one of those instances. For a moment, his attention caromed to Dr. Jill Bolte Taylor, the brain researcher he had interviewed about her groundbreaking work in catastrophic stroke. Taylor had experienced just such a medical emergency and yet had fought her way back to life and living in part by using her incredible base of knowledge to understand exactly what was happening to her physiologically. The resulting work transformed her field.

Pitcairn reflected amid a moment of awareness that even he was experiencing benefits from terrible trauma. Were it not for that inner healing, and all the practices he had been using to stay out of fear and worry, he'd likely be drunk right now, or trying to score some drugs, or in the middle of some related catastrophe.

Bringing his attention back to the screen as he looked for a good summary, a cross-reference to white squirrels appeared, which had too much allure to ignore. It turned out that Brevard College, less than an hour west of Asheville, had a largely unexplained colony of white squirrels. He knew immediately that whether he met Dr. Piron or not, he'd have to see the creatures. "Too good to miss," he muttered.

A few minutes later, he found a short piece that synthesized some of the ideas about post-traumatic growth. Research proposed that personal devastation or transformation was the proverbial fork in the road. If one possessed enough resilience, which could be inborn or learned, and sufficient nurturance from others, catastrophe could become a catalyst with profound implications.

Once again, his thoughts freewheeled as he reflected on Elise and her half-brother, the one a teacher in refuge, the other now dead through his own violent actions.

One final section held him in rapt concentration for long moments. "Cumulative trauma including that which passes between generations can and does damage entire cultures and lifetimes, becoming a seemingly hopeless downward spiral of tragedy. Still, there is a mysteriously tiny but incredibly powerful potential, fuel for what can become an explosion of cumulative growth with transformational power that is unbounded. If we can determine the mechanisms that translate trauma into transformation, an upward spiral of possibility can sweep people and cultures in the opposite direction. Hopelessness becomes a basis for most-profound possibilities."

Pitcairn recalled his dead sponsor's favorite line from the Big Book. "Cling to the thought that in God's hands, the dark past is the greatest possession you have—the key to life and happiness for others."

While Pitcairn remained agnostic, he could not deny the obvious connection.

A thought came to him just as exhaustion finally overtook him, and he collapsed into a disturbed sleep. *No one chooses resilience or nurturance. We are all innocent.*

▸19◂

PITCAIRN AWOKE WITH A START AND AN INSTANT FEELING OF panic that rushed through his chest, a visceral response to a nightmarish and all-too-real drinking and drugging dream. A gentle touch and voice cut through bewildering feelings and impressions.

"Are you okay, honey?" Nicky asked with gentle concern.

He looked up as he raised his head, and sharp pains shot through his neck. He winced as he tried to reorient himself. Nicky's face loomed near; beyond it he could see Elise watching with a quiet but attentive awareness.

"Kevin?" Nicky asked again.

"Fuck. . . ."

He looked down at his trembling hands. Turning them over, he could feel the energy coursing through his palms, either chi or fear, or both. It seemed like his palms ought to be sweating. He shook his head to clear away a confounding haze.

Then the details of the dream raced through his memory. He blurted it out without thinking. "Drinking and drugging dream. Too fucking real. I can still feel the rush of the cocaine." He paused. "Jesus. It's been so long since I had one of those, I forgot how real they can be, Nicky."

Tears rimmed her eyes as an unthinking prayer fell from her lips. "God, grant us the serenity to accept the things we cannot change, courage to change the things we can, and the wisdom to know the difference." She looked directly into his eyes. "We got you, Kevin."

The prayer and words slammed into him. He couldn't cry, but the overwhelmingness of the reminder that he was not alone forced him to take a deep breath to remember himself. Elise intuited it, and stepped forward. His attention turned to her. He was surprised at how much he trusted her.

"Breathe. Just breathe," she said softly.

He was aware of the presence and care of these two women, who were otherwise too psychologically close. He felt a need to flee, and could feel himself pulling away inwardly. Shutting down. He knew it was a trauma response. No doubt it was triggered by an inexpressible terror related to Maria Elena but linked at some unfathomable level by the neuro-chemistry to all the traumas across his life.

"Breathe. Just breathe."

He looked in Elise's eyes and flashed back to a dream near the end of the Crucifix Protests: a feeling of being held close to a woman's breasts, and of being loved.

He almost recoiled at the intensity of the feeling. Again, Elise sensed it.

"Lean into it. Breathe." She paused. "Breathe."

He began to tremble, but with just enough awareness to remember to breathe deeply without being reminded by Elise.

The trembling increased, and again he felt an overpowering urge to flee. He knew it was old trauma, but his emotions were not rational, and not within his control.

"Breathe. Ride the edge of those feelings."

He trusted. That which was unhealed was not rational, and could not be reasoned with because it was not reasonable. He had to be with the trauma, had to experience it until it released. A deep breath finally resonated somewhere inside, and a slight sense arose that told him he was returning to himself, a kind of re-embodiment. Self-remembering.

Breath followed breath. He was now aware of how firmly Nicky held one of his hands, and the intensity of Elise's presence. Slowly his breathing came easier.

Elise began to chant in a voice barely above a whisper. He closed his eyes and focused inwardly. Breath continued to follow breath. Slowly but surely, he moved away from the trauma and the terror.

After long moments, he opened his eyes. "Fuck. . . ." he uttered with reverence.

Nicky chuckled. "Best fucking prayer ever." Then she laughed again. "Right after 'thank you!'"

A surprising feeling of delight swept into him. The trauma faded. In its place he felt Maria Elena's absence, and his concern. A flood of thoughts about the night before followed.

"Pitcairn, come back to us," Elise urged.

He refocused on both of them. "Good catch. There is way too much happening here. Speaking of which, Elise, what just happened?"

"That is what it is to be lost to yourself, to be triggered by unresolved trauma. The history of your life, swept up in these matters with Maria Elena. Unconsciously blocked. Probably you were worn and tired enough that you could not suppress it any longer." She smiled at him gently. "A shaman might call this a soul retrieval."

Something in her comments rang with authority deep within him. He found himself held in silent reverie.

"Pitcairn, come back to us."

He blinked as a long slow breath coursed through him. He shook his head in disbelief.

"I guess the only way to really understand trauma is to have to find your way through it."

"Pitcairn, that's why our insistence in AA is on 'experience, strength and hope.' We can't give it to others if we haven't experienced it for ourselves." Nicky shrugged almost shyly.

"Damn, Nicky. That's brilliant."

He looked back and forth between the two women. "No offense intended, Elise, because that was all amazing, but I need an AA meeting." He turned to Nicky. "How about you?"

She brightened. "Oh, hell yeah!" she announced enthusiastically as she grabbed her phone to search for the local AA directory.

While she looked, Pitcairn glanced back at Elise. He shook his head. "How you came out of the same crucible as Grady is such a mystery."

She nodded with obvious awareness of the profundity of his statement. "Grace. . ." she said as her voice trailed away.

His nod matched hers. "Yeah. I gotta call Tony today. He's the only one besides you who understands Grace like that. The only one who gets it that I can experience Grace even though I'm agnostic. Or that I can simultaneously experience trauma, the intensity of current circumstances, and joy and delight. And that it will simply overwhelm my circuitry. Blow a circuit-breaker."

Her laughter splintered the remaining hangover of the trauma. "Fuck," she announced with amusement. "Pitcairn, we have so much to discuss."

"How in the world did I find you?" he asked.

A huge smile split her face. "Grace, honey. It's all there is."

A snort broke free from deep within him. "Got it. When you've seen the humor, you've seen the truth."

Nicky interrupted. "Pitcairn, let's get in the car. If we leave right now, there's an early meeting just to the west of Asheville. The High Steppers Group. Funny name. Loaded twelve-steppers. If we're lucky we can find a good cup of coffee before we get there. God knows the coffee at the meeting is probably pretty shitty."

"Have you noticed we're cussing a lot this morning?"

"Sacred profanity," Nicky replied instantly. "Hallelujah!"

He looked at her with still more surprise. "Do you know Leonard Cohen's song?"

"Oh yeah . . . the holy or the broken hallelujah?" she guessed.

"That's exactly what I was thinking. And there's far more going on right now to chalk it up to mere coincidence."

She looked at him. "That sounds like a strange faith for a guy who doesn't believe, Pitcairn."

He chuckled. "You and my old sponsor, Clint, and Tony, the heretic priest, and Maria Elena all seem to see me that way, Nicky."

"Who you are speaks so loudly that I cannot hear what you say."

Elise and Pitcairn both stared at her.

She smiled shyly. "Emerson."

"I can see there's a lot more to learn about you, Nicky." He turned to Elise. "Thank you. We have so much more to discuss, and I'll let you know as soon as we can make that happen. First though, AA calls. And there is nothing that cannot be made worse by me drinking or drugging. Then we'll go see the police to find out what's next."

She stepped forward and hugged him resolutely. "I will look forward to seeing you."

Nicky tugged his arm. "Let's roll, Pitcairn."

▸20◂

FOLLOWING NICKY'S MAPPING APP ON HER PHONE, THEY headed toward a coffee house in route to the meeting. As they drove, Pitcairn recounting the analogy of the tiger because he could sense the pace of things quickening with the dream being an obvious marker.

When he'd finished riffing on that and the nightmare, Nicky countered with her thoughts. "Pitcairn, it sounds to me like that tiger is a totem for powerlessness. After all, doesn't AA tell us that we are constantly seeking to convince ourselves we have control in the face of all the evidence that tells us we don't? That's the great illusion, right?"

He turned to face her for a moment as they parked in front of the coffee shop. "Nicky, that's spot on. . . again." She blushed at having been seen and acknowledged.

"Pitcairn, can I ask you a question before we get coffee?"

"Sure. Whatever's on your mind, probably best to ask while I'm temporarily in my right mind."

"How is it you were never prosecuted for killing the drug dealer?"

"Oh, you mean after I admitted to it in the interview on national television during that whole adventure of the Crucifix Protests?"

"Yeah. How can that be?"

"No good explanation, Nicky. At the time it happened, so many years ago, the cops couldn't have cared less that one more drug dealer was dead. Then when it fell out of my mouth in the interview, afterward I had to work through a lot of fear that it was going to catch up with me, which would be really ironic after all these years. Tony took me to an entirely different place about how we ought to view amends-making in AA."

Nicky interjected as her interest instantly piqued. "How so, Pitcairn? I mean, how can you make it right when you've killed someone?"

"Right? I so agree with that, Nicky. Tony said that I would need to think of amends differently. That the amends would be in the life I lived going forward. And that would be the Grace living through me. Passing it on to others for the rest of my life."

They were silent for a few moments before Nicky spoke again. "Wow. Just wow."

"Yeah. And I don't even know that I believe in Grace, but it makes sense as living an amended life. One day at a time."

"Pitcairn?"

"Yes, Nicky?"

"Can you buy me the biggest, strongest coffee now? After that shit, I really need it."

"You got it!"

After a quick visit to the coffee house, they drove a few minutes with their overly large cups of black coffee to a slightly rundown AA clubhouse where the twelve-step study group met, hurrying to enter before the meeting started. Pitcairn was instantly aware of the disproportionately large number of black men and women, a notable contrast to the other meetings he'd attended down South. He liked it, though he also noted the inevitable unplanned biases that would have led him to meetings and settings that were mostly composed of whites, no doubt reflecting a South that was still very race conscious.

He shook the hand of the greeter, a wiry old man with a grip like a vise. "Welcome brother. Glad to see you," the man said with genuine goodwill.

"Glad to be seen," Pitcairn replied with a customary response in the recovering community. The dark stories of addicts and alcoholics were filled with vanishing acts, some never to be seen again once the disease of addiction claimed them.

Agnes, a silver-haired black woman, called the meeting to order, then launched into the conventional practices that made every alcoholic feel at home: the Serenity Prayer followed by standard readings, and then a welcome to newcomers and visitors.

An old white guy named Rufus, who looked like a farmer, led the meeting and provided its topic.

"Let's keep it simple today, ya'll. I wanna know how you keep it in the day. It's one thing to say 'one day at a time,' but it's a whole different deal to live it."

Mischief twinkled in the man's eyes as he looked around. "Let's not bullshit each other. Not today. Tell the fuckin' truth. To us and to God." The old man paused, then added, "It helps us all to stay on the topic, but it's your meeting. Let 'er rip."

Pitcairn appreciated Rufus's approach. He cut right through to the tendency that too often unfolds in recovery meetings to parrot the party line. The best AA meetings for him were the ones where people opened up with their realities. And this group did not disappoint. Mostly people acknowledged their difficulty, some painfully, some humorously. One woman introduced herself, then admitted she had no success with practicing one day at a time and would listen to learn more.

Neither Nicky or Pitcairn felt the need to speak. In his case, it seemed vital to just take it all in since it was so relevant to his present circumstances. But then Agnes asked directly whether as visitors they wanted to share. Nicky shrugged, then Pitcairn realized it was a serendipitous opportunity for him to admit his present circumstances.

"My name is Pitcairn . . . alcoholic."

In the well-practiced call and response of AA, the group boomed back a greeting.

He told them about his drinking and drugging dream, and without divulging details of his circumstances, admitted there was a lot going on that was really pressing in on him. "I once heard that if you squeeze hard enough on any sober alcoholic or clean addict, that they'd get thirsty or tweaky. It's been a while since I last drank or drugged or felt the overwhelming feeling to need a drink or a drug. But I've never questioned that drinking or using will only make something worse. No need to convince me. But I'm glad to be able to say it out loud. Thanks for keeping the doors open and a seat ready for me."

Pitcairn noticed a young, powerfully built black man watching him carefully as he spoke. When he wrapped up his sharing, the man nodded an acknowledgement to him. Sure enough, when the meeting ended, the man came straight to him.

Extending his hand, he introduced himself. "Nat," he said simply.

"What's up, man?" replied Pitcairn.

"I heard about your girl last night. I'm a cop. The word's out, brother. And there are some of our guys who are looking to drop the full load on those mother fuckers."

Pitcairn felt gratitude rise within him. He took a deep breath. The power of the AA community overwhelmed him.

"You know who took her?"

Nat looked down, then looked him in the eyes. "Listen, I probably just said more than I should. I can't tell you what I know. But we got your back."

Pitcairn took another deep breath. "I'm headed down to police headquarters to check in. Anything else I ought to do?"

"Stay clean and sober, brother. We may not be your Higher Power, but there is one, and you can trust it."

Pitcairn laughed. "I believe that you believe."

"Good enough," the cop responded as he chuckled.

And with that, he and Nicky left the meeting which was quickly dispersing. He told her what had happened. She shook her head.

"Can't stop thinking about that tiger story."

"Good reminder, Nicky."

▶21◀

AS SOON AS THEY ARRIVED AT THE POLICE STATION, NICKY settled in with her phone to call the Harpies, and Pitcairn was quickly ushered to an inner office. The shift captain, a stout, no-nonsense woman, extended a strong hand.

"I'm Captain Harden, Mr. Pitcairn."

"Thanks for seeing me so quickly, Captain. And no need to call me mister; everyone just knows me as Pitcairn."

She nodded, then gestured for him to sit.

"Let me cut to the chase, Pitcairn. The FBI, ATF, and Homeland Security came into the mix during the night. It seems you stirred up a hornet's nest when you visited with those men at the Country Store."

Pitcairn leaned forward attentively. "Someone has been burning the midnight oil, captain. Sounds like there are more things going on than you can disclose."

She nodded with nothing on her face betraying her thoughts. He recognized she was quite a badass, which he appreciated. As the thought passed through his mind, he felt himself relax as he realized everything was in good hands. And more so, that there were forces at work far beyond him. The feel of it reminded him of the forces that began to unfold with the Crucifix Protests. Momentum was gathering.

Pitcairn flashed back to a debriefing he once had with Kari after an in-depth treatment session. A strange tapestry of recollections had emerged that day, seemingly linking the protests to his own childhood trauma. If he recalled correctly, it was the first time he had shared the story of the tiger in the jungle. Her words came back to him almost verbatim.

"That's the Tao, Pitcairn. There is always a flow, a current. It doesn't matter what you think or feel about it, it's best to just accept it and work with it, or at least to act with awareness of it. There is no point in fighting it. But you seem to have a better sense of it than many."

In that instant he knew it was this trait in him that others called faith.

"Pitcairn?" Harden's voice intruded into his reverie.

He shook his head. "Sorry, captain. Too much stress and too little sleep. I kind of blanked out for a moment there."

She smiled for the first time, then glanced away with her own distraction.

"Here's the deal, Pitcairn. You're right. There are a number of things going on that you would have no way of knowing. This situation with Ms. Maldonado simply forced our hand."

His journalist's instincts kicked in. "Of course. The Feds would have already made the connections with these guys and the Sufi bombing. They probably had someone embedded in the groups, right"

He saw a flicker in the captain's eyes that told him he was on the mark, though her countenance betrayed nothing. Pitcairn chuckled then.

"Okay, captain. Thank you. What would you suggest I do?"

"I would recommend you don't get yourself in the middle of this. Stay out of the way, Pitcairn. Don't go knocking on any more doors. Can you do that?"

"Sure," he muttered quickly. Then with a curt nod of acknowledgment, he added, "Absolutely. This is what my old AA sponsor used to call 'standing down the ego.' "

Harden stood and extended her hand. "Then stand down. Don't know about the ego. We will be in touch."

A few moments later, he was plopped into the chair next to Nicky, bringing her up to speed. All she could do was shake her head as she listened.

"Pitcairn, I get it that somehow things work out, and that somehow you have some strange juju, but this is totally amazing."

He shrugged. "No clue on how it can be. All I know is that I can't ignore the signs of a path when they show up. An old woman at a meeting in La Veta, Colorado, said 'The path is made with every step.' But it seems to me that it helps to be able to see that next step so you can take it. No idea how that happens. It just does."

"Why do you suppose everyone sees you as a man of faith, since you can't?"

He laughed out loud. "Nicky, your guess is as good as mine. Up in the mountains around here they used to talk about people having a knack. Kind of feels that way for me."

Her head was cocked as she studied him for long moments. "You want to know what I think?"

"Sure enough. Do me."

"Well, I remember a meeting I was at a few years ago. I was traveling to see family, and it was really stressful." She looked away as an obvious pang of pain passed across her face. "I do not have a good family. I'm estranged from them all. I've had to pick a new family in sobriety to stay clean and sober, but I am not healed yet."

He leaned a little closer as compassion rose in him, and nodded to encourage her to continue.

"Anyway, I was stressed and found a really interesting meeting. There was this young guy there who I'd written off as new in recovery. I sure did misjudge him. When he opened his mouth, he said that faith is not gullibility, that we're not supposed to blindly accept things, that faith comes from experience. Then he used a phrase that will stick with me forever. He said, 'We can't know it until we experience it. Then we can grasp it.' And I think that's what you've done. You seem to just lean into the shit, let it teach you, then you trust it. We call that faith, but you can't see it because it's just how you are."

Pitcairn stared at her so long he could see her beginning to get uncomfortable.

"Honey, there is far more to you than meets the eye. You finally helped me see myself, and you're spot on."

He leaned over and kissed her on the cheek. "Thank you."

She smiled shyly, then shrugged.

"Gotta write that down before it gets away from me." Reaching into his backpack, he pulled out his journal and wrote for a few moments. Nicky turned her attention to her phone and began sending a text.

When he was finished, she looked up. "Well, Pitcairn, what do you think we ought to do next?"

He chuckled. "Given we're on the back of a tiger, I'm not sure we have much of a choice. That said, I think I'm going to try not to get in the middle of anything."

Nicky laughed with him. "Fair enough. And beyond that?"

"I saw a coffee shop around the corner. Can I buy you a cup of joe? I'd like to call Tony and then check in on a few things in Albuquerque. That might keep me from worrying so much about Maria Elena. Do you suppose Elise will have more time for us this afternoon or evening?"

"Let me check with her. And now that you know I'm providing you with such wisdom, and that you're buying, I'd like a really strong latte."

"Deal," he replied.

▸22◂

THE COFFEE SHOP WAS FILLED WITH LOCAL ART, A STRANGE contrast to the police station. And it had a feeling of funkiness that seemed to be part of the Asheville scene. Pitcairn mentioned it to Nicky as they stood in line. She agreed and provided a simple framing for him.

"Appalachia meets wealth, and art meets grunge."

He laughed as they ordered, then they found a quiet corner booth. As Nicky reached out to Elise, he called Tony.

After bringing him up to speed, he paused for a breath. The priest waited a few moments before speaking.

"That's a lot, Kevin. How are you?"

Pitcairn chuckled to himself, realizing the impossibility of the question.

"Tony, I don't know how the hell I am. I'd guess a part of me keeps shutting down my emotions, old trauma triggered by new trauma, or maybe it's just a healthy self-protective thing. I know how worried I should be about Maria Elena, but I seem to bounce from obsessive fear and concern to something compulsive with Grady Donovan and post-traumatic growth. Throw in some strange moments of peace falling on me, and with Elise and Nicky, and the truth is I'm feeling kind of schizophrenic. Or at least I imagine this is how it would feel to be psychically split."

He paused to think. "Oh, and I had a drinking and drugging dream, which is generally a sign that all of it is working pretty hard on me."

"Hmmm . . ." began the priest. "Let me repeat my question now that you've unloaded all that. How are you, Kevin?"

A short laugh burst from him. "Brilliant parry, Tony. How am I really?"

He closed his eyes and tried to let go of everything.

"Well, amid all this mess, I did hear the voice again. Of course, it spoke simply. 'It's okay, and you're okay.' " He shook his head back and forth several times in acknowledgement. "Tony, somehow or other, I believe it. Don't know how that can be. On the one hand, Maria Elena is missing. On the other, I'm dragged against my will into some new spaces that I find captivating, bouncing between AA and the police and Zen mysticism. Could it be that in the midst of chaos, everything could actually be fine?"

Now the priest laughed. "Kevin, didn't you once tell me that Clint taught you that your well-being is not dependent on anything that is going on around you?"

"Yeah, he called it emotional sobriety, the ability to be okay no matter what. Though it wasn't in such fine language: 'Peace is what's left when the horseshit is gone.' "

"He did have a way with words, didn't he?"

"True that, Tony. West Texas plain English."

"Are you familiar with the writings of Alan Watts? Perhaps a book called *The Wisdom of Insecurity?*"

"Nope. I know the name, but that's it. A Buddhist guy, right?"

"Well, I don't know that most Buddhists accept him as one of their own. Watts walked his own path. But what he had to say about flux is useful."

"Flux?"

"Oh, we might call it chaos theory today, Kevin. Regardless, he maintained there was nothing like order in the world but that our egos are constantly trying to establish a feeling of order or control. Much like the monkey riding the tiger, the possibility of no control is very disturbing to us. So we incessantly grasp for anything or any mindset that will allow us to avoid the chaos. Also like your tiger analogy, the wisdom was in letting go and acknowledging the true nature of things. The Buddhists might say it is letting go of the attachment to the illusion of control. And the comfort of the illusion."

"Got it, Tony. The folks in AA would probably call it acceptance."

"Exactly!" the priest exclaimed. "I'm guessing acceptance is a fleeting matter, something that comes and goes just like the states of mind you are experiencing."

"That makes a lot of sense, Tony. I'm powerless over what is going on as well as my feelings about what's going on. I guess I'll just stay solidly in the program of recovery, keep dealing with the shit, and keep coming back as much as I'm able to what's right in front of me. First thing first, and next things next."

"That sounds right, Kevin. And let me remind you that your history and experience is a good indicator that you and things really are okay. Even though they may not seem okay."

"Tony, you are really good at this. You should be a therapist."

"You forget my degrees are in psychology."

"And you're a priest, which sure seems like a possible therapy gig."

"Pastoral counseling, we would call it, though I often think we would be better served by much more pastoral listening."

Pitcairn flashed back to a moment several years back when he'd learned that same lesson. "Tony, some time back, I had a guy asked me to sponsor him. Whenever we got together, I'd try to help and it would just seem to mess things up. Clint told me I should try to spend a whole meeting with him just listening. I did, and at the end, that guy told me it was the best sponsorship session he'd ever had."

Tony responded with a great belly laugh.

"Clint told me afterward that our egos just have to think we are doing something, or doing something good. Candy for the ego, he called it."

"Clint was clearly a homespun wiseman, wasn't he?"

"Yeah, Tony. But he ain't got nothing on you."

"Thank you for that, Kevin. Please call whenever you feel the need to talk."

"Will do, Father. I appreciate the time, and I appreciate you. See you later."

He hung up and turned to Nicky. She was beaming.

"That was fun to listen to, Pitcairn. Father Tony sounds almost like a sponsor."

"Fair enough, Nicky. I would have never guessed it, and it would have never occurred to me that a guy like me would end up with a priest as a close friend."

"Or that you and I would be having conversations like these."

He laughed and changed the subject. "What did Elise say?"

"She can see us tonight. So what would you like to do?"

Pitcairn's face scrunched up as he considered the question.

"I don't know, Nicky. The hotel in Greenville has our stuff. I need a shower. And a good meal. Then again, I need to track down a professor over in Brevard. And white squirrels." He shook his head. "Plus, I don't want to stray too far from here, and Maria Elena."

"That's a lot, Pitcairn."

"Yeah, but the worst part is I keep feeling like I ought to be freaking out about Maria Elena. Or feeling guilty about not freaking out." He shrugged. "Or doing something."

Nicky smiled. "Pitcairn, based on what you told Tony, it sounds to me like there is a whole lot going on with you, and inside you, and that you are riding the tiger just as well as you can."

He took a deep breath. "Thanks for that reflection, Nicky. I guess Bill W was right when he said we would never understand what was going on in the present moment until after it was finished.

"Let me change the subject for a minute. Don't you have something you need to do, Nicky? A job? A guy? Something? It's so funny that I know you so well in such a short period of time, but I don't have a clue about the rest of your life. Sorry to be so self-absorbed."

"No apology needed. I'm really lucky. When I got clean and sober after a long time helping my ex-husband build our business, the terms of the divorce take care of me really well. And to turn a phrase from AA, I've been happily and usefully single for a while. My kids have lives of their own. Rosemary and Betty headed back to Greenville. So you are my AA service work right now, Pitcairn. Plus, I get to be with Elise."

He grinned at her. "Thank you, Nicky. Now that I'm thinking about you, what kind of business did you build?"

"A large construction company in Savannah. My ex knows the industry, but I built the business. He had to hire three people to do what I did running things." A flush crept to her face.

"Well, that means we could wander off and do most anything, doesn't it? Do you suppose we could head back up to the Bodhi and clean up there? Then can I buy you lunch in Brevard?"

Nicky nodded. They finished their coffee and headed out.

▸23◂

PITCAIRN HAD CALLED AND LEFT A MESSAGE FOR DR. PIRON, hoping there would be an opening on her calendar. He was surprised by her voice recording, a down-home timbre that was curiously at odds with her profile yet comfortingly authentic. "Hi, this is Lulu. Sorry I can't answer now, but if you'll be patient, I'll be back in touch."

He told Nicky about her as they drove, including a quote he'd found from one of the excerpts on her work with post-traumatic growth. "Survivors of traumatic experiences can find a life of peace despite relentless storms. They can then live beyond those traumas. In doing so, they rise up and become beacons of hope to others."

"She sounds like someone we'd read about in the stories in the Big Book, doesn't she, Nicky?"

"Maybe one of our people," she replied. "Or maybe one of those who understands because of her own story."

"Curiouser and curiouser," Pitcairn said.

A few moments later, he went in a new direction with a question. "Nicky, do you think it's strange that the love of my life is missing and I'm off exploring? I mean, isn't that strange?"

"Great questions, my friend. Great questions. But aren't you practicing what the tenth step tells us?"

He glanced toward her. "Say more."

"I'm not talking about the usual stuff we hear. But when we clean up our affairs on an ongoing basis, the Big Book does tell us to resolutely turn our attention to someone we can help. Like . . . back to the now. Right?"

"Fair enough, Nicky. But it sure doesn't feel right."

"Feelings are not facts, Pitcairn. The point is to keep on living life on life's terms." She paused for long moments. "And to not get loaded."

He looked at her again. "Nicky, you just keep surprising me."

"Besides that, there is nothing you can do for Maria Elena right now. You're powerless, and other people are on it. And . . ." she added with emphasis, "the police did tell you to butt out. So let's roll. I'm happy to help you stay distracted by keeping you talking and busy."

A short time later, they saw a little cafe, Chicken Salad Chick, on Main Street just across the corner from Brevard College.

"Twenty-seven kinds of chicken salad – never heard of such a thing. What do you think?" Pitcairn asked.

"I'm game!" she replied gaily.

Midway through five kinds, all of which were very tasty, Pitcairn's cell phone rattled in his pocket. "Pitcairn here."

"Mr. Pitcairn, this is Lulu Piron. From your message, it would seem we have things to discuss."

"Please, just Pitcairn. May I call you Lulu?"

'Of course. That's just about the only thing anyone calls me. It appears to fit me."

He laughed, liking her instantly. She was so unassuming. "Are we fortunate enough to have a shot at meeting today? Just finishing a bite of lunch at Chicken Salad Chick right now."

"Good fortune, Pitcairn. I'm free at three o'clock. Will that work for you?"

"Absolutely! Where can I find you?"

"How about the lounge area in the campus center?"

"Perfect, see you there. Gotta go find some white squirrels in the meantime."

Lulu laughter was almost musical. "Good fortune again. If you cross the street and go to the brook running through the trees, you'll find them."

"Thank you, and see you shortly."

Hanging up, he smiled at Nicky. "Next things next. It's chilly but sunny enough. Let's go find those white squirrels."

She nearly leaped up with an enthusiasm that matched his. He felt a shot of guilt run through him as thoughts of Maria Elena arose. Pitcairn closed his eyes and took a deep breath, then sent loving thoughts toward her wherever she might be. Opening his eyes, he saw Nicky studying him.

He shrugged. "Had to pause and send some good vibes to Maria Elena."

She nodded, then led toward the exit.

Minutes later, they found comfortable benches in the sun a short distance from the brook Lulu had described. Almost immediately, two pure white squirrels careened down a tree in a mad chase that was delightful to watch. It reminded him of Lucy's cavorting. He made a mental note to call Zack to see about Lucas, and the dogs. For a time, he and Nicky simply sat with themselves, watching the comings, goings, and antics of the squirrels.

There were multiple backstories to the squirrel's presence in Brevard. Some said they were a genetic anomaly that just happened to appear. Another story said they had escaped from a traveling circus. Local Cherokee lore placed them as either a unique gift from the Great Father or a practical joke from the Trickster. Regardless, it was very easy to relax and take it easy for a time, even as Pitcairn continued to watch his mind cycle back over and over again to fear and worry, which he would note and let go of, then come back to the present moment.

When they'd had enough of sitting, chatting, and squirrels, they walked around the campus. It was a beautiful and idyllic place.

After a time, he stopped to check in with Zack. It was a timely call. There was little to report on Lucas's condition. At best, he was stable in his coma. At worst, the brain scans did not give a good prognosis. Still, when Pitcairn read between the lines, Zack sounded better than before. Pitcairn imagined that the stability of their home and proximity to Lucas was steadying if not reassuring.

He used the opportunity to chat with Zack about the journals. Much was surprising to Zack, who was not aware of much of the inner work his son had been exploring.

However, Zack was able to tell him about Teo. It was not related to those inner practices but was the childhood nickname Lucas had for Etido, the old man who had been such a presence for so long. Suddenly, the references in the journal made sense. It was clear that Lucas had woven much of what he learned from his unlikely mentor into his approaches. Pitcairn realized there was even more to the young man than he'd imagined. He would need to revisit the journals soon.

Just before three, they found their way to the campus center. At the coffee shop, Nicky opted for an afternoon triple shot of espresso, once again using her hand as a buzz indicator and concluding she was under-caffeinated. Pitcairn opted for a large iced tea, and was amused to realize he had to ask for a replacement when it came back saturated with sugar. They weren't kidding when they called it sweet tea.

▸24◂

NICKY DECIDED TO TAKE A WALK WITH HER COFFEE. PITCAIRN settled into an oversized easy chair in an open corner to wait. As soon as he ceased action and distractions, the voices of fear returned and ratcheted up almost immediately. He softened his gaze, located the distressing feelings deep in his core, and began to breathe steadily into them. Once again, the re-embodiment practice slowly brought the roaring vortex of thinking to a much more manageable level. He uttered a silent affirmation of thankfulness. At the same time, he reminded himself it was this kind of inner swirl that made the allure of alcohol and drugs so strong, always a good reminder for an alcoholic like him.

A few minutes after the hour, he saw a striking black woman with a clean-shaven head walking across the center. He was struck by how she held herself, her obvious confidence. While her attire was stylishly academic, her scarf and jewelry had obvious Caribbean colors and flair. Even though he had seen her photo online, he would not have easily recognized her. Partly it was because in the professional image, she had braided hair tightly wound around her head, and wore glasses that looked quite professorial. Yet nothing in the photo could have captured the poise that emanated from her.

Pitcairn stood as she approached and extended his hand. Much to his surprise, she grasped his hand and pivoted forward to hug him warmly.

"Lulu, you are not at all what I was expecting," Pitcairn offered as a greeting.

She smiled and laughed easily. "Pitcairn, you are exactly as I imagined you." Her eyes twinkled. "At least based on what I read of you."

"Ha . . . you're a researcher, so of course you did your homework."

"My Auntie Geneva taught me to always over-prepare."

He laughed. "And my long-time mentor and sponsor, Clint, told me I was prone to blind spots, and that I should make an ass of myself quickly so I could get it over with. You have a big advantage on me."

"It would seem to serve you well, Pitcairn." She handed him a file folder. "I brought you some materials that might be useful. Now let me get some coffee and I'll be right back."

He settled into the chair to scan the documents while he waited. There were three journal articles and a white paper that did not appear to have been published. Behind them were the first ten chapters of a book that looked to be in draft form, with a few graphics framing the information on post-traumatic growth. He glanced back to the title, which was noted as a working version: *Breakdown to Breakthrough*.

When Lulu returned, she placed her coffee on the table. Before Pitcairn could assist her, she moved another easy chair much closer to an angle where they could easily face each other. It felt strangely intimate. Once again, he was struck by her grace and poise.

Once settled, she took a luxurious sip of her coffee, sighed with pleasure and settled more deeply into the cushion. "Now, Pitcairn, you told me in your voice message about your interest in my work, but you didn't disclose the purpose behind it. Given your history, I think I should assume there is a story here that I need to know before we begin."

"True that, Lulu, though before we're done, I want to know more about your history. And especially I want to know how it is a world-class expert can get away with being called Lulu rather than Dr. Piron, or Antoinette."

Her laughter sounded brilliantly. "Let's get that one out of the way first. I was fortunate to come from a very educated family but one that held no pretentions. My parents knew how fortunate we were and didn't want it to go to our heads. They insisted on right-sizing us from the beginning. I was always Lulu, and my daddy made it clear if he ever caught me putting on airs, he would come find me and not spare the rod to remind me. So, I'm just Lulu. And just me."

"It would seem to serve you well, Lulu, and thanks for letting me in on it. Now, let me tell you what brings me to you."

He proceeded to share the entire story, holding back nothing including what had happened to Maria Elena. It was one of those occasions where he knew someone could be trusted.

"Goodness, Pitcairn! Would you like to talk about what's happening to Maria Elena? I'm not sure whether to be impressed or disturbed you're here with me now."

"Thanks, that's more than kind. I'd guess I'll need to tell you a bit about how a recovering alcoholic has been taught to navigate the world." He then shared with her the conversations he'd had with Father Tony, Elise, and Nicky. "So, Lulu, the truth is that I'm far better off thinking about you than being self-absorbed. When we're done here, I'm going to call Captain Harden and find out the latest information. It will be just about twenty-four hours, which means she'll be able to take more actions than she can now."

"Pitcairn, I appreciate you letting me in on that. Let's jump in then. Okay?"

"All the way in. Lay it on me."

Lulu proceeded to frame things with obvious expertise and relish. There was so much information she grasped so readily that he struggled to keep up.

First, she covered the basics of human development—that every child was born with a seemingly infinite desire to grow, though with an inevitably limited capacity to do so. There was just far more to experience and learn than could possibly be assimilated.

"It's no wonder babies and children sleep so much," Pitcairn observed.

"Exactly, they are saturated all the hours they are awake, and presumably all that sleep is needed to work through all the material they take in. During that time, the foundation for the future is being laid into place. If the development provides most of what they need, their possibilities are much greater than if they are impaired in building that foundation.

"Are you familiar with Maslow's Hierarchy?" she asked.

"Sure. Go on."

"If the essential needs for safety, security, and nurturance are provided, the upsides are dramatic. Self-realization, our highest potential, is built upon those pillars.

"Now, have you heard about adverse childhood experiences, also known as ACEs?"

"Familiar with the term but not the implications."

"Okay. Here's the most stunning conclusion: The greatest predictor of life success is the zip code you're born into."

It took a moment to register. "What?"

She smiled with delight. "Yes, Pitcairn. Without adequate resources or supportive matters in the first five to seven years of our lives, we are about fifteen to twenty percent less likely to complete an education, find meaningful employment, and establish secure adult relationships. Worse still, there is a much greater likelihood of chronic disease as we age."

Pitcairn was perplexed, yet something was connecting to earlier explorations during the Crucifix Protests. "Dr. Stephen Pfalzer?"

"Oh yes, Stephen laid some of our original research foundation into place, but our understanding has come so much further."

"But zip code?"

"Yes, Pitcairn. Zip code. Let me explain. During the critical early years, our development and even brain structure is altered by what we once called toxic stress, everything from hunger to violence and poverty, including lack of exposure to rich variables like language and experiences of all kinds. In high-resource communities, infants gain a huge advantage. Worse, when a child is constantly in survival mode, it has the reverse effect of undermining the foundations we most need to thrive."

"Okay, but I don't understand then how I turned out as well as I did. I was certainly not raised in optimal circumstances."

Excitement showed on Lulu's face. "Oh Kevin . . . Pitcairn, that's just it . . . that's where the state of our research presently stands, and here is what we hypothesize currently. By the way, all of this is in the materials I gave you."

"Cool! I've got a lot to study then."

"Yes, you do. Let me give you the shorthand version. I have a student meeting at 4:30, so we'll need to be done about ten minutes before then, though we can certainly talk on the phone when you want."

"Okay, but before we go on, why are you so enthused about teaching me?"

A smile split her face. "Pitcairn, it is who I am and what I do. In addition, you are clearly a man on a mission, and you may be able to cover some very important ground because of it."

He snorted. "I don't know how often I've been told something like that, Lulu. I don't see that in myself, but I'd guess it's who I am and what I do."

"It is indeed," she affirmed as she placed a hand on his forearm. "And from what I see, you are very good at it."

Sheepishly he looked away, then took a breath to settle himself. "Okay, continue Lulu."

"Now remember, we're talking about a whole population, not individuals, which is where misunderstanding always creeps in. We can't predict anything at the individual level, only that with any large number, the percentages hold up. We can't say Pitcairn did it, therefore others should be able to."

"Yeah, I get that. It's a problem that I run into often. It's like we want to deny the implications by finding a single exception."

"Exactly! Now here is what we do know. If a child is born with or is taught resilience by their families or caregivers, it can greatly mitigate the effects of trauma. Invariably, we also find nurturance, someone demonstrating caring for the child. With nurturance and resilience, that terribly important safety and security need is met, and beneficial human development is possible."

"I got it," Pitcairn confirmed.

"Excellent. I knew you would. Let me put this in another example." She paused to sip her coffee and collect her thoughts. "If we could clone you, the exact same you, and drop one hundred thousand of you in random settings, about fifteen to twenty thousand of the exact same Kevin Pitcairns would fail to thrive because of the circumstances around them."

"Okay. Still with you."

"We've also learned that a lot of mitigation can be applied to remedy some of the consequences. But it is far more likely to be successful if we make sure every child gets essential needs met, and that they experience nurturance and acquire resilience."

"Now to your bomber and his half-sister. Of course, we can't know their genetics, but both of them were exposed to generational trauma from their father. Let's be clear: Their father is not at fault. He was obviously traumatized in the war, and clearly did not receive any support from the military to address it. He passed it on, just like generational substance abuse can be passed on. Very likely, from what you've told me, Grady did not have a mother or someone else who could provide sufficient nurture and healthy resilience, whereas Elise did."

Pitcairn digested all that he had heard. Lulu allowed him time to do so, then glanced at her watch.

"What are you thinking, Pitcairn?"

"A question comes to mind. What about free will, and the power to choose?"

She laughed. "I bet you already know what I'm going to say, don't you?"

"Try me, Lulu."

"Free will is quite illusory. If the raw stuff of it is not in place, we do not find the capacity for self-actualizing. It's just not there. And the jury is out as to whether we can cultivate it after those essential developmental experiences leave us lacking. That's the state of the science right now. Yet we have a marvelous capacity for thinking we are able to choose, because we cannot see the soup of our own selves in which we are immersed."

He shared with her the tiger analogy, which she whole-heartedly supported. Then she resumed.

"Here's what we know. The ideal is to make sure every child gets the essential foundation one way or another . . . a parent, a family, a mentor, a community can provide that, can provide connectedness, nurturance. If we fail with any child, or if the child is traumatized through life circumstances, we want intervention and mitigation as early as possible. If we fail still further, or if an adult is exposed to something deeply damaging, we have tools which can mitigate and prevent a whole host of terrible outcomes. Our research is presently focused on finding ways to instill the raw stuff we've been discussing once we find out it's missing or damaged. There's that dated saying that a mind is a terrible thing to waste. What is truer still is that a life is a terrible thing to waste, perhaps the only thing in my mind that translates to sin, that we fail to provide the means for every self to actualize. That's my mission. What I have seen is that we are on the edge of having the understanding to create the tools that can take every traumatizing circumstance and bend it toward growth and transformation."

It was very silent. Her passion and words had stilled the space around them. It almost brought tears to his eyes. Pitcairn sensed a faint aura around her, though he wasn't sure he believed in auras. He softened his gaze and allowed the stillness to hold.

The moment came when he knew to speak. "Lulu, that was beautiful. You've given me so much to consider. Regardless, I'm a fan now. And when this story is told, I want to find a way to support you. No idea what that means, but this strikes me as too damn good to miss."

Lulu cast her eyes downward, perhaps collecting herself yet again or perhaps out of embarrassment at having been seen so clearly. When she looked up, there was a gentle smile on her face, and an aura still clung around her.

"Do you believe in auras, Lulu?"

A look of surprise came to her face. "Of course. Why?"

"Well, you're all lit up right now."

"Pitcairn, that is not about me; that is what you are seeing that is always present. Everywhere. There is nothing but subtle beauty emanating from everything."

"Holy ground, baby!"

She looked him square in the eyes. "Pitcairn, more so than you ever imagined. If you're not seeing the emanations of all that is holy, you're just not paying enough attention."

"Lulu, this feels a lot like conversations I had with Clint and now with Father Tony. You and I have business to do. Just don't quite know what that means."

She arose to go to her meeting. "You, my friend, are a godsend. If you'll hug me, I have to go. But I want to continue this conversation."

Pitcairn stood and wrapped his arms around her for a long embrace.

She stepped away and looked at him carefully. "Now, please go take care of whatever you must for Maria Elena. And when you have got her back in your arms, and before you leave this area, take her on a search for waterfalls. There are more beautiful waterways in this area than anywhere I've ever been. This time of year, a drive through the Nantahala River Gorge is perfect. Think *Deliverance*, the movie filmed in that rugged area, and then shift your mindset to holy ground. You'll find it all quite romantic."

She stepped in and kissed him on the cheek. "Then come by so I can meet her."

He nodded and offered a gentle goodbye.

Lulu walked away, and he returned to the easy chair. For a while, he scanned his surroundings, deep in contemplation. Everything had an aura that varied in color and intensity, and yet it was clearly present. After a time, he opened his journal and began to write. Especially he wanted to capture the stunning linkages from trauma to innocence. After all, if none of us chooses the zip code into which we are born, or the circumstances that may befall us, clearly each of us is doing the very best we are able to in the face of so much beyond our control.

▶25◀

PITCAIRN CALLED HARDEN AND WAS QUICKLY CONNECTED TO her. "What's the situation, captain?"

"First, Pitcairn, how are you?"

"Managing to stay out of your way."

"That's good, and better than most."

"I'm on your side, captain. As a journalist, I learned a long time ago to know when to push and when to stand down. Given my experience in recovery, I've also taken to heart that in a case like this, there's a lot I just need to accept and allow. Especially, to allow you to do your job."

"Much appreciated, Pitcairn. Makes it easier with what is already difficult. So we have nothing to tell you about Maria Elena, though you can trust me that we are on top of it. This is not the first time strange things have happened here in Asheville, given our interesting mix of activists, agitators, and no small number of misfits. We're just getting ready to start broadcasting missing persons reports and will activate some of our community action plans and teams. I'll be here pretty late tonight as will my whole team because we can expect a lot of activity as soon as things roll out. I would expect local media to move pretty fast, and given your profile, you should expect some calls. I'd appreciate it if you would not say anything other than confirming our statements. You know the drill. We don't need any misinformation or other problems."

"Yes, captain. I understand. You will not get any problems on my end. Can I come down in a few hours and check in?"

"Sure. I can't promise my availability, but if you're here, we'll figure it out."

"Understood. I'd guess seven-thirty or eight. Thank you again."

"Our pleasure, Pitcairn."

He looked up to see Nicky strolling toward him.

"That's a hell of a look on your face, Pitcairn. What's happening?"

"Police are moving into full activation, and I'd like to get over there in a few hours. In the meantime, Captain Burden expects it to be a media frenzy. And I can't stop thinking about what I learned from . . . and about . . . Lulu. Somehow this shit is all moving toward something interesting and maybe notable. I can feel it even if I can't explain it." He gazed at her thoughtfully. "What are you thinking, Nicky?"

"I'm thinking barbeque. . . ."

'Barbeque?"

"Yep, bigtime barbeque from BB's and Baby's, a dive that has a one-line marketing campaign, *We Mean Pig,* because like the whole history of this area, there are people who are willing to start a fight when you suggest something that isn't authentic."

He burst out laughing. "You want to say more?"

"Yep, you can argue about the style of the sauce, but the idea that barbeque could be beef or chicken—or turkey, God forbid—is cause for conflict. Pork sausage just squeaks in behind ribs and pulled pork, and BB's and Baby's is said to have perfected it to an art."

"Sounds like the people in New Mexico who will argue over the authenticity of enchiladas." He laughed. "And that Navajo tacos are an abomination!"

"Let's go find this place. I already called Elise to let her know we were headed toward her. She's looking forward to continuing the conversation, but she declined on the barbeque. Vegetarian, right? And besides that, Pitcairn, I understand we need to keep you distracted."

As they drove, they chatted about trauma and recovery. All the while, Pitcairn watched his mind flit from Maria Elena, to the pull of all he was learning about post-traumatic growth, and to the curious experiences with Lulu, Elise, and Nicky. And he could feel the edge of his own traumatic response to it all.

Despite the season, BB's and Baby's was surrounded by cars, although the line was short in front of the walk-up window. He noted picnic tables strung beneath the trees that ringed the place, most filled with people eating and talking. It looked like a very old building that had been serving food for a very long time, though it was well painted and tidy enough. A haze of wood smoke from the cooking fire hung in the air.

They kept it simple: ribs, coleslaw, and cornbread. It really was as good as advertised. Soon they were on the road again heading to the Zen center.

As they drove, Pitcairn's phone rang several times with numbers he didn't recognize. At a traffic stop, he handed the phone to Nicky and asked her to listen to the voice messages. It was yet one more strategy to keep his own traumatic response at a safe distance.

"The captain was right, Pitcairn. The word must be out. These media people sound like self-centered assholes. They say they give a shit with the first words out of their mouth, then off they go into their riff."

He laughed. "Remember, I'm one of them."

She looked at him with a frown. "An asshole you are not, Pitcairn."

▸26◂

BACK AT BODHI MANDALA AND WRAPPED IN THE COMFORT of the sitting room and Elise's presence, Pitcairn poured forth an update. Elise listened well, alternating between eyes closed with attention and periodic sips of tea when her gaze fell softly on him. An occasional gentle smile would cross her lips, invariably accompanied by a slight nodding of her head.

Finally, all talked out, Pitcairn asked, "Elise, what do you think, and what's next in your view?" A long pause followed as he took a few drinks of his tea and glanced over at Nicky, who smiled at him.

Elise took a breath. "Pitcairn, I'm really surprised you are so willing to ask for my guidance and listen to it. After all, we've not known each other long, and I'm the sister to a man who created a great deal of destruction."

He laughed. "Simple enough, Elise. AA has convinced me that quite often I will be out of my depth—or out of my mind—and that nothing in my arsenal of plans and actions will actually work, at which time I should ask for help."

She shook her head and chuckled. "Wisdom becomes you."

"Now that is yet one more rabbit hole," he chortled. "But as much as I'd like to follow that trail, I think it's probably a pointless distraction at this moment."

Elise and Nicky nodded in agreement.

"Pitcairn, there are times when there is nothing to be done or said. Stillness may be our only solution. It occurs to me that Tibetan chant may be just right. Their throat singing is a bit strange at first, but then it's almost like listening to the cosmic sound of Om. Perhaps it can take us beyond our words and thoughts."

Pitcairn started to speak. Elise hushed him. "Stillness. . . ."

"Right. Got it."

She was right about the strange chanting. He had to battle his worries for a time, yet there came a moment when his words and thoughts really did cease. It was in that instant he could see just how much was really troubling him. The contrast of inner turmoil versus stillness was revealing.

Later, the best he would be able to explain would be that the guy who called himself Pitcairn simply fell away. It was a novel experience. He'd never felt so settled . . . or so empty. He guessed it was the state of which mystics spoke, a place beyond self and beyond the world. He felt as if he was perched on the edge of emptiness, yet observing and experiencing it without thinking of it.

Much to his surprise, during more than an hour of being suspended in that odd ether, there was only one notable memory of the room around him. He had heard Nicky ask Elise if he was okay. She said simply, "He's being worked with." He was aware for a fleeting moment that there was indeed a flow at work in and through everything, and for the first time, he felt a deep, quieting comfort unlike any he could recall. Perhaps that was why he was able to slip back into the emptiness.

He returned to the room at the sound of more tea being poured, and opened his eyes slowly. Elise sat right in front of him gazing into his eyes. He hung there for a few moments, then blinked. She smiled at him and reached out to touch the side of his face, intimately but with great kindness. He took a very deep breath.

"Welcome back, Pitcairn."

All he could do was nod. There were simply no words, and he wasn't even sure he'd entirely returned to his body.

"Fuck. . . ." he managed to utter.

Nicky laughed gaily. "He's back!" Then she laughed again.

Elise leaned away and pointed to his refreshed tea. "Drink."

As he sipped the unusually fragrant liquid, she turned and opened a small vial of what Pitcairn recognized as some kind of essential oil.

"Give me your hands," said, then shook a few drops onto each palm. "Rub them together vigorously, then cup them over your face and breathe deeply."

The infusion of scents—some mix of mint and orange and cinnamon, he guessed—shot through him like a jolt. He opened his eyes wide in surprise.

"More tea," she said gently.

After a few moments, Elise announced again. "Okay, now really welcome back!"

He shrugged without words, then struggled to find voice. She hushed him again.

"Pitcairn, there is no need to try to explain the unexplainable. The experience is sufficient unto itself." She paused. "Actually, you probably can't explain it anyway even if you wanted to."

"Okay," he offered. "But can I at least try?"

Nicky and Elise both laughed with him as he proceeded to talk through the experience. Neither spoke until he simply ran out of words.

"You were being worked with," Nicky repeated Elise's words.

"That's as good an explanation as any. Now I need to stand and stretch. He rose and began to move after sitting for so long. After a few bends and twists and grunts, he announced. "Nicky, shall we head down to the police station? That seems to me like the next indicated thing." She quickly agreed.

"Elise, I feel guilty coming and going like this, but my sense is that it's time to re-engage."

"Rest assured, Pitcairn, I understand, and will be waiting to learn what you learn. Of course, I'll be sending good thoughts along with you."

He nodded and said quietly, "Thank you . . . so much."

As he turned to exit, Nicky added, "Life on life's terms, Pitcairn."

▸27◂

DRIVING INTO ASHEVILLE, NICKY AND PITCAIRN COMPARED notes on all that was unfolding. Simply put, it was a lot.

"Nicky, I need a little bit of AA grounding right now. It all feels pretty out of control."

"You mean you're powerless?"

He laughed. "Drop the mic, Nicky. Instant grounding just like that." He paused, "Okay, so let me reframe that. It seems I ought to have a better plan or something, rather than just bouncing from experience to experience."

She let the silence hang for a few moments. "Honestly, Pitcairn, it seems to me you are practicing as well as could be expected. Having your shit together in the middle of a shitstorm is probably not realistic. And actually, I think you're working through this really well."

"Thank you," he replied with a nod as they approached the police station. "It's after ten, but Captain Harden said they'd be here late."

"Let's go see what we see," Nicky responded.

Just as they stepped into the building, his cell phone rang. He didn't recognize the number and handed it to Nicky to answer as he turned his attention forward. Then he heard her sharp intake of a breath.

"Hang on, let me put him on." The look on her face telegraphed that she had just been gobsmacked, as she extended the phone to him with a look of amazement.

He grabbed the phone. "Pitcairn here."

"Hey brother, it's Nat from AA."

Pitcairn had to take an instant to reorient himself. Things had been swirling so wildly it took him a few long moments to remember the strong black man, the cop who had disclosed that things were proceeding."

"Nat?" he stumbled. "What's up?"

"We got your girl. She's safe."

Stunned, all he could he muster was, "What?"

"Maria Elena. She escaped. Some of our guys are driving her to the station. Where are you?"

"Wait . . . what . . . what happened?

He heard a warm laugh on the other end. "She coldcocked one of 'em. Caught him on the temple with a piece of metal she had on her that could pass for brass knuckles. Then she ran through the forest as fast as she could."

In an instant, Pitcairn remembered what she had said about the psychic, the protection her self-described talisman would provide.

"Are you shitting me?"

"No, Pitcairn. I wouldn't do that. I really can't tell you more. Just wanted you to know she's okay. Head on to the central station in Asheville."

He snorted. "Already here."

"No shit?" Nat asked with his own surprise.

"No shit."

"Man, that's enough to make you believe in a Higher Power."

Pitcairn laughed again. "Nat, that would have to be a Higher Power I cannot fathom."

"Listen brother, I gotta go. There's a lot happening right now. Stay tuned."

"Nat, thank you . . . thank you."

"Later," the man replied simply.

Nicky was watching his eyes openly curious. "Well?"

He shrugged in disbelief. "I guess Maria Elena knocked out one of her captors and got away. They're bringing her here right now."

Nicky began to cry. In that moment, Pitcairn realized she too had been holding herself together, or perhaps they had been both been supporting each other. He wrapped her in a big bear hug, and they rocked together wordlessly.

The phone rang again. With a quick glance, he guessed it was Captain Harden. With an arm still draped around Nicky, he lifted the phone to his ear. "Hello?"

The captain confirmed what Nat had just conveyed, then asked if he could come to the station. Maria Elena was due in another fifteen minutes or so. They were driving in from somewhere north of the city.

"Just got here, captain. See you in a few minutes."

Pitcairn and Nicky pulled away from each other to compose themselves. She wiped tears from her eyes. Her face was shining with light. She raised her hands in a sign of surrender. "Pitcairn, that tiger of yours is on quite a rip, isn't it?"

"You said it, Nicky. Let's go."

The captain ushered them into her office, and told them all she knew while they waited. "Pitcairn, I'm really impressed with Maria Elena," she said.

He nodded in understanding. "She can be quite a force."

Somehow Maria Elena had used the brass piece to coldcock the one man guarding her at the remote cabin where she was held, one of several that formed a small enclave. Then she'd followed a dirt road until she saw car lights down in a valley and bushwhacked her way to it, staying off the road while several vehicles passed until she saw a Subaru Outback approaching that she waved down.

Harden laughed. "Guess she figured no self-respecting, dirtbag would be driving a Subaru. Smart girl. And probably right. At any rate, a couple of local folks let her use their phone and delivered her to a couple of my people."

"Captain, that is one hell of a story."

"Glad it turned out so well. I'm really looking forward to meeting Maria Elena. My kind of woman."

He began to laugh. "Mine too."

▸28◂

THEY COULD HEAR A COMMOTION IN THE BACK OF THE STA-
tion. The captain told them it would take a while for all the interviews, adding that with the Feds involved, there was a lot of
ground to be covered.

She added, "Let me get her out of there for a minute to see
you." Then Harden disappeared.

Pitcairn stood with a nervous energy, stepped outside the office,
and tried to maintain a disjointed and distracted conversation with
Nicky while they waited. Moments later, he saw Maria Elena turn
a corner and break into a jog toward him as Harden stopped and
watched with a lopsided grin on her face.

As she neared Pitcairn, he was aware of a radiance shining
through her otherwise-disheveled appearance. She cast herself into
his awaiting embrace, and immediately began a breathless and excited account as his arms enveloped her. Driven by a nervous com-
pulsion, his attempts to quell her words only added energy to her
need to talk, so he just held her gently as she chattered.

Though he was unable to decipher it all, she gradually began to
settle down, and her words slowed until she slumped into him and
began to cry. Wracking contortions coursed through her. Pitcairn
remembered a long-ago television documentary showing how wild
animals would shake uncontrollably after a near-encounter with a
predator in a biological need to release the fear-based hormones
from their body tissues.

He gently began to rock her from side to side. After a time, she
leaned back to gaze up at him. Then she smiled softly, and he knew
the trauma was done with her for the time being.

He kissed her forehead, and nodded toward the captain behind
him. "You've got a story to tell now, Emmy. Give 'em hell, La Diabla."

Her hand touched his cheek. She shrugged with an almost-sheepish look. Glancing to the side to acknowledge Nicky, she took a deep breath, then turned and walked with resolve toward the interview rooms.

It was then that Pitcairn noticed Nat standing behind the captain. Nat grinned at him, then whispered something to Harden. She glanced at him and offered a quick curt nod. As Maria Elena disappeared with the captain, Nat walked toward them.

Waving them into the office again, he gestured for them to sit. "Cap says I can tell you what I know. They'll be at it for a couple of hours, so might as well lay it on you. Let's just call it an AA meeting," he chuckled.

Nat told them the things they already had pieced together. Maria Elena had been abducted from a stretch of the road in an open space between galleries. While they had immediately taken her cell phone and handbag, they had not searched her thoroughly enough. The brass piece woven into the hair at the base of her skull had escaped their notice. After some hours, when they left her guarded by a solitary man, she'd asked to go to the bathroom. When she came out swinging, he never knew what hit him. Then she ran until she came to the road and flagged down the motorist.

Nicky quickly commented: "That is some badassery!"

Pitcairn and Nat laughed. The cop added, "Everyone has been calling her 'gnarly,' which sure seems to fit."

Nicky excused herself, saying she wanted to let Elise and the other Harpies know. Pitcairn thanked her, then asked Nat if they could chat further. He agreed. They both knew it was one of those occasions where one alcoholic needed to talk with another one.

Twenty minutes later, Nicky returned with cups of coffee and a big smile. "Everyone wants to meet and hear the story. In the meantime, we've got your clothes coming up from Greenville. And . . ." she added with some swagger, "we got you a room for a few nights at the Grand Bohemian in Biltmore Village."

Pitcairn puzzled for a moment until Nat provided the context. "Best hotel in the city, and man, you and Maria Elena are in for a real treat."

Pitcairn shook his head, a bit stunned by the turn of events. Then he stood and gave Nicky a bear hug. "You are a real gem."

She beamed. "Only because I don't drink or drug, Pitcairn. Let's be honest."

Three heads nodded. As often happened with recovering alcoholics, there was no limit to the ways they could talk about the situation using the principles of their recovery.

▸29◂

THE DRIVE TO THE HOTEL WAS LARGELY QUIET. MARIA ELENA was all used up. Her head began to sag as she nodded off in the twenty minutes it took to get to the hotel. Before anything else, he took her up to the room. Their luggage was already there, and in the time it took him to park the car and return, she fell sound asleep in the huge bed.

While exhausted himself, he knew he needed to journal and to meditate. A torrent of feelings and words poured disjointedly out, like vomiting onto the pages. As was often the case, even if he couldn't discern an obvious clarity from the many subjects that poured into his journal, it settled him. Only then was he able to notice his surroundings.

The sitting room was separate from the bedroom where Maria Elena snored steadily. A huge bathroom with a spa tub was separated from the bedroom by large shutters that created an expansive, continuous space when opened. Standing and moving quietly, he peered out the window to see the shadows of Biltmore Forest in the darkness to the west. Turning slowly, he was aware of a feeling of deep gratitude rising in his chest. He had done nothing to deserve this, and nothing to retrieve Maria Elena from a dangerous situation. Somehow, a power greater than himself had resolved everything, far exceeding any reasonable expectations.

Returning to his journal, he noted: "A power I do not and cannot understand." Then he added, "X," which he then underlined several times. Only then was Pitcairn able to crawl into the oversized bed and sleep.

When he woke, he had slept so deeply that he felt like he had risen from the dead. It took a few moments to remember where he was. From the light filtering in around the edges of the curtains it was obviously daytime. He turned his head toward Maria Elena and saw her dark eyes steadily gazing at him.

"Hey . . ." he croaked before clearing his throat. "Hey," he repeated. "What good thoughts are you having this morning, Emmy?"

A hint of a smile crept to her face, though she remained motionless. He cocked his head with curiosity as he waited.

"Food. Bath. Nap. Then a long walk in Biltmore Gardens. Cito, my entire body hurts. And I have no idea how I feel about all this."

"That seems surprisingly reasonable."

"Not like me, is it?" she asked.

He laughed. "You know, no matter how long I know you, your resilience continues to amaze me. This whole deal could have turned out so badly, and yet there you are, worse for the wear no doubt but—there you are."

A somber look slipped onto her face. She was very quiet for long moments.

"Yeah. Here I am. I don't have any idea how, Cito."

"I know. I was writing about that last night after you collapsed. And when you get a good look at this room and this place, I'm thinking you are going to be even more amazed that despite everything, here we are."

"Hmmm . . . that reminds me of the book I read over the holidays by Viktor Frankl. The one with his lectures about finding meaning no matter what."

"*Man's Search for Meaning?*"

"No, Cito, the one before that: *Yes to Life: In Spite of Everything.*"

"What made you think of that, Emmy?"

She paused to collect her thoughts. "I'm just remembering something my Auntie Susan used to say. 'Life gives us moments, and for those moments we live.' "

He waited as she worked through what were undoubtedly very complicated feelings and thoughts.

"Cito, it's like the whole point is to have experiences, to experience life in every way imaginable." She struggled for an instant. "And maybe to be present for the experiences?"

Pitcairn waited again.

"Frankl says at one point that if he were to ask someone for the meaning of their life in a moment of great enjoyment of a symphony or beauty or art, in that moment, they would say, 'This . . . this . . . this . . . .' "

"Emmy, I think we are of like mind on this." He reached out to touch her cheek. "I love you."

Then she wept. It was all too much.

He waited and watched with his fingers lightly touching the side of her face.

When the wash of feelings passed, she took a deep breath, reached up to bring his hand to her lips and kiss it, then wiped the tears from her face with both hands.

Another deep breath, then she said, "Cito, baby, I need some breakfast!"

"Room service?"

"Hell yeah, and maybe we can get it next to that big beautiful tub too. I don't think I've ever had breakfast in a tub."

He leaned back to flip on a light, then stood to find the menu. While they waited for their food, Maria Elena gave him a more detailed account of everything that happened.

The kidnappers had driven by her, then leaped out and grabbed her from behind. With a hand firmly over her mouth, she couldn't call out, though she had struggled as they threw her into the back of their cargo van. Two of them pinned her down and held her until she stopped fighting. As soon as she accepted her situation, she began to plan. There was no talk, and she had no interest in asking questions.

"I was really pissed, Cito. I guess underneath that I was afraid, but mostly I wanted to hurt those bastards." She shrugged. "Now that I think about it, I was more focused on that than getting away, at least for a little while."

"Nat passed along what he knew. Turns out the psychic was right." He began to laugh. "Emmy, that's really a great part of the story, isn't it?"

"One of many, Cito. And how do you know Nat?"

"Oh, I've got stories to tell, but it's all about you right now."

"All right." A long pause followed as she collected her thoughts. "Cito, it's like a huge montage of feelings and disconnected thoughts, and somewhere in that mess are some things that actually happened." She took a deep breath. "And I guess if I'm really honest, a lot of things I imagined happened but maybe didn't."

"Emmy, you had an experience, and it's all valid. It's all real because you experienced it."

She cocked her head as she thought through what he'd said. "I think I disassociated from some of it. Big parts feel very distant, almost like they happened to someone else."

"Trauma is a strange thing."

Maria Elena snorted. "That is such an understatement. Strange as can be. And maybe more." A perplexed look came to her face. "I want to know what the hell is going on too. I mean, why did they take me? And what's the deal with all the Feds?"

"There's a bunch we just don't know yet, Emmy."

He started to say more, but her story spilled out of her still further. While disjointed, as most traumatic experiences prove to be, it was a really like a highlight reel of impressions interspersed with conjecture and musing. The delivery of their food broke the rhythm briefly. But afterward, they never thought to head to the bathtub. Maria Elena just kept talking, and Pitcairn kept listening.

▶30◀

THE MEAL AND THE CONVERSATION ENDED IN A TWO-HOUR nap. When they awoke, it was almost dusk. They had slept enough that Pitcairn could feel some energy had returned but not enough for him to have any interest in reconnecting with the world. It would have to wait. Maria Elena headed to the over-sized tub while he vanished into a long meditation.

"Cito, I'm really hungry," he heard her say. It took a few moments to bring himself back into the present and her presence.

"Damn, that was one hell of a getaway," he admitted. "Now, what did you have in mind, Emmy?"

"This place apparently has a really good, English-style pub. What say you?"

He laughed. "Let me wash up first. Then let's go for it."

The trip from their room to the pub was a revelation: Dim lighting, old wood paneling, and intriguing accent pieces were the signature style of the Grand Bohemian. Entering the pub made them truly feel like they were in another time and place, except for the television screens and the people paying great attention to them.

Pitcairn stopped to watch and realized it was a national broadcast of a coordinated federal raid that included the compound where Maria Elena had been held captive.

"Emmy?"

Captivated by the ambiance, she had not been paying attention to the screens.

"Cito! What the hell?"

The broadcast showed a split screen of multiple sites, large numbers of ATF and FBI agents, and uniformed law enforcement. Pitcairn and Maria Elena moved toward the bar and a small cluster of onlookers who sipped their drinks and talked as they watched.

As they got closer, he asked, "What's happening?"

A heavily tattooed man with a very large, handlebar mustache and a high and tight haircut glanced over. "Ruby Ridge all over again, dude," referring to the infamous federal assault on an armed camp in Idaho. His eyes darted back and forth from Pitcairn to Maria Elena. "You're them, aren't you?"

Other heads turned. "Cool!" said another man who had to be a body builder. A barrage of comments and questions followed and caused them both to shrink away.

The bartender, a study in awareness, intervened and nodded them down to the end of the bar. She was tall and striking, Nordic looking, and clearly in command. "I'm Ronnie, a nickname for Veronica. Sit. I got you." She smiled.

She turned to the group who were still chattering and gawking. "Cool is right, guys, so be cool," she told them. "I think they deserve some peace, don't you?"

Heads nodded vigorously though reluctantly, no doubt because they really wanted to hear the many details behind the news stories.

"Now what can I get you," Ronnie asked as she turned back to them.

They ordered club sodas and menus. Once they'd ordered, local pan-fried trout for Maria Elena, and a burger for Pitcairn, Ronnie brought them up to speed.

Earlier in the day, a coordinated effort began across five states: the area in North Carolina west of Asheville, the Upstate of South Carolina, North Georgia and Alabama, and southeastern Tennessee. Heavily armed agents had closed down escape routes at multiple roads and intersections while a combined assault had been undertaken at an undetermined number of locations. The full scope was still unclear but spokesmen for several law enforcement services said the groups had been under surveillance for some time. Though the groups were disorganized and had very diffuse leadership, they said, all were vested in what they called "The Cause." The Feds were calling it domestic terrorism.

Ronnie laughed at that. "Think Confederate flags, wanna-be militia, and general malcontents. A hillbilly mafia but without enough smarts to be anything more than random rabble rousing.

Except for the occasional time when they succeed." She paused for a moment as a more-somber look took hold on her face. "It looks kind of like the Oath Keepers, that far right group that hides behind the Constitution to advance causes that failed years ago. It's really pretty scary."

Pitcairn studied her. "Ronnie, that's a hell of an assessment. I'm thinking you're not just a bartender?"

She smiled somewhat shyly at having been seen so clearly.

"My daddy was a senior political adviser. Of course, I got my undergraduate in political science from Western North Carolina. Found the Blue Ridge country while I was there, so changed direction and picked up a master's from UNC Asheville in nutrition and physical activity. My real job is guiding rock climbing and river trips."

"That explains it," chuckled Maria Elena.

They introduced themselves then. Ronnie resumed her explanation.

"Maria Elena, it looks to me like you just stumbled into this clusterfuck, and that was all the cause the Feds needed to fully launch." She turned to Pitcairn. "I'm guessing her kidnapping forced their hand. One of the press sessions included an allusion to a journalist engaged in some discovery that changed their trajectory. That sound about right, Pitcairn?"

He nodded sheepishly. "I'd say that's a pretty reasonable guess." He paused. "It makes no sense why they would take Maria Elena, though."

"Oh," Ronnie replied quickly. "There was a commentator earlier who proposed what I said, that you stumbled into this. There's an organized core of really scary guys at the heart of this, and a bunch of fringy groups who don't really have their shit together. I'd guess that's who you bumped into. Clueless too, I'd say. If they had a lick of sense, they would have known they were starting a fight they couldn't finish."

He shrugged as he noted that Maria Elena appeared to be disassociating from the conversation. He gently placed a hand on her hip, a protective gesture which clearly grounded her.

"Any idea about the scope, Ronnie?" asked Pitcairn.

"Mostly peaceful, though one of the sites went full-on, guns blazing. That's why the guy over there mentioned Ruby Ridge. All the commentary is the most interesting. Died-in-the-wool southerners bitching about federal aggressions. Libertarians riffing on overreach. Traditional Republicans applauding the show of force. Democrats wringing their hands. And one hell of a peace, love, and granola protest raging right now in Pack Square in downtown Asheville with our usual collection of green activists, pacifists, bluegrass folk, and the Appalachian dope-smoking crowd. No doubt the wealthy folk around here are worried about property values, or in the spas sipping high-end drinks."

She shrugged. "It will all run its course. The global economy will be unaffected. Fox News will turn it into a few months of bullshit causes for defending the homeland from liberals. And . . . ta-dah . . . here comes your food. Just in the nick of time to keep me from ruining your night with my opinions."

"Ronnie, you are my kind of girl," said Maria Elena. "When we're done eating, I have some more-practical questions for you if that's okay."

"Honey, enjoy your trout. I think it's our best dish. Of course, I'm biased since I know the folks who farm the fish just up the road from here. Better still, part of their operation is restocking native trout all over Appalachia. If eating trout can restore the rivers, I'm happy to be a part of it."

The bartender pivoted away, leaving they to eat and watch images and messages move across the television screens. A short while later, Pitcairn felt his phone vibrate, and looked to see that it was Father Tony.

"Be right back, Emmy. It's Tony."

She nodded and smiled.

"Hey Tony," he said as he moved to a quieter part of the pub.

"Kevin, I've been concerned about you and Maria Elena."

"Sorry to not be in touch. It's been a bit wild, and then Maria Elena and I crashed big time. But we seem to be fine, Tony." He paused. "Much to my surprise."

"There is simply no telling how things will ever unfold, Kevin. I know we talked about that this morning, so we'll let it be. Would you like to tell me more? Mostly I just wanted to check in on you, and all the rest can wait."

"Not sure I can give a good summary right now, Tony. Still feel like I'm caught in some kind of vortex. Never dreamed following a story would drag us into a swirl like this. Can we talk about it in another day or so?"

"Absolutely, Kevin." A strained pause followed.

"What is it, Tony? I can tell you've got something more on your mind."

The priest sighed audibly. "I really don't want to add more to the mix, but I'm certain you would want to know."

Pitcairn waited.

"I've been in regular contact with Zack. Today the doctors determined Lucas is unlikely to ever regain consciousness. Zack has decided to disconnect him from life support."

Pitcairn felt a massive stab of pain in his chest, like a harpoon to the heart. Involuntarily, he closed his eyes and wrenched his way through a breath. And then another, and another. It felt like more than he could bear, no doubt a culmination of emotions from which he had divorced himself for too long. He knew from long experience that his only real choice was to stay present and to breathe, that the feeling would allow him to neither flee nor collapse into it. Father Tony was quiet all the while.

Finally, he was able to speak. "That hurts, Tony."

"Yes. Yes, it does." Silence followed before he spoke again. "Acknowledging the pain is a powerful prayer, one we too seldom practice. And I know you know this, Kevin, but it bears repeating. For reasons we cannot know, you are one who must bear witness to the heartaches in the world. It will find a voice through you. As always, that message will be powerful."

"I know. But I'm never prepared for the blows when they come, Tony." He felt himself shake his head. "I'll hold space for it, because I'm not really sure I have a choice. But it's a lot to be with."

"Yes. Yes, it is. I won't give you any platitudes. If and when you need to talk, please call."

"I will, Tony. Thank you. I'm glad you told me even if it's heartbreaking."

"Will you tell Maria Elena?"

He snorted. "She'll know something is up as soon as she sees me, and I'll have to tell her. Thankfully, she's stronger than anyone I know."

"Both of you are in my prayers, Kevin."

"Thanks, Tony. I'll call you soon."

"And Kevin, please remember that a heart breaking is painful and unfortunate, but broken open hearts heal the world."

He felt a nagging need to explore the idea further with Tony but realized it was more important to be present to feelings rather than taking refuge in his own thoughts and thinking.

"Tony, thank you. I gotta go, but we'll talk later."

"I understand," the priest said as they disconnected.

Pitcairn waited for a few moments collecting himself. Then with a deep sense of resolve, he walked back to the bar. Somewhere in his thoughts, he was aware that it had never occurred to him to take a drink, even in this setting. He noted to himself that it really was quite miraculous, and that somehow everything would eventually add up.

Maria Elena and Ronnie were chatting intimately. The bartender nodded at him as he approached. "Here comes your guy, Maria Elena." Ronnie moved away discreetly.

Maria Elena turned toward him. Instantly, her countenance changed as she sensed his distress. "What is it, Cito?"

He leaned into the edge of the bar. Looking at her steadily, he said softly, "It's Lucas. He's not going to make it, Emmy."

A stunned look flashed to her face. Pitcairn imagined a flood of emotions. It looked like she wanted to howl in pain. She checked herself. Instead, a low visceral groan came from deep within her. She didn't break eye contact with him, and he gently placed a hand on her arm. Her eyes signaled many thoughts racing through her mind. Then she said simply, "We need to walk, Cito."

She stood as Pitcairn turned toward Ronnie to settle the tab. The bartender cocked her head and nodded, clearly intuiting that something was happening.

"I got you. Come back when you can."

Maria Elena hit a brisk speed immediately while he kept pace easily with a long stride that was well-accustomed to walking when psychically disturbed. They looped through a retail district sprinkled with restaurants, though the number of customers made clear it was not the height of the season. She found a path along the

Swannanoa River as it spilled through the heart of Asheville. The uneven ground slowed them some as they proceeded wordlessly.

Finally, they came to a pocket park with a few benches beside the river. Maria Elena steered toward them. She perched on the edge, leaning forward, hands between her clenched thighs. Pitcairn positioned himself hip to hip with her and placed his hand gently at the base of her neck, his arm draping downward.

After a moment, she collapsed her torso over her knees as sobs wracked through her. He sat with eyes closed, breathing and feeling. There was nothing more to be done.

▶31◀

PITCAIRN AWOKE IN THE DEEP OF THE NIGHT WITH A STRANGE dream suspended in his awareness. He and Maria Elena had walked for quite some time along the river after their tears were spent. They exchanged few words, though their closeness felt profound.

Upon returning to the hotel, they had called Zack, who was devastated. He had not decided when to proceed but deeply appreciated the help he was getting. Father Tony had coordinated a support group from the community. Bonnie, the nurse, was a steady presence for him. For a man who had been become so isolated, the connections were beautiful. He admitted he'd become very attached to the presence of Lincoln and Lucy, which Pitcairn understood.

Pitcairn and Maria Elena were grateful for the support he was receiving, and planned to speak with Zack again over the weekend. She assured him they would make every effort to return before Lucas died.

After the exhaustion of so many emotions and experiences, they had collapsed into a deep sleep. Yet the dream was so real that waking early was inevitable.

For years, the nightmare of his violent experience in Evansville, Indiana, had haunted him. In an alcohol and drug-induced haze, Pitcairn had strangled a drug dealer. But his experience with the Crucifix Protests had brought him a deep and different understanding of the event. The nightmares had shifted, and there had been a growing presence of loving and nurturing dreams. It was all a reflection of the deep healing that had come to him.

His dream revealed a gauzy, opaque space that was dimly lit. He could not see very far; it was almost like peering into a fog. It felt like the space was incredibly expansive, maybe even unlimited. No matter where or how he moved in the space, he could not gain any clarity about direction or point or purpose. It was not a feeling of being lost, and certainly not claustrophobic. He felt comforted and reassured, like he could trust it all, though he could not see or sense the full scope of his surroundings.

Then it all shattered, from no apparent cause. The veil parted and revealed a shimmering image of a gathering of people. They were clothed differently but he could not really make out the form. Regardless, he felt completely at ease, as if he were being welcomed. The image continued to shimmer, then slowly faded as the opaque quality returned. The impression it left was one of initiation.

Then for what felt like an endless amount of time, he simply rested in the veiled place. Nothing to do. There was nothing to be done. It was as if he was beyond words and thought.

Awakened and writing about the experience in the dimly lit alcove of the hotel room, he was struck by the reassurance he felt. Even though nothing was clear, somehow all was well, and he was fully a part of something.

He did an online search and discovered that in the Jungian orientation, it was a very archetypal dream, something he could not recall ever experiencing before. The interpretations he found suggested it was a glimpse of the realm of the soul, which perplexed him. He was of two minds about souls. Either they explained a great deal that he could not otherwise fathom or they were an artifact of the make-believe that human egos needed to make sense of everything, despite the fact that it was all nonsensical.

He made a note to talk to Tony about it, then quietly let himself out of the room to again go walking. He went along the river path, though in the opposite direction from the night before. For once, a walk was just a walk.

When he returned, Maria Elena was in the shower. He could hear her singing to herself. While not exactly upbeat in tone, it seemed that a night of rest had allowed her to find a psychic reset.

He knocked as he eased into the bathroom. "Que pasa, mi amor?"

She poked her head around the glass wall and gazed at him with a soft smile. "Breakfast, baby. Then we really need to see the gardens at the Biltmore. A morning in the middle of all that loveliness will be a really good thing given everything that has happened."

"Emmy, that sounds perfect. Then maybe this afternoon we can regroup. There are a whole lot of moving parts right now."

She smiled again then slipped back into the shower.

* * *

Maria Elena had been right. Strolling the wandering paths of Biltmore Gardens had been restorative. Though it was the off-season, they found a lovely grove of camellias with blossoms in a wide variety of colors. A nearby bench proved to be a perfect respite. Then they meandered through the greenhouses with their many exotics.

Lunchtime brought them to a bistro on the grounds where their solitude continued. Back at the hotel, they stopped to watch the continuing news of the federal raids filling the big screens of the pub: more than a hundred arrests, four deaths including a DEA agent, extensive seizure of weapons, properties, and assets. A video showed a burned and smoking compound near Huntsville, Alabama, at which armed conflict had broken out.

"Violence begets violence," said Pitcairn in a tone filled with heartache.

Maria Elena looked at him. "What can we do, Cito?"

He nodded. "What we are able to do—to be agents for change and to mitigate violence, in every way we can." He gazed at her. "That's my mission with my writing, Emmy . . . and why I have to bear witness to it all—no matter what."

They went to a comfortable, secluded corner, and Pitcairn moved to bring them coffee.

"Emmy, how are you at this point?"

Her eyes moved about outwardly scanning, though she was clearly inwardly searching. "I'm okay, Cito. I'm okay." She nodded as if in affirmation to herself. "I think I need to see your therapist for some trauma work."

"Understandable." He thought for a moment. "You might also benefit from some time with Elise. She's pretty remarkable. Completely at odds with what one would expect as the sister of a terrorist."

"Hmmm . . . that might be a good start. Sooner has got to be better than later, right?"

"I would think so, Emmy. How about we weave that into our plans."

"Plans?" she asked.

"Well, we'll need to figure out when to get back home to be there for Zack. I assume you'll have some follow up with the Feds. You've really got to meet Lulu, and I really need to learn more from her. Plus there are the white squirrels to see." He laughed. "How could we not do that? And I need more time with Elise too. I think I've got an angle on what I need about this post-traumatic growth, but there is clearly a lot more to learn."

Maria Elena shook her head. "It's complicated."

"You know me, I've got no evidence it's possible to keep it simple. And I can't imagine going home without spending a little time with the Harpies. They've been stellar throughout this whole mess."

He lifted his phone. "And the whole free world wants to talk to me, though I guess Tony and Mortenson are at the top of that list."

"Easy for me. No phone. Feds didn't return it to me. Of course, I probably need to call a few folks to let them know I'm okay."

"Looks like they must have all called me," Pitcairn said. "And it looks like it's going to snow tonight."

"Snow? A lot?"

"In the high places as much as a foot, down here a dusting."

"Cito, how about we just stay put until Saturday afternoon? I think I might just rest."

"Can do. And I can catch up on some of this mess in the meantime."

"While you go do that, I'm going to go take a nap, Cito."

He leaned over and kissed her gently. "See you when I see you, Emmy."

▸32◂

WHILE MARIA ELENA RESTED, PITCAIRN FIRST CHECKED HIS news feeds. As a consequence of the federal actions, President Barack Obama would be addressing the nation at 8 p.m. Saturday. That would be worth watching. It seemed to Pitcairn as if the tensions and vitriol were escalating across the nation, and perhaps around the world. Somehow a dark underbelly was emerging, which was all the more reason for what would follow with Maria Elena and him.

He turned his attention to the long queue of voice messages, many without identification. It proved to be quite a mix: requests for interviews and several remarkable options for Maria Elena including talking with a representative of Oprah Winfrey. It was clear that a spiritual opening was emerging, though he had no idea what to make of it. The Feds wanted to meet with Maria Elena the next day. Nicky and the other Harpies wanted to meet up as soon as it would fit everyone's schedule. Lulu left a gentle message and expressed her concern for how they were being affected. Clearly a cusp of a wave was sweeping them along.

At that moment, he flashed back to his dream in Albuquerque—the Jeep in a descending pirouette into an ill-defined whirlwind, carrying Maria Elena and him into its sweep. In a moment of clarity that pulled him into a still, quiet reverie, he knew their path was somehow coming together. Despite a pang of anxiety for Maria Elena's well-being, he remembered Tony's assurance that he could trust not only his own path but hers as well. He felt himself nod in affirmation, then picked up his journal and began sketching an outline of the next few days.

He was so absorbed in thinking through next steps that he didn't realize Maria Elena was awake and watching him from across the room. She smiled.

"How did I ever find a guy like you, Cito?"

He laughed loudly. "Emmy, it's all a tiger in the jungle of reality, and somehow we ended up strapped together to its back."

"That is the most unromantic comment ever!"

He shrugged, then added, "Okay, how about this. In a past life, you made a commitment to stay with me across time until I was finally the man you knew I could be."

"Total bullshit but romantic," she replied with mock disgust and resignation. "Enough on that, I'm powerful hungry again, Cito. It's like these experiences are burning up a whole lot of energy. Do you want to go back and see if Ronnie is around? She's pretty cool."

"Sure enough. And while we eat, we can talk about your upcoming interview with Oprah."

She had started to turn to the bathroom but stopped in her tracks. "Oprah?"

"Yep. No idea how her people got my number, but you are a very hot topic right now."

Maria Elena sat on the edge of the bed and stared at him.

"Oh, and the Feds want to see you tomorrow."

All she could do was shake her head in disbelief. Then a puzzled look came to her face. "Cito, I just realized I had the strangest dream during my nap. There was some kind of a protest, but it was really quiet. The marchers reminded me of the guys who took me, but they were warped and twisted. They were marching between lines of people silently watching. They were like the angels in that great German film we saw, *Wings of Desire*. Fully present but devoid of judgment or opinion. Just watching with great compassion. It seemed like the watchers far outnumbered the marchers, and they kind of faded away into some vast background."

As she spoke, Pitcairn realized a potential connection to his own dream just the night before with the shimmering gathering of people in different garb. He told her then about his dream, and also the realization about the Jeep dream.

"This is just too weird," she said, clearly perplexed. "Can we go spend some time with Elise? From what you described, maybe she can work with us on this, Cito."

"Let's do it," he agreed. "For now, let's see if we can get a bit of this sorted out over some good food."

They quickly pulled themselves together and headed for the pub. As they passed by large windows, they could see that snow had begun to fall. They stopped to watch, completely captivated, for a few, long moments.

"It's really pretty, Cito. And maybe perfect timing, a coating of pristine, white snow to overlay the catastrophes of the past few days."

At the pub, Ronnie waved and pointed to a secluded corner booth. A few minutes later, she came over with menus and offered to bring them up to date. They were eager to hear more, though only after placing their orders.

Ronnie attended to a sprinkling of customers, then returned and pulled up a chair.

"It seems clusterfuck is an understatement." She smiled kindly at Maria Elena, clearly a gesture of consideration. "Obama is going to address the nation on Saturday night. That douchebag Donald Trump is all over his Twitter feed making ridiculous claims which are generating all kinds of agreement from every fascist in America. All over the South, there's agitation. Supporters on the fringe of reality are calling for marches to protest federal overreach and the trampling of individual freedoms. The only one that seems to be gaining real traction is in Montgomery, which is as ironic as anything I can fathom. Imagine a gathering of wannabe secession-ists and hate-mongers marching through the heart of the mecca of American civil rights." She shook her head in amazement. "Looks like most of the federal engagement has steadied, but na-tional guardsmen have been deployed in a number of places."

She alternated glances at each of them. "How's that for an update?"

Maria Elena spoke first. "I just can't figure out how I was pulled into the middle of this."

Ronnie quickly replied. "That's the story of transformation, honey. Fate appears, and destiny is created by how we engage fate." She shrugged. "I'd guess you don't get a choice in it."

They looked at Pitcairn, and he smiled. "Emmy, it's that tiger in the jungle again." Then he turned and explained to Ronnie, who burst out in laughter.

"Perfect!" she proclaimed. "And someday I get to tell my grand-kids about hanging out in a bar with you two as a whole new movement began."

"Don't you think that's a bit of a stretch, Ronnie?" Pitcairn asked.

She cocked her head in mock amusement. "Dude, I have been all over the web since we met, and if there is anyone who would stumble into a hot mess like this, it is you." She turned back to Maria Elena. "And honey, you are guilty by association, which would appear to be a really good thing."

Maria Elena looked stunned. After a long pause, she asked, "Why do you say that, Ronnie?"

"Have you ever heard the quote, 'Well-behaved women seldom make history'?"

A strange look crossed Maria Elena's face. Pitcairn could not contain his merriment.

"I gotta go back to work but look forward to chatting some more. Your dinners should be up shortly."

As Ronnie walked away, Pitcairn lowered his gaze at Maria Elena and whispered, "La Diabla!"

▸33◂

AFTER DINNER, THEY HAD TAKEN A LONG WALK IN THE SNOW, which proved to be more than a dusting as it slowly accumulated. Chilled by the cold and damp from the snow, they had dropped into a local coffee shop and art gallery. The many beautiful pieces provided some uplift for the weariness that continued to return. It was as if in finally settling, the effects of the wear and tear had quieted them both.

"Cito?" she asked as he sat deep in thought.

He looked up from his drink. She noted the careworn features of his face. As much as Pitcairn had a seemingly endless psychic energy for difficult circumstances, she knew it came at a much greater cost than he would acknowledge. A slight smile arose, and she could feel the warmth of their connection.

"I'm feeling really sad."

He nodded in agreement. "Me too, Emmy. Me too."

"We're not done with this, are we?"

A stifled laugh snuck from him. "Emmy, baby, we're not being given an option. I'm remembering what Eckhart Tolle said in his book *The Power of Now*. That we would be done with it when it was done with us." He chuckled. "Or maybe we should just ride the tiger until the tiger comes to a rest."

She thought for a moment. "How are you, Cito?"

Long moments passed as he considered all that had unfolded. "This shit asks a lot of me." He shrugged. "Then again, why not me?" He smiled again. "And why not you, Emmy? We're living such charmed lives. Who are we to be excluded from difficulties?"

Back at the hotel, they had collapsed into bed. Admitting their weariness allowed them to rest.

When Pitcairn woke, he was aware of her closeness without opening his eyes. He stayed very still, noticing each of them breathing, motionless for a few minutes before realizing she was awake as well.

"Touch me, Cito," she whispered.

He rolled toward her, eyes still closed, and began to gently move his hands over her body. Light touches with no particular pattern, following some inner intuition, every part of her body a next potential touchpoint. Within minutes, she began to make soft sounds of pleasure, her body beginning to move ever so slowly.

Long, slow caresses, more meditation than sex, it was as if the whole of the world fell away into timelessness. Beyond thinking, until a moment came when a slow sigh escaped her.

Stillness then returned. He was unwilling to break the moment until he sensed her moving toward him. A gentle lingering kiss to his cheek, then she whispered again.

"Breakfast, baby . . ."

His laugh broke loudly. "Emmy, you are amazing!"

"And hungry, Cito. Powerful hungry again."

"Well, the good news is that Nicky told me about what she said would be the best breakfast we would ever have."

"Oh? Do tell," she asked.

"Nope, it's a surprise. We have to get there when they open so we don't end up with a long wait and you get even more hangry. So get your ass in the shower."

"Come with me. I want to wash you from head to toe." She smiled and winked.

A short while later, they found themselves the first to arrive for seating at the Early Girl Eatery, an unassuming storefront that advertised organic, farm-to-table fare. They took a bay-window seat, and began looking at the menu. Eclectic would describe it well, and if the promptly-served and outstanding coffee was an indication, they were in for a treat.

Pitcairn struck up a conversation with their server, a young woman with turquoise hair and the unusual, old-fashioned name of Mamie who generously walked them through the menu. They learned that she had been raised in a small former plantation town in South Carolina, and had fled at fifteen when she asked a court to emancipate her from her racist parents. She'd earned her GED and was now working her way through Western North Carolina University with aspirations to be a veterinarian. It was a bit of a drive, she said, but the program and scholarships were very good, and the tips in Asheville made driving back and forth worthwhile.

After considerable deliberation, they decided to go with the flow and be non-traditional. Maria Elena ordered the Yam Scram, scrambled eggs with sweet potatoes, local sausage and shitake mushrooms. Pitcairn couldn't resist the Bow to the King, southern fried chicken on battered french toast made from cinnamon buttermilk biscuits. Both meals would prove to be outstanding, and Mamie dropped in and out at mostly perfect intervals.

As the snow continued to sprinkle down, they planned their day, first swinging by the Feds' makeshift office to reclaim Maria Elena's phone, then dropping in on Elise if she was available. Pitcairn would also reach out to the Harpies and Lulu to see what plans could be made to meet. It was a leisurely breakfast that could easily have been longer had they not begun to feel guilty as the line of customers grew outside.

"Interesting that so many folks are willing to stand in the snow and cold, isn't it?" Pitcairn observed to Mamie.

"Damned good tucker," she countered with an exaggerated drawl.

"Sounds about right," he replied, then pulled a fifty-dollar bill out his billfold. "Good luck, Mamie. Looks to me like you have a great future ahead of you."

"Oh . . . that's too much!" she exclaimed.

Maria Elena interjected, "No Mamie. You've got a spark in you, and we can support you, so let us do so."

The young woman blushed and slipped away.

"Emmy, that was sweet and perfect."

"Yeah, but she couldn't let it in yet. I hope things work out well for her."

"We've done our part, now let's get this table to someone who's been crazy enough to stand outdoors waiting."

While Emmy debriefed with the Feds, Pitcairn settled into a chair in the outer office and slowly worked his way through a variety of notes he had jotted to himself. There was a certain serenity that always came from shaping disparate items into a plan. Even if he didn't follow it, at least some temporary order came out of what had become something akin to chaos. Then he made a few phone calls, struck by how things were falling into place.

"Timing is everything," he said aloud to himself as Maria Elena approached with a young man. She smiled. "I heard that. And here we are. Perfect timing."

The man extended his hand. "Agent Timothy Rousseau. It's a real pleasure to meet you, Mr. Pitcairn."

Pitcairn chuckled. "What the hell has she been telling you?" Then he added, "And you can drop the Mr., just Pitcairn will do."

"Oh, I knew about you from our casework. Maria Elena just filled in a few blanks. I admire your writing."

Pitcairn felt surprise register on his face. "Which writing?" he asked.

"I may be in law enforcement, but I'm a huge advocate for non-violent approaches to achieve it. I don't know if I can go as far as you do with the idea of innocence, but there's nothing but good that will come from our attempts to deescalate all the troubles in the world. It seems much more practical to me."

"I told Tim you'd appreciate hearing that," Maria Elena said.

Pitcairn nodded thoughtfully. "It's unusual to find people who can support the ideas, even if from a practical point of view, Timothy. Mostly everyone seems to expect retaliation and punishment. And it just goes on and on. Every now and again, it explodes. Everyone in the culture pays attention just like they do when they see a car wreck, then they check back out and go right on about their business of inflicting it on others."

The agent nodded and extended his hand again. "Take good care of this woman. She needs a good break after all this."

Pitcairn glanced at Maria Elena, who shrugged sheepishly.

He stood up as Rousseau smiled once more and turned quickly.

"Curiouser and curiouser," Pitcairn said to Maria Elena.

"You have more stories to tell?"

"Let's head on out. Elise wants to meet you. While we drive, you can catch me up on your debriefing. And I can catch up on all these curious things."

▶34◀

THE CONVERSATION WITH THE FEDS HAD BEEN LARGELY A RE-counting exercise with a few more details added. It took Maria Elena only ten minutes or so to describe it to him.

"What's next?" he asked.

"I think I'm done with it until they call me for more, Cito." She paused. "I'm ready to be done with it."

He looked over toward her and noted a tired but settled look on her face. She glanced back at him. "What?"

"Glad you're done, but it's not done with you, Emmy."

"What?" she asked again with some exaggeration.

"You'll be meeting with Oprah on Tuesday."

A dumbfounded utterance fell from her, "What? . . . WTF, Cito."

His eyes stayed on the road with its increasing snow cover as they gained elevation outside the city. "Yep, you really are one very hot commodity right now."

He then described the call, the travel plans that were being made for them, and the other pieces that had fallen into place: Afternoon would be with Elise, dinner with the Harpies who were driving up to see them, a Sunday meeting with Lulu and return to Atlanta, a Monday flight to the West Coast and Oprah's studio, then finally back to Albuquerque in time to be with Zack and Lucas.

"Damn," she responded.

"That was why you heard my comment about timing. Emmy, it just all clicked into place."

"The Tao," she said. "Life flows like a current, and we're just along for a ride."

"Can't wait to see what the flow brings with it."

He thought for long moments before going on. "Emmy, I just can't help but think there is something trying to happen." He remembered the words of his therapist, Kari. "Watching for what wants to happen."

"That's a funny phrase, Cito."

"Yeah, it's from the Good Witch," he laughed.

"Hmmm . . . I like that. Maybe it's perfect for meeting Elise," she added as the compound unfolded before them. "And Lulu."

"Emmy, we are not in charge. Let's see."

At the Zen center, Elise came out to welcome them. After a quick nod and hello for Pitcairn, she wordlessly wrapped her arms around Maria Elena and held her gently. With her knowledge of how trauma can hold people against their knowledge and will, Elise did not release her until Maria Elena had relaxed into her.

"How did you know?" she asked as they finally leaned away from the embrace.

"Oh, honey, I can't even imagine how hard this has been." Elise clasped Maria Elena's hands. "We're going to take care of you now, if you'll allow me."

Maria Elena nodded almost shyly, and with some surprise. Then she looked to Pitcairn.

"Told you she had a way." Then he hugged Elise as they turned to go inside.

The first order of business was a detox tea that Elise said was a local remedy long used by the Cherokee people, a concoction of bark, twigs and berries. The aroma was earthy and calming. Then they settled onto cushions as Elise wrapped blankets around them and added sage to the wood stove.

"Let's just be here together for a few minutes," she said as she closed her eyes.

The stillness was punctuated by the sounds of the woodstove. The quiet rose up and enveloped them in the dimly lit yurt. Then Elise began a very gentle chant.

Once again, it was not clear how long they sat. It reminded Pitcairn of a long-ago flotation in an isolation tank, when he couldn't say afterward where he had traveled to, only that he'd been far away.

When Elise finally spoke, it took him a moment to find himself. Then she asked a simple question: "Maria Elena, please tell me what you were feeling."

Pitcairn kept his eyes closed but could hear Maria Elena's long, deliberate breaths.

"It was really strange, Elise. I felt like I was watching from outside myself. First, it was the men who were holding me captive. I wasn't afraid, just curious. Nothing really made sense, it was all really kind of ridiculous." She chuckled. "Maybe it is all really kind of ridiculous."

"How so, Maria Elena?"

"Oh, I don't know. It's like we have to play out the script in order to see . . . and to learn . . . and to grow maybe?"

Pitcairn couldn't resist looking at her. Her eyes were closed, her head was cocked, and there was slightly perplexed look on her face. He was captivated watching her, and couldn't imagine looking away.

"The funny part is what came after that, though." She took a very measured breath to steady herself. "Then I remembered . . . well, I don't really know if it was a memory, but I was back in the room where my daddy . . ."—she breathed audibly three times— ". . . where my daddy first touched me."

Pitcairn could feel the sharp edge and strength of her emotions.

"Good, Maria Elena, good. Use your breath to stay present," said Elise.

After a few pressured moments, she went on. "I never knew how gentle he wanted to be." A short exhale followed. Eyes closed, she shook her head. "I've always remembered him as a monster, even though we seemed to set that right, and I know what he did was wrong." Now her eyes startled open and she looked steadfastly at Elise. "Oh . . ." she began with a break in her voice. "Daddy was so twisted, but Elise, it was the best he was able to do."

"Just breathe, Maria Elena. Stay with that," Elise encouraged her.

She took a very deep breath as her countenance softened. "Elise, it's like I was watching it but with understanding I never knew before. And now . . . it all makes sense in its own terrible, contorted way."

Elise nodded.

"It all makes sense. So do the kidnappers." She turned to Pitcairn. "Cito, that's the innocence you've been describing, isn't it?"

All he could do was shrug in disbelief. "Emmy, baby, you may have gone beyond what I can get my head around." He paused to consider his words. "I think you just experienced it."

He turned to Elise. "That was beautiful, and amazing. Did you do that?"

Before she could reply, Maria Elena spoke forcefully.

"Oh . . . the dream . . . the dream with the watchers! Cito, it's the message in the dream!"

She turned back to Elise and excitedly described the dream. The warped and twisted marchers moving between lines of people silently watching in complete non-judgment.

"Elise, they are all the same feeling: the vision I just had, and the flashback to Daddy, and the dream! They feel the same."

Elise smiled at her, then turned and grinned at Pitcairn, who described his own dreams, the shimmering gathering of people. In the moment, it felt completely parallel to Maria Elena's experiences.

"Elise, what the hell did you just do?"

She laughed gaily. "Oh no, I'm not taking any credit for what just happened. At best, I'm a spiritual midwife, if even that. No, just to remind you, that is what my shaman teachers would call a shamanic healing, or soul retrieval." A strange look came to her face. "Though I have to admit it is pretty uncommon that both of you would be swept into it."

Pitcairn looked at Maria Elena. "I had a soul retrieval too, Emmy. While you were captive." He raised his hands with an open gesture signaling his own surprise.

Turning to Elise, he filled her in still further on the voice and their common experiences.

"Kevin," she began before taking her own deep breath. "Maria Elena, you two are being called."

"Called to what?" Maria Elena quickly asked.

Once again, she demurred. "I can't answer that. Only the two of you can. All I can do is encourage you, and perhaps to support you with my own inner work."

Then she turned to Pitcairn. "Kevin, what you just saw and described is post-traumatic growth."

It was if she had shocked him, it startled him so greatly. "Shit
. . ." he said, then lapsed into quiet.

"The same traumas that could have harmed Maria Elena have
now been transmuted into great healing and understanding. That
is metanoia, a profound change of heart. Suddenly, experiences
become a springboard rather than deep, enduring damage. Sometimes they cross generations, and relationships."

He frowned. "And it fired out of the past and into the present,
and then into me?"

Elise laughed again in delight. "Your guess is as good as mine,
but there is no denying what just happened." She looked to Maria
Elena. "Right?"

"It could not be clearer, Elise, though I have no clue what's next."

"Kevin and Maria Elena, you do not have to know anything.
You just have to follow the echoes."

"Echoes?" they both replied in unison, and laughed.

"Sure, you may never know the source of the sound that has
been echoing from past to present and now beyond, but you can
trust the echoes. They will lead you well."

They all lapsed into an extended quiet. Then Pitcairn said, "I
have a feeling we are done for now, Elise."

"For now, Kevin, but never done. The echoes will not cease now."

"Emmy, we've sure got a lot to work with now. And more coming
at us for sure. But now we need to get going and track down the
Harpies for dinner." He looked back to Elise. "Can we call you as
we need to?"

Her quick response surprised him. "I couldn't imagine otherwise."

"Thank you does not seem to be enough, Elise," Maria Elena said.

Elise smiled yet again. "This is what I do, Maria Elena." She
turned to Pitcairn. "Sometimes it seems this is a balance to my
brother, light and darkness. That's another conversation, though.
You two need to go."

Their parting was gentle and sweet.

▶35◀

THEY WERE SILENT AS THEY DROVE BACK TO THE HOTEL UNTIL the buzz of a text caused Pitcairn to look and laugh.

"It's Nicky. They want to meet us at a funky place in downtown called the Vortex." He glanced over to her. "Of course, it would be called the Vortex!"

Maria Elena just shook her head, the parallel not really registering given the depth of her reflections. "Cito, I'm really surprised how little pain there was in that awareness. My whole history of working through the incest and the family denial . . ." Her voice trailed away. "You know as well as anyone how painful that has been, yet it was as if it was all swept away with the realization, and the clarity. How can that be?"

Pitcairn began to speak just as she continued.

"For that matter, how can La Diabla, who punched her way violently out of a terrible situation, suddenly have dreams and ideas about non-violence and innocence? This makes no sense, Cito."

He considered her question. "Emmy, it reminds me of what happens when someone is struck sober. Like you said, a moment of clarity comes, and there is an immediate transition to a new point of view and a new way of being."

He turned his head and studied her. She looked back to meet his gaze.

"Regardless, I'd say it qualifies as some kind of what Carl Jung called a psychic change in you."

"When did you study Jung?"

"Oh, I didn't. But he had a lot of impact on AA's approach. Maybe if we'd understood enough back then, he would have been able to speak to post-traumatic growth as well. Seems to be the same angle."

He checked the time as they neared the parking garage. "You have time for another luxurious bath before we go to dinner." A memory rushed back from the past. "You know, Clint always said the result of the Twelve Steps and a spiritual recovery would be that what used to be malignant in our lives would be rendered benign and no longer harmful to us. That seems to fit right into the reframing the trauma work does, as well as into my own remaking." He paused. "Maybe yours too."

She nodded, though her thoughts clearly still held all her attention at depth.

* * *

They parked up the street from the Vortex and strolled down the sloping hill through the heart of Asheville's funky district. Art galleries, a head shop, a tea house, and a CBD dispensary slipped by. A couple of men, bearded and dressed for the cold, played a violin and a guitar in front of the restaurant. They were a perfect complement to a place that looked classic shabby-chic, a part of the whole scene of the city.

As soon as they stepped in, Nicky saw them, raced over, and swept Maria Elena up in a giant hug. Then she leaned back to look at her. "You look good, honey." She turned to Pitcairn, leaned into his embrace, and kissed him on the cheek. "You too."

She led them to a table in the dimly lit back where Rosemary and Betty hopped up to give hugs all around. Then they quickly settled in.

"I'm impressed you drove up through the snow," said Pitcairn.

Rosemary snorted. "Hell honey, if moonshine and crack couldn't kill us, a snowstorm ain't nothin'."

"Besides that, Pitcairn, we have a Higher Power, what do we have to fear?" added Betty. "Now catch us up!"

"Christ almighty, Betty . . . ," said Rosemary. "Let them look at the menu first."

Betty rolled her eyes, then laughed with a conspiratorial look. "I am a gossip whore!"

Her simple acknowledgment caused laughs all round. After ordering, the Harpies all looked to Maria Elena expectantly. She began to recount the entire experience. Amazingly, the women listened without interrupting. At one point, Pitcairn observed this was what AA called "the language of the heart," which was the spirit of the Twelve Steps. They listened to Marie Elena respectfully and diligently, knowing it was extremely important for her to tell her story, and for them to hear it.

When the appetizers came, two charcuterie boards and enough crusty bread for a small army, the breaking of bread did nothing to alter the rhythm of the story. At moments that begged for an acknowledgment, there were now quick interjections—including when Maria Elena punched her captor and ran.

"God damn, girl, you go!" Rosemary said with a flourish.

The rest of the food arrived, and even as Maria Elena continued to share, the meal began to feel like a family affair as tidbits and quick comments were traded. When they came to the afternoon just passed, she turned to Nicky.

"Elise is amazing," she said almost reverently.

"She is that, sweetheart," Nicky replied. "What happened?"

Not before Betty offered with very real appreciation, "Maria Elena, you are a walking miracle."

"Why do you say that?" she asked.

Betty teared up, and everyone became very attentive to her.

"A big part of my story is abuse. I've worked for years to find peace with it all. Granted, when I was using, I kept putting myself in harm's way." She caught herself. "Oh, I'm not saying you had anything to do with this, Maria Elena, just that it can be really hard."

Maria Elena smiled generously at her.

"I'm sorry to hear that, Betty. But I guess that makes us both walking miracles."

Rosemary jumped in. "When this shit gets real, we get real." Then she thought for a moment. "Or maybe when we get real, this shit gets real. Never thought of it like that." She placed a hand gently on Betty's forearm and squeezed reassuringly. "Go on, Maria Elena."

Pitcairn was very curious how Maria Elena would describe the time spent with Elise. He wasn't entirely surprised she didn't share all the details. But he was aware of the care with which she periodically looked to Betty, and he imagined she was passing on the healing she had experienced.

The chatter swept them up after that. Pitcairn could see that Maria Elena was glad to no longer be the focus of the conversation. Of course, the Harpies needed no invitation to fill the space.

At some point, Nicky asked Pitcairn, "So what's next?"

He decided to play fully into their love of gossip. "We'll be flying to the West Coast on Monday. Maria Elena has an interview with Oprah."

"What!" Rosemary and Betty simultaneously erupted, then repeated. "What?"

Maria Elena giggled and shrugged toward him, "Your turn, Cito."

The conversation continued to be entertaining all the way through dessert. Sensing that they would soon be parting ways caused them to linger, reluctant to say goodbye. In the end, Maria Elena simply announced she was "all tuckered out."

When they'd left, Nicky turned to look back somewhat wistfully at the signage. "The Vortex was more like whirling dervishes tonight," she said. "I'm really going to miss you two." She laughed. "It has been real real!"

After quick hugs all round, they settled in for the short drive to the hotel.

"Cito, I'm really tired."

"It's been a lot, Emmy. I do want to watch Obama's speech, though. You?"

She hesitated. "I don't know. I'm not sure I can keep my eyes open."

"What will be will be, Emmy."

▸36◂

THEY BOTH SLEPT DEEPLY. MARIA ELENA HAD FALLEN ASLEEP before the president's address. Pitcairn was disappointed that Obama did not offer more than fairly obligatory remarks. Perhaps he'd expected too much. The result was that he had woken early feeling somewhat emotionally hung over. Then again, sleep was not a strong point for him under any circumstances.

He'd taken a long walk and contemplated the call he wanted to make to Father Tony. There was so much information and so many experiences to pass on. It occurred to him it might be best to meet instead as soon as they got to Albuquerque.

When he came back, Maria Elena was sitting quietly in an easy chair. She looked almost childlike, and Pitcairn guessed that all the inner scrubbing had reshaped her in ways that would inevitably show in her appearance.

"You look wonderful, Emmy."

She stood with arms extended upward to hug and kiss him. "Baby, I'm excited to see some white squirrels!"

"Not me?" he asked playfully.

"Always! Though I've seen a lot of you, and I've never seen a white squirrel. Which begs the question, why are there white squirrels in Brevard, North Carolina?"

"A good question. Apparently one that everyone asks. And as I understand it, there are several theories. One involves escapees from a traveling circus, which strikes me as the one I'd most like to be true. Another is some genetic mutation, which is kind of boring. The other proposes some local brought them in from somewhere. The real answer is, no one knows."

"Oh well, a mystery is a good thing. Speaking of which, what do you feel like for breakfast? And as a side note, I'm ready to be

157

back home and eat some really good huevos rancheros. I need a red chile fix."

"There's got to be a Mexican beanery around here someplace, so maybe we can get close to meeting the need."

After checking out, they found a small Mexican cafe whose huevos were not New Mexican style but nevertheless very good and filling. The drive to Brevard was relatively short. Since they were well ahead of schedule for meeting Lulu, they detoured to several of the waterfalls Transylvania County was known for. With the cold and snow, they couldn't wander far on foot, but the falls were still wonderful to see.

In Brevard, they stopped for coffee to go, then headed to the common area where the squirrels could be found. With the ground covered in fresh, deep snow, they would be harder to spot, and Pitcairn feared they might just stay laying low in their nests and cubbies.

A few minutes later, though, Maria Elena squealed in delight as she saw one of the creatures slowly creeping down a tree trunk. The squirrel heard her, and looked up to stare toward her.

"He's looking at me, Cito!" she announced with pleasure.

A moment later, another squirrel inched its way down the same trunk, and the two of them began to cavort around it.

"How do they do that, Cito?"

"What's that?"

"How can they jump and dart and still stick to the bark?"

"Somewhere I read they have paws that pivot like hinges, and they grip like the loops and hooks of Velcro." He demonstrated with his hands.

Then the squirrels flung themselves into the snow and raced up another tree. Pitcairn and Maria Elena could hear them barking and see the movement of pine boughs, but there were no other sightings. After getting chilled, they hopped back into their vehicle to warm up for a few minutes then drove to the student center.

After both getting lattes—high-end joe, Clint used to call it— they found a nice sunlit corner to sit amid the soft buzz of voices that filled the space. At ten to one, Pitcairn saw Lulu approaching. He nodded toward her and Maria Elena looked up.

"Cito, she's not at all what I was expecting," she said. "What a beautiful woman. And those brilliant Caribbean colors are stunning."

"Yeah," he replied. "And she's wicked smart too!"

They both stood, Lulu first kissed Maria Elena on both cheeks European-style, then leaned into Pitcairn's embrace.

"I can't tell you how much I've been looking forward to meeting you, Maria Elena, and to this conversation, personally and professionally."

Maria Elena blushed.

"I brought my tea with me, so let me sit and we can get started."

She pulled out a file and offered it to Pitcairn. "More materials that you may find useful." Then she turned to Maria Elena. "Please, dear, tell me how you are and what you've been through."

Maria Elena was startled, and it showed. "I wasn't expecting that, Lulu."

"Oh, to not first attend to what you've been through would be the height of malpractice. Given what I know, your well-being is a necessary starting point." She looked to Pitcairn. "And then you, buddy." She smiled at him. "You've been traumatized too, whether you know it or not."

With that she turned back to Maria Elena. "I'm all yours now. Tell me whatever you need to."

Maria Elena took a deep breath, then launched into the recent events. As she spoke, Pitcairn was once again aware of how important it is to tell our stories, over and over again, until things worked out. While she rambled her way through, including far more detail about the time with Elise, both he and Lulu listened attentively.

When Maria Elena had finished, she looked toward Pitcairn. "Did I miss anything important, Cito?"

"Emmy, I love you. That's all I have to add."

Her eyes teared up, and she blushed again. Looking up at Lulu, she waited expectantly.

"That was perfect, Maria Elena. Just perfect. And I can see you are on your way to being bettered through this whole messy affair."

"Bettered?" asked Maria Elena.

"Oh yes, it is our breakdowns that can lead us to breakthrough. And you are already well on your way. The time with Elise was perfect, and now telling me your story adds to it, though I do have a suggestion if you'd like to hear it."

"Of course! Should I write these down?"

Lulu smiled. "It looks like Pitcairn is already ahead of us on that account," she said as she noted his journal. "And I do want to know how you came to be Cito to Maria Elena."

"First, though, please track down Stephen Levine's excellent book, *Unattended Sorrow*. He and his wife, Ondrea, spent many years working with HIV patients, and he also happened to be in recovery from addiction. They were the keepers of the death-and-dying work from Elizabeth Kübler-Ross, and he took a Buddhist approach on how we heal. It's filled with useful practices that both of you can use to good effect. He said the whole point is that life and our experiences harden our hearts and callous our souls, and in order to be revived, we must always attend to those wounds. I cannot recommend a better set of tools."

They both nodded. Pitcairn added, "This sounds like really good research material too."

"Absolutely," Lulu replied. "Now, Pitcairn, how about you? And how is it you are Cito?"

He laughed. "I'd like to just say I'm good to go, so I don't have to tell you how this has felt." Pitcairn paused. "I'll fill in my side of the story, but I have to say this whole deal has really stretched me. And at the same time, it has been really fruitful."

"Fruitful?"

"Oh yeah! Look, I'm so grateful this turned out as well as it has. And I'm deeply disturbed by all the violence that runs through it, and the effect it has on Maria Elena. But damn, so much about post-traumatic growth has been revealed, and everything you shared with me last time we talked has been so powerful. Then experiencing the healing work of Elise is mind blowing."

He took a breath to collect himself.

"And how do you feel, Pitcairn?"

Another deep breath came without a thought. And another.

"I'm all in, Lulu."

She and Maria Elena laughed in response.

"Honey, you're going to have to say more than that," Lulu said.

"Man, oh man . . . it's heartbreaking, and magical, and captivating all at the same time. It's like I've spent my whole life looking to understand this mess of my life, and the messiness of all life, and now this great revealing." He stopped for moment. "So, I'm grateful and humbled. My heart hurts. And somehow, I'm soaring."

He stretched his arms above his head. "How's that for an explanation?"

Maria Elena leaped in. "I love you and your badassery, Cito!"

Lulu stared at him carefully. "What happened to you during Maria Elena's abduction? How did you manage it?"

It took him a few moments to collect his thoughts. "Honestly, it alternated between being really disturbing and difficult, with flurries of head-spinning, and times where a really strange peace held me. I remember what it's like to be caught in a trauma cycle, and my best guess is that I've made some progress with healing." He shrugged. "There is no good reason I was not more fucked up by it all."

Lulu nodded thoughtfully. "I think you may be right. A lot of healing, but I will still strongly recommend Levine's book."

"Now Pitcairn, perfect timing for you to explain the meaning behind Cito."

He shook his head. "When I was a kid, I was little Kevin. And mi amor here translated that to Kevincito, Cito for short." He shrugged and smiled at Maria Elena. "It's the sweetest thing in the world."

Lulu beamed at them, then looked to her watch. "Time is flying. So let me give Maria Elena a bit of a summary of what I passed along to you last time, Pitcairn."

After an overview, she added some very somber points. "The first thing we must do is to acknowledge that much trauma comes from low-intensity experiences repeated over time, everything from exposure to violence and neglect to chronic hunger and poverty. The data are so very strong, yet it's so easy to overlook the effects because they're so commonplace. Second, anything we can do for children, to prevent or mitigate, is paramount. A lifetime under the shadow of unresolved trauma produces many unfortunate outcomes. More broadly, as you'll see in Levine's book, there is much we can do for everyone affected by trauma, whether the intense forms, Trauma with a capital T, or the low-grade forms, trauma with a small t."

Lulu took a long pause and sipped the remains of her drink.

"Here is where the magic begins. Since the same experiences that produce trauma can produce post-traumatic growth, we need a positive exploration, one that seeks to produce the benefits out of what is otherwise potentially very dark. If we can pin down the means to bring transformation out of tragedy, that can change our world. Even if it prevents one bombing, or a September 11 episode, or a single armed conflict, the possibilities are unfathomable."

Maria Elena looked perplexed. "Lulu, this is so much to digest. Can you simplify what post-traumatic growth looks like?" She pursed her lips. "For individuals and for a community or a society?"

Lulu nodded vigorously. "An obvious difference is you, Maria Elena. Or Pitcairn. Or Elise. And all the effects you are having on those around you. But Pitcairn, if you'll hand me the file, I'll read you what I wrote that has not yet been published." He gave her the file, and she quickly found the piece.

"Post-traumatic growth tends to appear in four ways. Sometimes people find new opportunities and possibilities that were not previously available. New paths emerge. A second area is that their relationships are profoundly altered. We often find this in the service they might offer to others because of the compassion it has brought forth. A third area of possible change is an increased sense of one's own strength, or one's ability to demonstrate that strength. An '*if I lived through that, I can face anything.*' And a fourth aspect of post-traumatic growth can be in the realm of one's appreciation for life or in one's viewpoint from a spiritual perspective."

She looked at them before continuing. "Surely you can see yourselves in those descriptions. And all we need to do is look to the recovery programs, or any number of non-profits, or community development efforts to see where those individual transformations can very quickly create groundswells of change."

Pitcairn snorted. "Bill W's story, Emmy."

"His experience and the creation of AA is a perfect demonstration of how one person's post-traumatic growth can change a culture," Lulu acknowledged.

"Now, that's a lot, and there's so much to read. I'm going to suggest a change of pace for both of you as you drive back to Atlanta. Here's a map I put together for you. If you leave right now, you can see two waterfalls en route. You know, beauty and nature are restorative, and western North Carolina has more waterfalls than anyplace in the U.S. Then there's a stunning view of the Piedmont at sunset from Caesar's Head State Park as you cross into South Carolina. You'll be out of the mountains and onto the main highway before nightfall."

"That is so sweet of you, Lulu!" exclaimed Maria Elena.

"Oh honey, with what I know about the need for restoration after difficulties, I could not possibly let you get away without giving you that chance."

She stood and wrapped Maria Elena in a warm embrace. "I really like who you are, Maria Elena." She turned to Pitcairn. "And I can't wait to see where you go with this." She hugged him in turn, then smiled generously at both of them. "Please drive safely, and take care of each other."

With that, Lulu was gone.

"Wow," Maria Elena said as she looked at Pitcairn. "That was something, Cito."

"It's all been something, Emmy. I have no idea what to write at this point."

"Cito, first things first, and next things next. Let's go see those waterfalls!"

▶ 37 ◀

THE DRIVE THROUGH THE CAROLINAS TO ATLANTA HAD BEEN a wonderful change of pace. With a late-morning flight the next day, the transition provided a much-needed respite. They'd had salads for dinner, and Pitcairn took a long walk around the airport's Gateway Center. Maria Elena took a long hot bath. Then they both poured themselves into bed early.

Pitcairn woke with another dream firmly in his thoughts. While Maria Elena continued to sleep, he took his journal and Lucas's, and headed to the lounge. There was little activity there. He sat with a hot coffee near large windows looking out into the manicured central courtyard.

The dream was entirely unfamiliar terrain, a mountain landscape with a stream running over and through smooth, rounded stones. The rock that soared above and filled the watercourse was suffused with a beautiful, reddish undertone, though it seemed like volcanic pumice in texture. He could almost feel the roughness as he wrote of it. Yet the most striking feature was leafless but starkly beautiful white-barked sycamores that lined the banks as far as the eye could see. Each was ornately gnarled, and they stood like silent, ghostly sentinels. The stream also stretched into the distance and felt like it could go on for an infinity. All was still. The burbling of the waters dancing over stone was the only sound. The feeling of infinity was reminiscent of the earlier opaque dream, which he noted as a parallel.

As he wrote, he suddenly realized he had dreamed of this stream and landscape for longer than he could recall. It was intimately familiar, as if he'd been clambering along its rocky banks forever. Then he also remembered a single, large iridescent blue mountain jay unlike any he'd ever seen that studied him from a perch in a nearby sycamore.

Deep in his bones, he knew he was to follow the waterway, and that the jay was an observer to his journey, not so much a guide. He also knew there was a distant destination to his trek. While the entire scene was fresh and new, it was deeply entwined inside him.

He looked to see the time on his phone, and debated whether to call Tony. Then again, if the priest was not yet awake, Pitcairn knew that most nights, he would not have his phone nearby, so it would not disturb him.

"There you are, Kevin," the priest's voice rang clear and true.

"Hi Tony, I know it's early, but you answered, so I'm guessing the time is just right. Right?"

Tony's warm humor came through the line with a chuckle. "I didn't know when to expect your call, but I have been expecting it."

"A whole lot of ground to cover, but can we start with a dream I just had?"

"Of course. It will let me play amateur psychologist."

"Tony, you are not an amateur at anything. Besides, you do have a degree in psychology."

"Well, there is that, isn't there?" He chuckled again. "And I do trust dreams. Since we're asleep, we couldn't possibly make such things up consciously. Carl Jung believed, and I tend to agree, that they are the psyche's guidance bubbling up to teach and lead us through metaphor and symbols. Now tell me your dream."

It only took a few minutes for Pitcairn to relate both dreams, and afterward, the priest said simply, "Those are big dreams."

"Big dreams? Come on, Tony, big?"

A guffaw burst forth over the phone line. "Well, that's what Jung called them, and he was as good an authority as we have."

"Jung? Are you kidding me? He made up more language than most of us even know. Big dreams? That seems very under-realized."

"What can I tell you, Kevin. Jung was way beyond me, and I'd guess he had a good reason to avoid some notable descriptor."

"Okay, enough of my rambling on that point. What do you think?"

"You know, Kevin, it is interesting we've not really talked much about Jungian psychology, though I guess now is the time." He paused. "A more contemporary psychologist would say that you have seen the psyche's vision for your soul's journey home."

Pitcairn pondered what he'd just heard. "And . . . ."

The priest continued. "Our present understanding is that the soul, also known scientifically as the psyche, has a plan for bringing us home to ourselves."

"You know I'm not exactly a good candidate for believing in a soul."

"True enough, Kevin. Yet you continue to follow this calling, do you not?"

"Fair statement," he replied.

"I'm curious, Kevin. How does Maria Elena fit into this dream? After all, it certainly appears the two of you are into this together."

"Huh, that's a curious question." He stopped to think. "Do you suppose she's the jay? As I say that out loud, it seems to ring true."

"I don't know, Kevin, Perhaps you should remain curious about that and allow it to clarify itself. And speaking of Maria Elena, would you like to bring me up to date on your experiences since we last spoke?"

"Oh . . . that's a long story, but here goes."

Pitcairn proceeded to connect the many strands of the story, while the priest listened attentively. When he was done, Tony was silent for some time, which Pitcairn knew sometimes was his style.

Kevin," the priest said, "I'm going to refrain from any suggestions on what this all might mean. I'm confident you will follow this path because that is who you are, and what you do. My only suggestion is to make sure you tell Maria Elena about the dream, and especially that she may be the mountain jay."

"Will do."

"When will you be back in Albuquerque?"

"We fly back from the interview with Oprah on Wednesday. I'd guess we'll be back on the beam by Friday."

"Does Zack know of your plans? He'll want to know so the plans can be made for you to be there for Lucas."

"We'll call him in a little while."

"Kevin, one more thing occurs to me. Would you reach out to Kari and make an appointment. Something tells me you need a good therapy session right about now."

"That's a really good idea, Tony. Anything in particular you're thinking?"

"No, it's just a sense that it would be useful."

"Got it. And I need to get to some AA meetings too. I'm good, but a little sobriety insurance is always a better idea."

"It will be good to see you, Kevin. Would you like to join me for meditation and tea on Friday morning?"

"Perfect. Just perfect."

"One last thing, Tony. Last time we talked, you said that saying it hurts is powerful prayer. What did you mean?"

"Ah . . . of course." The priest breathed audibly. "Kevin, everything is prayer. No exceptions. When Jesus told us to pray without ceasing, it was an affirmative prayer. The magic elixir is in our awareness that we are always praying, consciously or unconsciously. Our lives are prayer being lived, Kevin." He laughed gently. "And it doesn't matter what we believe. When we say we hurt, when we acknowledge pain, or most anything else, we're just telling the truth out loud."

"Damn, Tony! That takes me right back to the Twelve Steps, 'Admitted to God, ourselves and another human being. . . .'"

"There you go again, Kevin. Connecting the dots in a most profound way."

A belly laugh shook through Pitcairn.

"Tony, I gotta go. This is all just too too much to get my head around."

"Oh, but you will," countered the priest.

"I will what?"

"Get your head around it." Tony paused. "It's what you do, Kevin."

"Ah . . . well, maybe it gets done to me would be more accurate."

"Kevin, I'll look forward to wherever our next conversation takes us. Safe travels."

Pitcairn refreshed his coffee, noted that a few people were stirring, and returned to his seat. Pulling out his journal, he began to write. As always, there was something deeply comforting about collecting his thoughts. Sometimes things became clearer; always things made better sense.

When he was done, he threw his things in his backpack and headed out the door for another long walk. If anything, walking made things even clearer than journaling. It occurred to him that the long flight would be a very good time to read more of Lucas's journal.

▸38◂

THE FLIGHT TO LOS ANGELES TOOK ALMOST FIVE HOURS BE-cause of extremely strong head winds. Pitcairn and Maria Elena talked about the dream, which she found intriguing though not definitive for her. Regardless, she was curious about the idea that the mountain jay could be her.

"Cito, I really like the idea that I'm on the journey with you. Which would mean that you are on the journey with me." She paused to think. "It fits."

After a long silence, she mentioned what lay ahead for them.

"I can't quite get clear about what Oprah will be like."

"Don't know, Emmy. I'd guess you'll both hit it off."

"Why do you say that?"

"It just seems like you're her kind of guest."

"Which means what, Cito?"

"A helluva story to tell. A real spark in your personality. A passion. Besides that, she's damned good at what she does. She wouldn't even ask you for an interview if she didn't already think there was a good angle to it."

Maria Elena sank into contemplation. Then, as expected, she allowed herself to sleep.

Pitcairn pulled out the final journal from Lucas. Having learned so much, he was now quite interested in the final days of the young man's life. Starting at the last page, he worked his way backward. As before, he mostly found routine journaling. Then toward the beginning, he found a reference to the previous month's "ceremony" and its profound effect on him. Taking the previous journal from his backpack, Pitcairn quickly looked a month earlier.

Toward the end of the year, Lucas had traveled to far northern New Mexico, a setting off the grid near Chama. There he'd taken part in an ayahuasca ceremony, the ancient, shamanic tea and practice that first induces vomiting, then a hallucinogenic state. Advocates call it an authentic spiritual practice while the federal government considered it use of an illegal drug.

The activity fit with others Lucas had been involved in for which he'd been expelled from college. His writings as he prepared for the ceremony were quite reverent. While Pitcairn had never sought out an altered state for anything other than to get loaded, he knew that the state of mind one brought to the spiritual practice was extremely important. It seemed like Lucas was on solid footing, and as Pitcairn read between the lines, that he'd been in the hands of a capable practitioner.

Lucas's journaling entries during the few days after the ceremony were fairly scattered. Pitcairn could see that he had been wrestling to bring meaning from the hallucinations.

Then Pitcairn found a long commentary weaving together notes that seemed to come from a lecture the Dalai Lama gave at the College of Santa Fe with a reading Lucas had found and his experiences with ayahuasca:

"Tibetan mystical traditions wish to transform the world by bringing forth from a well of ancient practices. Dalai Lama says at the heart of violence we inflict upon others and on the natural world is our self-absorption. Because we cannot see the many points we have in common across creation, we perceive the world and people as *other*. When we see *other*, we are able to justify mistreatment of many kinds.

"That's what I saw in Ceremony. That there is no separation. It's like that analogy I heard in the lecture with Charmaine Glennis. That the Hawaiian Islands look separate, but when we go beneath the surface of the water, we see all is one. That was the wavy lines I saw across all forms during Ceremony.

"Dialogue changes that says Dalai Lama. But Charmaine said it was the contact we experience, the contact that is central to dialogue. That we can't unthink or untalk our biases and stigma. We have to come into contact with the *other* so we can experience the falling away of misconceptions. We don't find understanding, we let go of misunderstanding.

"That fits with Ceremony when dark forms vanished from background and the wavy lines became more distinct. Somehow, it's all a big beautiful design."

"I love this kid," Pitcairn whispered to himself. "So much heart." Then sorrow swept over him as he remembered that Lucas would soon be gone from the Earth. "What a shame it was that one such as Lucas was collateral damage," he whispered again. Then he lapsed into contemplation until returning to Lucas's writings.

"So much to ruminate on. First, we think we are separate, and are drawn to community and communication to try to overcome that sense of separation and isolation. Yet these are only gathering of selves that cannot overcome separation. Amazingly though, if we persist with diligence and practice, we can find communion. Coming to union? Oneness?"

Once again, Pitcairn closed his eyes and lapsed into contemplation. Some time later, after what may have been deep meditation or sleep, he felt the nearness of Maria Elena as she sang softly into his ear, "Come out, come out, wherever you are . . ."

He fluttered his eyelids multiple times in relocating himself, then turned to look her in the eye. A large, gentle smile greeted him, and her dark, limpid eyes in which he so often lost himself.

"Where were you, Cito?"

He thought for a moment before responding. "First things first, Emmy. I gotta pee. But while I do that, I think you should read what I found in Lucas's journal." He nodded his head in affirming his words to her.

Maria Elena immediately felt his somber tone and nodded as she smiled more softly.

When he returned, tears were rimming her eyes. "My God, I wish I'd had a chance to spend more time with him, Cito."

"Yeah, me too," he replied sadly.

"By the way, who is Charmaine Glennis?"

"Ah . . . she's a psychologist and anthropologist who has been working in rural communities in Northern New Mexico for years. She's kind of off the grid but has done a great deal with developmental work with the folks who live there."

With that, the announcement came that they would soon be landing, and their attention turned to practical things.

▸39◂

OPRAH'S STAFF HAD ARRANGED FOR A LIMOUSINE TO TAKE them to a hotel near her estate in Montecito. The drive took ninety minutes along the captivating Pacific coast. Caught in their own reflections, they had little to say to each other.

At the vintage, mission-style Montecito Inn, they were quickly settled into an executive suite. Their point-of-contact, Leandris, had arranged for flowers, snacks, drinks, and a file of information on what to expect. She would meet with them first thing in the morning for breakfast and to plan their time with Oprah. In the meantime, they were encouraged to enjoy the inn's amenities.

"Cito, let's walk down to the ocean!" Maria Elena said.

"That sounds perfect, and I haven't been walking enough, so let's roll."

Fifteen minutes later, they found themselves on classic California bluffs above the water. Gnarled evergreens, classic temperate-climate blossoms, and gusty ocean winds welcomed them.

"Cito, we are living a charmed life, aren't we?" Maria Elena asked. "Our life in Albuquerque is almost idyllic, and we get to experience the Carolinas and now this." She shook her head. "All amid this incredible mess. I don't know what to make of it all." She paused before adding, "And I get to interview with Oprah?"

Pitcairn wrapped her in a big hug and kissed the top of her head. "Baby, we were born to run!" Then he stepped away to hold her at arms-length and look at her soberly. "Somehow, what Clint always said seems to be true. He always said if we cleaned up our insides that our outsides would fall into place. And then if we persisted, it would go beyond good to better and better."

They turned to look out over the windswept ocean. "Looks like we can get down to the beach. What do you say?" he asked.

A few minutes later, they were strolling along the edge of the surf, searching for shells and looking at the landscape and the homes lining the bluffs. Later they made their way to the inn's restaurant for local seafood, then made love with the ocean scents and breezes floating in from open balcony doors.

Maria Elena's final words before they drifted off to sleep were simple and profound. "We are so not in charge, Cito."

It needed no reply.

* * *

Pitcairn woke early, and as Maria Elena continued snoring lightly, he left her a note and took the file for her interview to a quiet area of the expansive lobby. There he drank coffee, read, and journaled. Much to his surprise, she joined him a short while later.

"Emmy, looks like I need to remind you that you don't do early," he said playfully as she leaned down to kiss him.

"Well, I've never had an interview with Oprah either. Some things change, Cito."

He laughed as she turned and walked over to get some coffee. As she quietly sipped it, he reviewed with her what he had learned from the file. She listened and nodded often as she slowly awakened.

"Any suggestions for me?" she asked.

He thought for a moment. "Emmy, you don't need any guidance from me. Be yourself. She's going to love you just the way you are. Tell the truth. See where it goes."

"See where the tiger goes, right?" Maria Elena countered. "We are so not in charge," she repeated from the night before.

* * *

Breakfast and the limo ride to Oprah's compound were uneventful, though the estate's far-reaching vistas and manicured grounds were beautiful. The preparations with Oprah's staff were pretty much what they'd expected.

Yet when Oprah swept in to greet them, it was anything but normal or expected. Immediately it was clear she had a way about her that was captivating and authentic. Her warmth quickly settled them, which Maria Elena acknowledged after the greetings.

"Oprah, you are not what I was expecting," she said.

Oprah smiled gently. "How so, Maria Elena?"

She stopped to form words, then added somewhat tentatively. "In my family, which goes back a long way in New Mexico, they would say *de la gente*, that you are of the people."

"Thank you. Very much. With all this," she gestured around her, "it's terribly easy to lose myself. A few of my people have permission to remind me regularly." She smiled more broadly.

"Now, we are going to take as much time as we need. We plan to air this on Friday because it's so timely."

"Wow," Pitcairn said. "That's really fast."

"Indeed it is, Mr. Pitcairn." She paused. "Of course, you'll be in a separate studio to watch and listen. We'll make sure you have anything you need to be comfortable. And let me add that I really appreciate your writings."

He felt a surge of feelings in response, immediately noting that it was an old story of fearing being seen, then leaned into it. "Thank you. I'm glad you know about that."

Oprah smiled, then reached out to hold Maria Elena's hand. "Here we go, Maria Elena."

As they moved away, Maria Elena looked back over her shoulder. She was beaming. A surge of love raced through him as well as a deep appreciation for the part on this stage of life that was sweeping her forward. He was suddenly aware of what Kari called an inflection point, a moment like a tidal turning when flows surge in a new direction. That feeling would continue to pulse through him as he followed the interview remotely. He had no idea how he could sense it, and yet a turning was certain.

The interview began simply enough. Oprah asked Maria Elena to describe the kidnapping. It was interesting for Pitcairn to just listen from a distance without being part of the story. It was incredibly captivating.

Then she asked Maria Elena to provide a little more backstory about the bombing and the search for answers. She was able to weave in more of Pitcairn's circumstances as well, including the

Crucifix Protests. Oprah acknowledged the importance of the entire story, and promised to come back around to innocence and post-traumatic growth before they were done.

Then Oprah asked the gut-clenching question: "Please Maria Elena, tell us how this felt, and how it feels even now."

"Oh my," she began, as the feelings began to emerge and she caught herself with a steadying breath. Oprah placed her hand on Maria Elena's, which clearly grounded her. "Never in my wildest dreams could I have expected something like this. Never." She closed her eyes. "It's like everything you ever feared comes crashing together. And your brain goes into overdrive, first trying to think through how to get away, then slashing back to what you did wrong, then dealing with the possibility of dying or being harmed, then it plays over and over." Her eyes opened, and an edge came to her voice. "Then your animal brain kicks in, and you realize you could kill, or even chew off your own arm if necessary to get away." Maria Elena laughed. "Then you say to yourself, 'That's crazy, girl!' "

"Yet you had the presence of mind to prepare yourself, didn't you?"

A guttural exhalation burst forth from Maria Elena's mouth. "No, no, there was no presence of mind. It was more like my mind lurched to the idea of using a brass piece I had woven in my hair as a weapon. The animal brain got really sneaky and contrived ways to use it."

She laughed and rolled her eyes. "We'd found it on the West Mesa in Albuquerque, and a psychic in Greenville, South Carolina, urged me to weave it into my hair like a talisman for protection."

She laughed again at how crazy it all sounded. Oprah laughed with her, but before she could follow up, Maria Elena leaped forward in her thoughts.

"I mean, who could dream these things up, Oprah? It's surreal. I'm not a survivalist, but clearly the desire to survive called something forth from deep inside me. I remember the words of that woman, the Slovenian deep-water diver whose name I can't remember. An awful life story, and diving saved her. She said, "When you've been to the very edge of the abyss and found what makes you want to return to the surface—to live—you have everything to lose.""

The silence that Oprah allowed then was deafening. Pitcairn hoped they would not edit it down; it was so profound. Then Maria Elena found her voice again.

"From that moment on, it's like I was hyper-focused. On each moment. And each moment was focused on surviving, and on everything that happened. Right up until the moment I collapsed into the Subaru that I flagged down after I was free. I have no idea how much time transpired. The need to live was all I could hold in my brain."

She shuddered, like an animal shaking uncontrollably to release the hormones of trauma. Once again, Oprah steadied her by reaching out and touching her gently but firmly. For a moment, it looked to Pitcairn like Maria Elena was absent, disembodied. Again, he hoped they would not edit the pause out; it was so powerful.

"You know," Oprah said seriously, "a new meme has surfaced just in the past day. It's inspired by you and what you've done."

Surprise came to Maria Elena's face. "What? What meme?"

Oprah grinned with delight. "Yes, Maria Elena. You are affecting countless women, even though that was not your aim.

"Live dangerously. Underestimate her." Oprah smiled as she uttered the meme.

Maria Elena couldn't contain herself. A snort burst from her, followed immediately by tears. She was speechless, so Oprah stepped in.

"Do you have the brass piece with you?"

Mischief showed on Maria Elena's face as she nodded like a little girl who'd been caught. She extended her hands behind her dark locks of hair to slowly remove the piece. There were long moments of silence before she showed it in the palm of her hand.

"May I?" Oprah asked as she tentatively extended her own hand.

Maria Elena nodded and gently offered her the talisman.

"A fleur-de-lis? What is it?"

She told the story of finding it on the West Mesa. And their guesses as to its origin. She stared at it for a long moment. "I love lilies. An ancient, sacred image."

Oprah offered it back with an addition. "And a lifesaver, honey."

Maria Elena nodded somberly. Then looked at Oprah. "It's all very improbable, isn't it?"

"Serendipitous, if not grace."

Maria Elena was obviously struck by the comment. Another pause followed that Pitcairn knew would play poignantly if unedited.

"Grace," Maria Elena said and shook her head with a perplexed look.

Oprah leaned toward her. "Yes. . . ."

"I'm just remembering how it felt as I floundered around in the woods hoping I was going to live." A painful silence punctuated the moment. "I felt so lost. So abandoned. Alone. But I kept stumbling forward. Hopeless but hopeful." She looked at her host with a spark in her eyes. "Serendipitous, if not grace?"

Oprah suddenly grinned. "You know, Emmylou Harris has an album called *Stumble Into Grace*. That seems to be your story, honey."

"I like that idea. Stumble into grace. It fits, doesn't it?"

Oprah nodded as her brow furrowed. "What's next, Maria Elena. It seems you are emerging as a voice for women fighting a very good fight—a necessary fight."

A stunned look crossed Maria Elena's face, then she again seemed to find her footing, though Pitcairn would later observe that it looked like the footing found her.

"No, not a fight," she said with conviction.

Oprah looked surprised as a smile again emerged on her face. "No? But Maria Elena, you fought your way to freedom. That's what everyone is seeing in you. That's the heart of the meme, isn't it."

"No," Maria Elena affirmed assertively. "No. I did then what I had to do. But I've since had a dream." She paused as a thought appeared. "Maybe the time of fighting has to pass away. This is a new world. We need a new approach."

Oprah was captivated. Pitcairn could see that the information was coming from beyond Maria Elena's conscious self.

"A new approach?"

Maria Elena proceeded to describe her dream. Again, some kind of psychic footing seemed to find her.

"I don't exactly know where I'm going with this, Oprah. Bearing witness, maybe. Bringing the power of observation to the troubles around us. Not unlike the wisdom of Martin Luther King Jr. And maybe women are now finally positioned to lead from that place of non-violence."

Oprah asked for more clarity. Maria Elena shrugged with a perplexed look. "I don't know, but I can't stop thinking about the movie *Wings of Desire*. Do you know it?"

Oprah beamed. "It's a favorite, and beautiful. Please tell our listeners, Maria Elena."

She recounted the story of the silent angels, the watchers, and the incredible feelings of sorrow and compassion it evoked. Then she added, "Maybe it is like that. An entirely different kind of fighting . . . a different way of being."

Oprah reached out with both hands, and the distance closed between them. "Maria Elena, some say the power of non-violence is because it provides such a potent contrast to violence."

A gentle look swept across Maria Elena's face. "Well, there is more than enough violence already. So the last thing we need is 4 billion women adding to it."

An almost-ethereal pause came, lighting up her face, a look and a feel that Pitcairn knew in an instant would translate across the airwaves.

"Oprah, it's not that violence won't occur." She shook her head as she lapsed deep into thought.

"Let's be honest. I didn't hit that man to harm him, though he was certainly hurt. I knocked him out to save my own life." She paused and cocked her head as a look of chagrin passed over her face. "Okay. I did lash out. I did want to hurt him. I was scared and angry. But somehow or another, we have to find a way to get past the violence. To transcend it. To stop it just as quickly as we can. And then to do whatever we must to try to make it right."

Again, an unnatural poise took hold. "Here's another example. Martin Luther King Jr. did not set out to harm others by changing our world through civil rights. But a whole bunch of people had their lives irrevocably altered. Many will say to this day they have been harmed by civil rights." She huffed and laughed. "We've just seen how a whole bunch of white people still feel harmed by the Civil War. But make no mistake, what motivated Abraham Lincoln and MLK was not to injure others. It was to set things right. Right?"

A look of astonishment came to Oprah's face as she rose with her hands still firmly in those of Maria Elena, who stood with her. An embrace followed.

Then, leaning away with arms still entwined and an amazing intimacy between them, Oprah added. "I can't wait to see what comes of this, Maria Elena." She kissed her on the cheek. "Thank you, and bless you!"

Pitcairn was suddenly aware that he too had been swept into the moment with them. He had to force himself to take a breath. He could feel the movement beneath it all.

▸40◂

OPRAH HAD OTHER COMMITMENTS, SO THEY WENT BACK TO the hotel immediately afterward. During the ride, Maria Elena was a chatterbox. Pitcairn just listened. Afterward, she suddenly exhaled.

"Cito, I need a cigarette."

"You earned it, Emmy. We can probably solve that pretty quickly even though this is California, and we'll have to make sure we don't get incarcerated for it."

She cocked her head and looked at him lovingly. "Okay, but first, how did I do?"

"Baby, even Oprah underestimated you." He laughed. "You are magnificent. I can tell you a lot more, but let's find you some cigarettes and a place to settle, so we can talk about it. Then maybe a nice long walk on the beach."

After dropping into the corner store, they crossed the street and headed away from the shops and people. She lit a cigarette and inhaled deeply.

Exhaling, she said to Pitcairn, "Now we need to find a homeless person who wants cigarettes so I can get rid of them."

"I don't understand how you can do that, Emmy. I'm from that if-one-is-good-ten-will-always-be-better school of addictive behavior."

"Oh, it's easy. I hate smoking, Cito."

"Like I said, I don't get it." Then he added, "FYI, this is Montecito. I don't think we'll find any homeless people."

She smoked half the cigarette, then stubbed it out to drop in a trash can. On their way to the beach, though, with a little bit of wandering, they managed to find a man who looked like he was a bit on the margins and was happy to take her pack of cigarettes.

They descended the bluffs to the beach and moved easily along the waterline, just chatting. During a lull, Pitcairn segued to what he really wanted to discuss.

"You were really rocking with your comments about a different kind of fight. I could feel the energy of it, and the clarity. Setting aside for a moment how cool it is that you've become a meme, what's up with that?"

Maria Elena looked down and carefully studied her steps as they moved along the beach. "Thanks for letting me think that through for a bit, Cito. All I can tell you is I'm really clear about the truth of what I said, but I really have no idea where to go with that."

She stopped and looked up at him. "Do you have something coming clear?"

"Nada, Emmy. Nada."

A rock jetty ran out into the water just ahead. Maria Elena nodded toward them. "Want to play on the rocks?"

"Hell yeah!" he answered without skipping a beat.

Clambering on the rocks was almost like a playground for them. But finally, Maria Elena sat down on an ocher-colored knob, closed her eyes, and lapsed into silence. Pitcairn joined her, scanning the water in a kind of visual meditation.

A while later, he heard her phone buzz. She took a long, satisfied breath, then scanned the messages. He could sense a rising discomfort in her. Maria Elena looked up and stared in the distance with a hint of tears skimming her eyes.

"What's up, Emmy?"

"It's Pattie," she began in a distracted tone. "She flies into Albuquerque tomorrow. They'll be taking Lucas off the respirator on Saturday. She wanted to be there, and wants us there too."

Her jaw muscles were tensing and releasing. "Goddamnit, Cito."

He didn't reply, merely held himself steady beside her, feeling his own heartache, wishing again there could have been some way to know Lucas better before this.

"He'll be cremated on Sunday. Pattie wants us to drive with her and Zack up to northeast New Mexico. There's a river canyon where she buried Etido a long time ago. They think that's the best place for his ashes to be scattered."

He nodded. "It's going to be a hell of a weekend, Emmy."

She turned and looked into his eyes. He could see a fire of resolve burning in them.

"I don't know how this plays into a new kind of approach, but it does. And I'll be damned if I won't see this through. Now I need to walk." She stood and moved back toward the sand.

They walked until just before dusk, saying little more. Then, chilled by the ocean air, they found a small restaurant that featured cioppino, the Italian-style fisherman's stew. Sitting near a fireplace that blazed warmth and comfort, small talk about their return home was all they could manage.

▸41◂

THE FLIGHT BACK WAS UNEVENTFUL. APPROACHING THEIR HOME on Gold Street in downtown Albuquerque, Pitcairn was struck by the scent of burning piñon wood and a pang of homecoming. It was a quintessentially New Mexican smell.

As they came in the door, Lucy and Lincoln were beside themselves with joy. A brief note on the kitchen table from Zack said he was at the hospital with Pattie and that they would return for dinner. Then as Maria Elena began to move efficiently about the house, Pitcairn leashed the dogs for a neighborhood walk.

When he returned, he heard Maria Elena, Zack, and Pattie in the kitchen. The scent of beans and red chile suffused the air, making it feel all the more like home. Something about the smell of food translated into a sense of security.

As he entered the kitchen, he was immediately struck by how haggard Zack looked—and in strange contrast, by how invigorated Pattie appeared.

Maria Elena stood, leaned up to kiss him, then gestured to her seat at the table. "Cito, let me take care of dinner while you chat with Pattie and Zack. I can chime in from the stove."

Pitcairn quickly shook hands with Zack, who was deep in his own inner quiet, then hugged Pattie, who began a steady recounting of her travels and then their conversation. As Pitcairn listened, he kept ruminating on the difference in their appearances. Clearly, circumstances had crushed some part of Zack's being, while more or less the same life had enlivened Pattie.

As Maria Elena began serving dinner, the conversation turned toward reflections on Lucas and his life. The first item was beloved dogs that had been a part of his childhood and early life. Pitcairn could not help looking toward the boxers curled up in their beds in the corner. Then a lengthy characterization of Etido, whom Lucas had called Teo, the strange character who had deeply affected them all.

Pattie looked at Pitcairn as Maria Elena finished placing bowls and corn tortillas on the table. "Can I say grace?" she asked.

He nodded, and gestured for Maria Elena to join them.

Pattie began, "There was this great, Christian mystic, Meister Eckhart, who said that if the only prayer we ever offered in our whole life was 'thank you,' it would be enough." She closed her eyes for a moment. "Thank you. Thank you."

She looked at Zack. "I'm sorry if that's hard to hear, given what's happened to Lucas."

Pitcairn sensed that a crack in Zack's grief almost appeared. Then he cast his eyes downward and offered a nod of acknowledgment.

Sometimes we just can't go to where the pain calls us, thought Pitcairn. After a gentle silence, Pattie shifted the conversation.

"Etido found something in New Mexico. And now with what has happened to Lucas, it seems I have to get his memoir out in the world, if for no other reason because Lucas would appreciate it. He's nagged me over the years to tell the story. Maybe when we drive up to the canyon to release Lucas, I can tell you more." She paused wistfully. "It was many years ago that Etido died there. And where I buried him." Her heartache was palpable. "It's so bittersweet that Lucas will join him."

A somber quiet overtook them. It seemed reverent to allow it. Then at some point, the conversation resumed with Maria Elena recounting all that had unfolded during their travels, both east and west.

Friday was very busy. By evening, when they settled in to watch Maria Elena's interview with Oprah, she and Pitcairn were both tired. Zack and Pattie joined them, and after a day spent sitting with Lucas and making final arrangements, they were likewise weary—soul weary.

Fifteen minutes into the broadcast, both their cell phones began to blow up with texts. Maria Elena ignored hers so she could focus on the program. But since Pitcairn had seen the entire recording, he attempted to multi-task, shifting focus from the messages to the program. Periodically he simply watched Maria Elena, who was deeply immersed. He noted Pattie and Zack both occasionally glancing at her as well.

At the first commercial, Pattie spoke with a reverence in her voice. "Sweet Jesus, Maria Elena . . . this is remarkable."

Maria Elena blushed and looked down.

"Emmy, the meme is just exploding on the web, baby. 'Live dangerously. Underestimate her.' It's everywhere. Scattershot for sure, but there is some serious tipping-point-shit going on here."

That triggered some chatter among the three of them. Zack just listened. Pitcairn wasn't sure he was even able to be present, so deep was his trauma with Lucas and all that had preceded it in his life.

Then the program resumed. When they reached the point where Maria Elena reframed a new approach—not violence but awareness and watching—Pitcairn knew from the feel of it that some deep echo of truth was being spoken into the culture. Sure enough, when he next searched the meme online, the amount of traffic and reflection was off the charts.

Oprah's closing was as they had experienced it in the studio. "I can't wait to see what comes of this."

But then they had edited in her final observations after Maria Elena left.

"A new kind of fight. That sounds to me like the new heaven and new earth so many of us have been seeking to call into being."

Oprah smiled beautifully. "So it is. And so it shall be. Nothing but the best for all of us."

Maria Elena stood up quickly. "I have got to pee so bad. Be right back."

Pitcairn wasn't surprised; he knew she would also be able to collect herself after the experience. "I think," he said, "that we need to eat some of that chocolate pinon pie Maria Elena baked. Serious shit calls for good pie. So does celebration."

Before long, they were all gathered around the kitchen table. The conversation ran in so many directions it was impossible to track.

After a while Maria Elena said she had peeked at her cell phone earlier. "Cito, if your phone is like mine, we are going to need some serious help from someone."

Pattie quickly interjected. "I got this. After Monday, I have nothing to do." Then she turned to Zack. "I'd like it if you'd stick around for a few days. I'm not sure returning to your secluded life is going to be good for you, honey."

Zack nodded, more in compliance than enthusiasm.

"Actually, how about if I get started in the morning?"

"Okay by me," Pitcairn replied. "Emmy?"

"I have no better plan. Besides that, I'm probably going to have an emotional hangover tomorrow. This has been a bit of a roller coaster ride." She paused, looked to Zack, and added, "And tomorrow is part of that ride. Not a bad thing, just a necessary one, including the trip to the canyon on Monday. Despite all this, Zack, we are here for you. And for Lucas." She paused again and then smiled at Pattie. "Sweet Jesus. That seems to sum it all up. I'm going to bed."

Pitcairn stood to hug her. "The dogs need a walk. And so do I. Emmy, I'm going to sleep in the office on the couch. I'm headed over to see Tony pretty early. We've got a lot of ground to cover. Won't want to mess with your beauty sleep."

They kissed. Then he wrapped Zack and Pattie in a giant bear hug.

▸42◂

PITCAIRN HAD DECIDED THAT WITH TONY'S AGREEMENT, HE'D bring along Lucy and Lincoln. They walked to the center, since neither the boxers nor he had been getting their usual lengthy walks.

It was a clear, crisp morning, and very invigorating. Father Tony met him at a side entrance, an elongated, wrap-around portal supported by massive vigas with multi-colored latillas layered above them. Tony kneeled and laughed as Lucy swarmed him, while Lincoln sidled up to lean into his leg after her energy had dissipated a bit. Then he stood and offered a generous hug to Pitcairn, who returned it in kind.

Tony pointed with his head. "Come in. The fire is well stoked, as is the coffee." The dogs sniffed around, then settled near the large kiva fireplace and promptly fell asleep.

"We should be more like dogs, Kevin."

He smiled back and wrapped both hands around the large mug of coffee the priest had provided. "In AA, there's a saying from the Big Book we use quite often, 'We relax and take it easy; we don't struggle.' Though there's wide agreement it's a simple concept that is not so easy in practice."

They both lapsed into silence. For whatever reason, this time and space with Father Tony was one place he was able to readily follow AA's guidance and rest easy.

The sounds and smells of the burning piñon, and the gentle snoring of Lucy and Lincoln created a kind of white-noise effect. Soon Pitcairn was deeply aware of the stillness. Though his eyes remained open, his gaze unintentionally softened. A short while later, the priest took a long, audible breath, and the spell lessened.

"Tony, I don't have a clue where to begin."

"When in doubt, just start talking and trust the flow, Kevin."

"First, did you see Maria Elena last night on Oprah's program?"

"Oh yes, and what a message she carried."

"Message?"

"Of course, the story is quite a story, and that's as far as many will get in terms of what they understand. But . . . her reframing of violence was quite powerful."

"Tony, I know you aren't exactly an online geek, but are you aware of the whole meme of *Live dangerously. Underestimate her?*"

"Center staff gave me quite a bit of information. They've been monitoring it all along, largely because what it is triggering aligns so well with our mission and purpose."

"Right. Of course it would." He gestured openly with both hands. "There's no telling how and when things will gain traction, Tony."

"Looks like a wave for you and Maria Elena to ride, Kevin."

He chuckled in response. "I'll tell you what, man, we are so in this together that I'm pretty amazed. Somehow that girl and I are like quantum entanglement."

"That is the perfect analogy. Somewhere at the level of the Spirit, or quantum mechanics, or the Tao, you two are called, and called together."

"What the hell do you suppose is unfolding, Tony?"

"No idea. No idea whatsoever, though it does very much remind me of the cultural groundswell that came with the Crucifix Protests. As you know, you could never have predicted that entire watershed, which continues to this day. The most profound parts of the Gospels continue to be advanced even if the frequency of crucifix events have waned. And it continues to shake some of the church communities to their very foundations."

Pitcairn thought for a moment. "Okay, you're being cagey, Tony. I know you have some thoughts about what's happening. Are you going to fess up to them or not?"

A belly laugh shot from deep within the priest. It was such a jolt that Lincoln looked up and gazed in the priest's direction. Lucy slumbered on.

"Kevin, I think Maria Elena's interview was like the first emergence of the crest of a wave. All the movement in the social media realm tells us momentum is growing. Since it is counterpoint to the entire violence side, everything that burst forth with the federal sieges and actions, you can bet there is more to come."

"Fair enough. Though I noticed you didn't offer any thoughts about me and my badass beloved. So. . . ."

"Kevin, the dream you had about the two of you in the Jeep in pirouette tells us that you're on this ride together. You are entangled—in a good way, good entanglement like Representative John Lewis always frames good trouble. And you will be hard pressed to stay off of the cusp of the wave."

"That feels spot-on, Tony."

"Then let's trust that it will come clear. Now tell me more about what happened. There is so much at play. I am intrigued. Plus, I care a great deal about you and Maria Elena."

With that Pitcairn began the story of everything that had transpired since they arrived down south. At first, it was chronological, then, as with most stories, the pieces began to connect themselves in the telling.

At one point, they paused to refresh their coffee. Mostly Tony listened, though on occasion he asked for clarification.

At the end, Pitcairn asked, "So what are you thinking, Father."

The priest smiled, "It is not lost on me that you punctuated that by using my formal title at the end." His smile grew. "But I will not fall prey to your plan to get me to play a role which you and I have agreed I will never play with you. We are friends. I know I'm a confidante, and that you trust me, but first and foremost, we just talk."

"You and the Good Witch of the High Desert are in cahoots together, Tony. She is very careful to not give me advice. Why the hell is that? Why do the two of you both take that approach?"

"Oh, Kevin, it is so clear you are being taught, and guided, and called from within. Perhaps Kari and I are just wise enough to know to stay out of the way of your spiritual journey."

Now a belly laugh bounced from Pitcairn. "Tony, need I remind you of the irony that we keep returning to—that I am the last person on Earth who would believe himself to be in any way spiritual. Sober, yes. Spiritual, not so much."

"Kevin, didn't you tell me that a number of the folks you just described in your story are reflecting the same thing at you?"

Pitcairn's overly-active brain seized up. The priest was right. "Tony, I just saw it. Felt it really. My thoughts stopped in their tracks when you said that. And I can't help thinking about Bill W and what he wrote about it. That we cannot see some of the most important things about ourselves. Right? You're a psychologist, so how do you frame this?"

"Yes, Kevin. The shadow parts of us that we cannot see, or cannot acknowledge, or cannot allow to be true. Both you and Maria Elena have had so many traumas and been so deeply convinced that you are flawed or damaged by a culture that is invested in making people feel small, that it is exceedingly difficult to realize that the Divine lives in each of us fully, with no limitations."

A very long silence followed.

"That's what Marianne Williamson meant in her writings when she said that the world is not well-served by playing small."

"Yes, yes, yes, Kevin. Something is working very deeply with and through you and Maria Elena. I suppose you could find a way to stifle it. The better strategy would be to lean into it."

Pitcairn felt the resolve shoot through him. Apparently, it showed in his countenance. He could see it on the priest's face just before Tony spoke.

"Kevin, the difference between fate and destiny is based entirely on what we do with what life brings. I can see you are already leaning into it." He chuckled. "Perhaps not exactly willingly, though it seems it has fallen upon you—to use the phrase you so often like."

Pitcairn nodded. "Okay. Okay." He stood. "Let's do this. Lincoln. Lucy. Let's roll."

The boxers scrambled up and shook themselves vigorously. The priest snuck a few treats from his pocket and fed them to both dogs.

"Always good to bribe the critters, Kevin."

The men embraced for long moments.

"See you at the hospital at one o'clock, Tony. And thank you for all the support you've given Zack. You and your people are good people."

Tony nodded as they parted.

Before he had left that morning, Pitcairn had provided the cell phones, email information, and passwords written down for Pattie. When he came back home, after the dogs had scrambled to the kitchen for the food she'd set out for them, she walked up to him and whacked him firmly above the heart.

"Buddy, you and Marie Elena have got a whole lot of shaking going on, some of which is pretty amazing. But first, she's still sleeping. Much deserved I might add. Let's talk over breakfast. There's one thing in particular you need to know."

▸43◂

MARIA ELENA DID NOT APPEAR UNTIL AFTER ELEVEN O'CLOCK. She was terribly groggy, so he and Pattie did not tell her she had been invited to lead a counter-protest in Richmond, Virginia, the following weekend.

A group of hard-core, southern agitators angered by the federal actions were going to march down that city's Monument Avenue, and it's long string of Confederate statues. It was exactly as Ronnie had described it in Asheville, a mash-up of state's rights supporters, anti-federalists, and racists.

In Richmond, a non-profit community organization called The Mission had long worked to promote harmony and healing across the South and beyond. It had latched onto Maria Elena's ideas driving the emerging movement as well as the meme: Live dangerously. Underestimate her. They wanted her voice, and her presence. The Mission, which really was anchored in an old mission on the river bluffs in downtown Richmond, had put out a call for an army of watchers. They indicated that the numbers already were swelling.

Pitcairn shook his head. "Look, I can't quite believe this, but I can't really deny it. Let's hold off until tomorrow to tell Maria Elena. We have enough in our day already."

Pattie agreed, and their attention shifted to preparing to go to the hospital. Zack returned from a coffee shop a short while before they needed to leave. Maria Elena had taken a leisurely bath, eaten lightly, and was fairly subdued. It was a somber drive in the Jeep across Albuquerque.

When they entered the room in which Lucas had been moved for this final day, they were floored. It was brightly lit, and Father Tony and Bonnie, the nurse, were already there. Yet it was not the room that made such an impression. Rather it was the hundreds of flowers that surrounded them. Bouquets and plants were like a colorful halo wrapped around Lucas. The color and scent were overwhelming.

Maria Elena was first to speak. "Sweet Jesus, what the hell?"

Bonnie offered an open-armed gesture. "It seems the community, and the Center—Father Tony's people, went a bit overboard."

The priest shrugged, but Pitcairn was aware in that moment that this gesture had penetrated deeply into Zack. Pattie was weeping, but Zack looked as if he was experiencing a moment on the road to his own private Damascus. A thought shot through Pitcairn's mind from all the explorations into trauma. *Metanoia—a profound change of heart.*

Zack was speechless and motionless until Bonnie embraced him. Then he collapsed into her. Pitcairn guessed that years of sorrow were bursting loose from deep within the man. No one spoke, and Bonnie knew how to hold that space with him.

Pitcairn's only thought was that this was one more expression of watching. Bearing witness, as so many seemed to want to describe it. Ground made sacred merely by being present and engaging it. He thought back to something Tony had told him long ago. He had observed that the burning bush story for Moses was an analogy that applied to us all, and applied all the time, that there was nothing but holy ground made holy by our awakening to it. Perhaps that was what Maria Elena had sensed in her comments to Oprah.

He felt Maria Elena nudge him from his reverie. The physician had entered the room, a slender, gray-haired man with an enlivened presence. He hugged Zack even as Bonnie continued to embrace him.

"You can call me, Erv, or Doc," he said. "Or if you're more comfortable with some formality, Doctor Erv." He smiled.

Mixed greetings followed. The doctor was clearly very at ease. Pitcairn imagined that his practice with hospice had brought that forth in him, or perhaps it was his countenance that brought him to the field. Regardless, it had a gentling effect.

After everyone had settled, Doctor Erv told them what they could expect as they disconnected Lucas from the medical machinery that kept him alive. Also, that at any point they could change the pace, or ask questions, or voice any concerns.

"We just don't know about pain when someone is in this state, so we administer a steady low dose of morphine in his IV as a precaution. No reason for anyone to experience pain unnecessarily." He looked at Zack. "The morphine has a very slight depressing effect on breathing, so you'll see his vital signs slow, which would happen regardless." He smiled again as a strained look came to Zack's face. "Not to worry though, it does not really hasten his passing, only eases the way."

He allowed a long silence to suffuse the room before he continued. "Zack, do you want any prayers, or are there any rites you'd like before we begin." He glanced to Father Tony.

Zack shook his head in the negative, then croaked. "Please, go ahead, Doc."

Bonnie rose, taking a moment to squeeze Zack's shoulder, then began with the doctor's guidance to slowly remove Lucas from life support. Sure enough, when all that remained was the IV and the monitor for breath, pulse, and heart rate, they began to see a gradual slowing of vital signs.

While Pitcairn had seen people's passage before, he was always captivated by the process of life ebbing away. A slow decline followed by a lower level of stability, then another slow decline and another lowering stasis. Over the next forty minutes, Lucas departed. At the very end, when vitals flat-lined, Lucas shuddered three times as if trying to shake himself back into life. Then his time was at its end.

No one moved. It was still except for the distant, white noise of the hospital and the city beyond, punctuated by gentle sounds of sorrow. Doctor Erv slipped out, but Bonnie stayed steadily beside Zack.

Maria Elena eased herself up, lightly touched Pattie and Zack, and left the room. Pitcairn guessed that she needed time and space to process her own emotions.

Tony spoke then. "Zack. Pattie. What do you need now?"

Pattie answered softly. "I'd like to just sit with Lucas for a while. Zack?" He nodded his agreement wordlessly.

Pitcairn, Bonnie, and Tony knew it was time to leave them. Outside the room, they hugged. He told them he was going to take a long walk home, that he needed some time as well. He texted Maria Elena, who said she would make sure Pattie and Zack had a ride home.

Heading across the street, Pitcairn walked with long, steady strides. He planned to meander his way home. The unplanned route and the sights along the way would be an excellent backdrop for his thoughts and feelings to play out.

▶ 44 ◀

THE EVENING HAD BEEN VERY SOMBER. PATTIE DECIDED SHE needed to cook, and prepared a large, Oklahoma-style meal of fried chicken, black-eyed peas, a bean salad, and the always-ubiquitous cornbread. Regardless, they ate lightly, and much of the meal ended up in the refrigerator.

Sunday morning, after a disjointed night of sleep, Pitcairn woke early. Much to his surprise, Maria Elena arose shortly afterward and joined him for coffee at the kitchen table. She too had slept poorly.

"Cito, there was a whole lot stirring inside my dreams, none of which I can remember, but it feels like it was a really busy night. Does that make sense?"

"Sure enough, Emmy. Sometimes there's a lot of stuff that has to get worked through. And we do seem to have a lot of it lately."

"Can I go to the West Mesa with you this morning?"

Surprised, he countered with his own question. "Sure, but what's up with that?"

"I don't know. Maybe I just need to spend some time with you and the dogs. Things may not be normal in our world, but we can at least try to find some normal."

"Makes sense, Emmy. And I can tell you all about our next adventure."

"Adventure?" she asked with raised eyebrows.

"Pattie was really busy sorting things out for us, and one of them you need to know about. Get your hiking boots on, and I'll tell you all about it."

It was a short drive to the high-desert trailhead that would take them along the basalt escarpment. Lucy could barely contain her energy; it had clearly been too long since her last morning hike on the mesa. They struck off briskly under an uncharacteristically heavy cloud cover that had trapped the previous day's warmth close to the ground. While not the typical cold morning, there was a comfortable, seasonal chill.

After the first turn in the trail, they followed a long tongue of the mesa to the east toward the city's lights lining the river valley from northern to southern horizons. Against that twinkling backdrop, Pitcairn described the invitation from the Mission in Richmond. Much to his surprise, her response was subdued, almost pensive.

After a number of steps, he asked, "Emmy? What are you thinking? I sort of expected a larger response from you."

She laughed. "Of course you'd expect that, Cito. But everything just keeps getting weirder and weirder. I have no idea how to orient myself to it. I guess I'm weirded out by the weirding."

"Now that is a great line! And I don't disagree."

He stopped to watch for Lucy who had vanished into a craggy area. She burst out a moment later like a shell from a cannon. Who knew what strange things motivated her.

They walked for quite a distance before he asked again. "What's the plan?"

"Oh . . . I'm doing it. I'm just mulling over what it might mean."

"Well, that has quite a ring of certainty."

She stopped and looked at him. "Cito, I can't not follow the call. Right?"

He leaned into her with an easy hug. "Let's do it."

She laughed and slowly scanned the panorama, the faint light of the breaking day in the east, a fading dark in the west, clumps of brush and stunted junipers slowly taking shape in the dim landscape.

"There is something about this mesa."

He waited to see what she would say next.

"It feels like it just absorbs you. And whatever you bring with you."

"My experience too, Emmy. I've always imagined that across time, people have been drawn to this place. Probably all the little caves and grottoes have been small refuges, places for retreat or vision quest."

"You know, we need to go back to the cave we were in when all this started. The day I found the talisman."

"You don't mean today, do you?"

"No. No. Maybe after Richmond?"

"Sounds like a deal. Want to head back? There's a crossover trail ahead. I'm not sure you've ever been on it with me. Lots of ups and downs. Very fun on a bike."

"Sure. Breakfast. Then we can check in on Pattie and Zack. Busy day. They're supposed to pick up Lucas's ashes later today."

On their way back to the Jeep, they talked about what to expect when they drove to the northeast part of the state on Monday. While Pitcairn knew of the open, high plains, it was an area neither of them had traveled much.

"I hope Pattie will tell us more about Etido. He sounds like quite a character, and quite an influence on Lucas," Pitcairn said.

"And Pattie," she added. "I mean, she's written his memoir. That's something."

"Good observation, Emmy."

"Maybe we can get Zack to talk about Lucas. I think he needs to talk."

"Perfect. And we need to just listen, I'd guess."

"Watch, baby. We need to just watch," she countered.

► 45 ◄

SUNDAY WAS INDEED FILLED WITH MANY TASKS. AND BEFORE day was done, Pattie had sorted through the many calls and emails. She gave them a lengthy, annotated list, and promised to talk them through it on Tuesday or Wednesday before she and Zack left.

Pattie had talked him into coming home with her to McAlester, the small city where they had long lived in southeastern Oklahoma. It was where Lucas had grown up, and Pattie thought it would do him good to revisit the places and the times as part of his healing.

He had protested initially, right up until the moment she looked him in the eye and said, "Zack, if you just go back to Eastern Europe, isolate yourself and work, you are going to suffer." He did not disagree, so Pattie added, "I can't let you suffer more, Zack. And Lucas would not want that either." Perhaps too the need to work his way through the death of his son had become clear to him.

After a good breakfast Monday morning, Maria Elena packed lunch. Their trip would take them into fairly remote areas across the high plains to the valley of the Canadian River. Pattie was fairly sure of the state highway that would lead them to the canyon where Etido was buried, and where they would release Lucas. She also admitted they might have to explore a bit if her memory was not as good as she thought. When they were finished, she thought they should drive to Wagon Mound, a small community that rested at the bottom of a promontory shaped like a Conestoga wagon.

"Etido found a little cafe there that makes great pies from scratch. Actually, it's the only cafe in Wagon Mound." She chuckled loudly. "I know Lucas visited there, part of his quest in following Etido's journeys. It would be a perfect conclusion."

Once they were on their way on the interstate through Santa Fe, Las Vegas, and then into the expansive grasslands, Pattie began reminiscing about Lucas. He'd had quite a childhood, and before long Zack began to add his memories. That inevitably brought up stories of Lucas's mother, Diana, Zack's deceased wife. It was clear from the feeling of the conversation that Zack had many unresolved sorrows from her passing as well. While he was not a man who would easily cry, his emotions tinged many of his comments. In contrast, Pattie wept on several occasions.

Pitcairn remembered. *Loss, is loss, is loss.* And on more than several occasions was aware of his own feelings of loss, which he attended to with his awareness and breath.

As they turned off the main highway to cut into the heart of the prairie, Pattie said she would tell them more about Etido on the trip back. Then she began to watch the terrain, remembering her own long-ago trip with the old man. For some time, it was gently rolling grassland, the endless plains that made their way across the heartland of the entire country.

In preparation, Pattie had studied a road map which now rested in her lap. "If I had not been working on Etido's story, with so much of it fresh in my mind, I don't know if I could remember enough to bring us to the right place." She grew quiet. "It's almost like I'm reliving that final trip with him. Not déjà vu exactly, and with the strange feelings of this being Lucas's final trip." Her voice faded away.

A few miles later, she exclaimed. "I remember that big barn there on the left, and the chewing tobacco advertisement on its side, and those two grain silos. But . . . I don't remember for sure which of these crossroads ahead will take us there."

She looked at the map again. "Then again, we can always crisscross them until we find it," she said with a hint of humor in her voice.

Sure enough, the first small highway running due north was not correct. The crossing of the Canadian River was unremarkable. Then they cut east on a county road until the next small highway, which they followed south.

"This feels like it might be it," Pattie said enthusiastically as the road began a long, winding descent into the valley. Her head pivoted left and right. Then she proclaimed. "Those bluffs! And all those cottonwoods! I'm sure that's it."

Pitcairn glanced at her in the rearview mirror. Clearly, she was deep in her own memories, many of them linking Lucas and Etido.

"Down here, there will be a dirt track that runs along the bluffs. It's not very far now."

Sure enough, it was as Pattie remembered it. Soon they came to a stop just above the placid waters of the Canadian. She pointed toward an alcove in the bluff. "That's where Etido is. Right there." Then she wept again.

With Maria Elena arm in arm with Pattie, they walked up the silty slope. Pitcairn stayed at Zack's side as they followed. A few steps from the base of the bluff, Pattie turned and began to describe Etido's last few days here. The silvery boughs and limbs of the cottonwoods swayed softly in the sunlight beneath massive skies.

"Our fire was right here," she pointed. "And when he slipped away, I remember coyotes howling." A pause followed. "It was not a coincidence."

Then Zack spoke. He'd been quiet for so long that it was a surprising sound. "Thank you, Pattie. You were right. This is exactly where Lucas would want to be." He looked to the rise in the soil where Etido's remains rested. "And I think this is what Etido would want." He glanced back them. "I still miss him, Pattie."

She offered a sad, winsome nod. "Me too, Zack. Me too."

Pitcairn opted to walk the river for a time to stretch his legs. The others found a comfortable part of the slope and settled down cross-legged. Zack cradled in his arms the urn that held the ashes of his son. Pattie sat beside him. Pitcairn nodded as he turned to follow the river.

When he returned a short while later, the others were telling stories again punctuated with laughter. Lunch was spread around them on blankets. He joined in and listened until Zack reached a moment of resolve. He stood and said simply, "It's time, Pattie."

Everything became very still. Zack lifted the lid of the urn and stared into it. He turned and moved up the slope. Bending, he began to sprinkle his son's ashes around the area where Etido rested. He stepped back, as if to survey his efforts. Then he turned and walked to water's edge where he cast the remainder into the air and river.

Zack turned with an odd look on his face. "What about the urn?"

No one answered. It was his decision. Suddenly he spun and cast the urn into a pool in the river. Facing away, Pitcairn saw him nod gently.

When he returned, Pattie and Maria Elena wrapped him in an embrace. Then Pattie announced. "Now we need to celebrate Lucas and Etido with pie."

There was a lightness in the Jeep as they drove for an hour to the cafe. While the apple and blueberry pies were not especially noteworthy, a lemon meringue was outstanding, and the home-made crust was even more exceptional. Their conversation was heartfelt.

Once they hit the open road as the day began to fade toward dusk, Pattie shared her thoughts about Etido.

"He was quite an unusual man. A wanderer like you, Pitcairn. He started out a fisherman in western Canada but got a calling that sent him onto the road. Fell into some significant learning with a teacher in Chicago. Really kind of meandered his way into Oklahoma. And into our lives. Especially me and Lucas."

"How so?" Pitcairn asked. A question she pondered.

"Well, I think you'll want to read his story. The short of it is that somewhat mysteriously, he took me under his wing to teach me what he had learned. Really, though, what he taught me was what he came to embody. To this day, it is a part of my world."

She added ruefully, "Etido entrusted Lucas into my care to bring him along in the same teachings. It's why Lucas was seeking. It's what brought him to New Mexico. He was following the spiritual path of Teo."

"Oh, Pattie, that's gotta hurt now that Lucas is gone," Maria Elena interjected.

"Not really," she promptly replied. "It lives on in his journals. And now it lives on through both of you, though you didn't know Etido, or Lucas either."

There was a long silence.

"Stumble into grace," said Maria Elena with a kind of reverence.

"Apparently, that is true," replied Pattie. "The way will find a way."

Pitcairn heard the phrase and knew in an instant it would be part of what he would write about this entire affair. Already it was taking shape in a corner of his mind as he drove. The way will find a way.

▸46◂

THEIR PLANS AFTER PARTING CAME TOGETHER VERY QUICKLY. Pitcairn and Maria Elena would travel on Thursday through Atlanta, once again, to catch a connection to Richmond. Pattie and Zack would head home Wednesday, after securing a promise from Maria Elena that they would visit them in Oklahoma. Pattie agreed to send a copy of her manuscript to Pitcairn, who could already sense that it was still more of the information that was coming together around post-traumatic growth and innocence.

Maria Elena decided to delay any interviews or appearances until after Richmond. She said she knew in her gut that everything needed to wait until then. Besides, so many items already needed their attention in these few, fast-moving days.

Pitcairn made advance plans with his editors at the *Albuquerque Chronicle* and the *North Country Reader* for a series of articles. Somehow, he also managed to squeeze onto his calendar an end-of-day session with his therapist, Kari, for Wednesday. Given all the pieces of the puzzle that were flying around, he was not surprised that on both mornings, he woke very early to walk and to write. He knew to trust the strange inner process.

When he plopped somewhat wearily into the easy chair in Kari's office in the Nob Hill district of Albuquerque, the flow of things was just on the verge of what felt like clarity.

"Hola, Pitcairn," she began.

"Hola, Kari. Which witch are you today?" he asked with amusement. Kari enjoyed his reference to her as a witch, and had woven the notion of light and dark witches into her frame of reference with him. Both necessary parts of the whole, she liked to remind him.

"Ah . . . today I am all the colors of the spectrum of light that fall between black and white. And you, are you able to entertain them?"

He laughed. "I always forget that gray is not the color between black and white on the spectrum of light. And yes, I'm pretty damned open to the possibilities given all that is unfolding."

"Let's begin with a moment of silence," Kari said as they both closed their eyes. After a few seconds, she took an audible breath and spoke again, "Tell me about the possibilities."

"Before I start, you do know you are the only meditation teacher I ever heard of who thinks seconds are enough time for a meditation."

An exaggerated look of exasperation appeared on her face. "Kevin, you and I both know that whatever that Great Reality is that your Big Book references, it only needs an instant to restore and reawaken us."

"Except I don't believe in a Great Reality." He paused for a moment of reflection. "Though I do have to admit all the things that are happening do not seem to be random." With that he launched into an overview of all that had transpired. Kari listened attentively, making an occasional note in her file.

When he felt satisfied that he'd framed it all well enough, he asked, "What do you think?"

She had closed her eyes, presumably to listen for her own inner guidance. Then she gazed at him, her eyes sparkling. "Mother Mary comes to me. Speaking words of wisdom."

"Really, the Beatles and *Let It Be*, Kari?"

The glint in her eyes grew brighter. "The Divine or Sacred Feminine, Pitcairn. From which powerful women and feminine energy have always appeared across all time and all wisdom traditions. Even in you, Kevin. Big, strong guy with a depth of the feminine that is striking. The ability to follow a calling that you do not even believe. The intuition."

He was somewhat stunned by this moment in which she seemed more oracle than therapist. He'd experienced it sometimes before with her but never so pronounced as this.

Kari continued. "The dream, Kevin, the Jeep dream. You and Maria Elena are being drawn together into new relationship. A new path. A shared purpose."

"And that is . . ." he asked, tentatively.

"Maria Elena was so clear with Oprah. The time of the old male paradigm of power and leadership is waning. The feminine approach is a new paradigm. A wisdom paradigm."

"I need some help here, Kari. Any examples?"

"Of course, though they are just not well-known. I'll share a more prominent one, then I'll tell you a more proximal one."

"Okay," he said.

"Few know that it was the mothers and grandmothers who brought to an end the generations-long standoff between the factions in Northern Ireland. Behind the scenes, unbidden, they approached the male leaders on both sides and told them very simply that they no longer wanted their children and grandchildren to die in violence. They spoke with the authority of the Sacred Feminine. They spoke truth to power, and power necessarily listened. It took, and soon peace came."

Pitcairn was deeply attentive. "Go on."

"There is a story Charmaine Glennis loves to tell," she began.

"Wait . . . Glennis . . . she just came up in the writings I read from Lucas!"

Kari laughed and beamed. "Pitcairn, that is interesting, and all the more reason for you to hear this story."

"No disagreement from me."

"I'm sure you know there has been a terrible opioid problem in northern New Mexico. Its epicenter has been Española, but it did not begin there. It began in Chimayó."

"Chimayo? Really? Opioids in the same place as Santuario de Chimayó?"

She nodded vigorously. "Yes Kevin. It began in the same place as the healing earth found in that holy place. Of course, it would. Right?"

He knew that across generations, pilgrims had sought out the sacred place in Chimayó that was known for miraculous healings, but this story was new to him. He shook his head in disbelief but gestured for her to continue.

"There was so much death the opioids brought to Chimayó. It changed one day, though. And it was Glennis who pieced together the story beneath the story. The grandmothers grew weary of all the devastation and one day approached the brotherhood within the Catholic community. 'Where are you?" they called out to them. 'Our children are dying. For God's sake, where is your faith?'"

Kari closed her eyes and lapsed into silence. Pitcairn waited.

When she opened her eyes again, they were filled with light. "Kevin, it took a few months, but one day, word spread that the faith fathers would be leading community marches and efforts to drive drugs out of the village. With that march, there was no longer tolerance. They reclaimed their people. And their community."

"And it relocated to Espanola?"

"Sadly, yes, Pitcairn. But to this day, Chimayó has been restored. There is a funny part of the story, though."

"Yeah?"

"One of the grandmothers went back to the faith leaders to ask what had happened and why it took some time." She shook her head. "They had to get the drugs out of their own brotherhood in order to have any authority in the community. The grandmothers had spiritually shamed them into action."

"Kari, that is really a great story. Is it true?"

"Do you mean factually or spiritually?"

A belly laugh erupted from him. "Touché, you witch! Point well made. It doesn't matter. It is the story of restoration. And Chimayó was saved for itself."

Her silence was all that was needed.

"Okay. So, what wisdom for me?"

The therapist again closed her eyes. "Kevin, please share all of this with Maria Elena. The two of you are in this together. A community is rising up. The Sacred Feminine is going to reclaim this world. That is not one woman. It is not women. It is the emergence of a feminine energy that will mend that which is broken."

"And the guys?" he asked.

She beamed again. "Well, Kevin, you are a guy's guy. Between the two of you, there is a bridge of spiritual opportunity."

He had no idea what to say. "I feel like I'm in the *Matrix*," he replied.

"I am no oracle. And you are no shape shifter. Still, I will trust."

▸47◂

THEIR FLIGHT TO ATLANTA THE NEXT DAY HAD AN ALMOST surreal quality to it, given that it was only a short time since their last flight to the city. Granted, they were only passing through this time, but so much had transpired. Regardless, Maria Elena slept and Pitcairn studied, wrote, and meditated.

The Harpies would join them in Richmond, an unexpected surprise. Nicky had said they wanted a road trip, and Richmond was a great reason.

After a quiet night at their hotel, Pitcairn and Maria Elena's breakfast meeting with the organizers at the Mission's dining hall was surprising. The Mission's leaders had brought together a group of lay community organizers from up and down the length of Appalachia. There were a few from as far north as Burlington, Vermont; a strong presence from the traditional civil rights communities that included Montgomery and Birmingham, Alabama, a belt running from northern Georgia all the way up through the Shenandoah Valley of Virginia; and sprinklings from the West and points far and wide.

Unknown to the larger world, in response to the rising tide of racism, misogyny, nationalism, and fascism, a number of community-based people, about a third of them men, had been preparing. A small but innovative team with great tech savvy from Chattanooga, Tennessee, had created the Live Dangerously, Underestimate Her Foundation with GoFundMe sites, and had begun submissions to copyright and trademark everything they could. They'd also snatched a large number of online domains. It turned out they had been behind some of the strong current of memes.

The attendance Saturday was guessed to be in the thousands, though no one knew for sure, compared with the expected few hundred marchers at most. Regardless, slightly fewer than a hundred team leaders were prepared to engage anyone and everyone who wanted to participate as watchers. What impressed Pitcairn more than anything else was that there was no evidence of a single celebrity among them. And while he could not be certain, it sounded on the face of it like an incredibly diverse group coming together for a non-violent response to violence.

He whispered to Maria Elena, *"De la gente."*

She nodded appreciatively.

That afternoon, the team leaders would come together to finalize their strategies for Saturday's gathering. Maria Elena would be asked to speak to them. And much to his surprise, so would Pitcairn. Kari had been right about the credibility he represented for men.

There was little for them to do but listen. Afterward, they were given a tour of the Mission grounds by three docents who lived there. All three had been born and raised in the Richmond area, and were joined together by their common desire to *make right in the world*, as they called it.

After lunch in the community commons, there was an extended prayer and meditation vigil, followed by a period of rest. By mid-afternoon, and the meeting of leaders in the Mission gardens over-looking the river valley, Pitcairn was incredibly impressed. The only group he'd ever seen organize with such effectiveness had been as an embedded reporter with Mormon women responding to torren-tial rains and terrible flooding in Boise, Idaho. They had been a force, just as these organizers were. Fortunately, while the day was cold, as would be the weekend, the skies were blue and the winds calm. It made for an idyllic view of the city from high atop the bluffs.

Pitcairn first impression as the team leaders gathered was of their composure. None came across as firebrands. As he saw a number of interactions, from some who obviously knew each other to others who were introducing themselves, it was all being done with groundedness. Since they were largely community organizers, they would know the power of connection and relationship.

When two of the local leaders, a Latina named Cecelia whom they had met that morning, and Ray Lee, a slender, white man who immediately came across as professorial, stood side by side to address the gathering, a hush came quickly to the audience. As they sat in the wings on a wooden bench, Maria Elena whispered, "Cito, they have purpose. You can feel it."

He looked at her and offered a curt and affirming nod. Then whispered back, "Common purpose."

Cecelia began very simply. "Welcome to the Mission. Welcome to a common pathway for which we here in this community have long prepared." She paused and scanned the audience. "To our way of thinking, there is no better place for this work than Richmond, a city that has long stood on the edge of the many concerns that have so long divided this nation." She smiled. "Please look around you at all these faces." She paused for a much longer time as she allowed visual connections to be made. "What you see is a portrait of our many viewpoints. While we are all bound to create a cultural commons that extends to anyone who wishes to be a part of it, the Mission's mission . . ."—she laughed at the phrase—". . . the Mission's mission, and our entire body of work reflects our innermost desires to bridge the divides. To do so with non-violence that allows for a different kind of conversation, one that is rich with listening, consideration and compassion. Not just tolerance, though that is immensely valuable, but real engagement between every kind of person."

She turned to Ray Lee who said only: "All those faces you just observed are every kind of person."

The team leaders scanned the audience again, and the recognition and appreciation was a felt thing.

"Before I introduce Maria Elena Maldonado and Kevin Pitcairn . . ."—all eyes turned toward them—". . . we have a few logistics. Each of you have been given a folder of information. It's simple enough. Each of you has a partner and an assigned location along the route of the march. There is a tip sheet for dos and don'ts."

"No surprises, I'm sure. You all know these things. Not just non-violence but an emphasis on watching, observing, letting go of judgment. Anything you and your partner need to do to hold others in that space, use your judgment and your practice tools."

"Our team will be circulating among you to talk with each of you about any questions you have. The main reassurance Ray Lee and I want to offer is that the Mission has established a very good relationship with local political leaders and law enforcement. In our conversations with them, they have assured us they trust us. While they are not happy this demonstration has come to Richmond, they know our work well, and we have their full support. Like it or not, a commons has come to Richmond."

"Ray Lee, will you introduce our guests?"

He nodded and gestured to Maria Elena and Pitcairn, who stood and began moving forward.

"You all know Maria Elena from last week's nationally broadcast interview with Oprah, and from the meme *Live Dangerously. Underestimate Her*, which our friends from Chattanooga have really pumped." He turned and pointed to two women and a man seated to the side, who all nodded at the acknowledgment. "And you know Kevin Pitcairn from the Crucifix Protests and his writings. Please welcome them."

The audience response was interesting. Some light applause, a great deal of welcoming smiles, plus a few people using the universal joined hands associated with the blessing of Namaste.

Maria Elena spoke first. She and Pitcairn had discussed this moment at great length.

"All of you know about violence. I've known it in subtle and not-so-subtle forms my whole life." She held the moment which was pregnant with meaning. "But I've had a vision. Actually, a number of epiphanies. All I know is what you heard me say to Oprah." She shook her head with humility. "This is not the fight we know from the past. Not that kind of fight. We need a new way. Bearing witness. Seeing others differently. Seeing the problems differently. Oprah called it a new heaven and a new earth. I don't know about that. But I know that we need to be done with the old fight. Or it needs to be done with us. Its time is at an end."

She turned to him and gently reached out her hand. "Cito?"

He'd been watching the almost-electric effect of her words, and set aside all the remarks he had planned. Pitcairn knew this was not the occasion they had planned.

"I'm with her," he said with good humor, eliciting a ripple of good-hearted laughter. He knew from his many experiences in AA that the power of well-timed laughter only added to the potency of her words.

"I'm with you. Every bit of my doubting self is with you. We didn't plan for this. But it seems to have planned for us." He took long moments to consider what to say next.

"Earlier this week, we sat with a young man, Lucas, as he was taken from life support. For us, his death was a powerful illustration of what needs to come to an end. Before that, Maria Elena and I have learned more than we could have ever imagined about the roots of violence, and the terrible human experience in which it is wrapped."

He turned to look at Maria Elena, who smiled back at him.

"The old fight needs to be done with us."

Cecelia stood again and thanked everyone. "Here come our people to answer your questions. See you tomorrow."

Like a multi-headed creature, the garden-full of organizers divided in many directions. More than a few sought out Pitcairn and Maria Elena. The conversations amid the beautiful setting went on for some time.

Finally, they thanked Cecelia and Ray Lee, then walked from the grounds into the surrounding city. It was only a dozen blocks to the restaurant where they were to meet the Harpies. Since they were running early when they arrived at the Harvest, they sat and reflected over tea.

They heard the women before they turned the corner. Rosemary's loud voice careened toward them, "For Christ's sake, Betty . . ." The rest was lost as her voice apparently dropped. Then Pitcairn stood as he saw Nicky appear with the other two right behind her. Greetings soon flew amid hugs.

Once seated, Rosemary spoke first in reference to a common point of agreement in the rooms of recovery. "AA makes for strange bedfellows, doesn't it?"

They all laughed as Nicky jumped in. "Maria Elena, I loved you with Oprah!" Betty followed with a quick affirmation. "Now, catch us up."

Betty added in a conspiratorial tone. "And give us the dirt too!"

Rosemary rolled her eyes and groaned. With that, Pitcairn and Maria Elena began to tell the women everything that had come to pass, breaking at several points to chat with their waiter and place their orders.

There was much chatter about the *Live Dangerously. Underestimate Her* meme. Rosemary thought it was wimpy. Nicky loved it. And Betty seemed to just be happy hanging out in the middle of all the excitement.

When much of their meal was finished and the catching up completed, Nicky asked about the day to come. Before either of them could respond, Rosemary let Pitcairn and Maria Elena know they had not come alone: Another ten people from the recovery community in and around Greenville were en route.

"A couple are ambulance chasers, of course, but they're all in."

Pitcairn let Maria Elena take the lead. He knew his was a supportive role in many ways. It was a long conversation. Somehow, they were all deeply bonded in a very short time. Trauma engaged and transcended would do that.

Finally, the day was done. They made their way back to their hotel. In a very short time, they were sleeping deeply.

▶48◀

SURPRISINGLY, PITCAIRN AND MARIA ELENA WERE SO WORN out they both slept until almost six. He woke loggy-headed from the unaccustomed deep, unbroken sleep. Maria Elena admitted as she lay in bed with him that she was nervous.

"Cito, what if this all runs off the rails?"

He replied softly. "It's the tiger, Emmy. We're just going to ride the tiger. Other than our awareness, there's nothing we can do."

"Do you want to go for a walk? Or are you headed for a long bath?"

"I'm going to soak, soak, soak."

He leaned over, kissed her on the forehead, and hopped up to dress and get moving. "There's a local bagel shop not far from here. How's that sound?"

"Lovely, Cito. Thank you."

With that, he pulled himself together and headed out. For once, a walk was just a walk, to reframe that great psychological notion from Sigmund Freud. It was chilly, but he had no trouble warming as his pace increased. And, relatively at ease, he could simply take in the sights. After forty-five minutes, he got the bagels and returned to the hotel to clean up for the march and the counterprotest.

At nine-thirty, ninety minutes before the expected start of the march, they arrived at the front end of the route down Monument Avenue. They'd agreed to stand on a side of the pedestal of the statue of Confederate leader J.E.B. Stuart. Already, hundreds of people were positioning themselves along the route. The team leaders were organizing people as they arrived.

Cecelia met them at the statue and welcomed them with a hug: "What a wonderful day to carry our message to the community and beyond." She called their attention to local and national news crews already positioning themselves.

"Are you worried, Cecelia?" Maria Elena asked, signaling her own concerns.

"No, no, no," she replied, "Our plans are in place. What will now be will now be. Fate has presented us with this moment. We shall see what destiny we can pull forth from it."

With that, she kissed Maria Elena on the cheek as she grasped her by both shoulders. "*Gracias, mi linda. Gracias.*" She placed a hand on Pitcairn's forearm as she turned and moved away.

He sipped on the coffee he'd brought as the watchers gathered and were deployed along the avenue. Again, he was struck by how well organized was the effort. As the numbers swelled to what would eventually be estimated at six thousand observers, he experienced the overwhelming feeling of presence that had come to him at the first Crucifix Protest in Albuquerque.

"Emmy, can you feel it? This is just like the feeling we had at the park when we saw the three crucifixes."

"Yes. A groundswell." She looked up at him. "Cito, I'm so glad we're a part of this. It matters."

He agreed, and continued to scan the crowd with great interest. Though they didn't know, news cameras were showing their faces over and over to audiences near and far. It was only when a young couple approached with their two teen-aged daughters for Maria Elena's autograph that they grasped the implications. The older girl was a bit aloof, but the younger one unzipped her coat to proudly display a sweatshirt with a brightly imagined *Live Dangerously. Underestimate Me* emblem.

Maria Elena glanced at Pitcairn with a stricken look. He grinned reassuringly at her, which encouraged her to turn back to the family. As she took a pen from the woman to sign the girl's notebook, she was interrupted by the father: "Thank you for your example for our girls. They need strong role models."

She paused to let the words sink in, then looked back and forth at both daughters. She had no words to express her thoughts, though as others approached both of them over the coming hours, she would begin to find a voice for the unsolicited goodwill. Instead, she offered a thumbs up, then finished the auto-graphing.

Afterward, she studied Pitcairn's face and the grin still stuck there. He could see she was processing the experience deeply, and imagined that for someone who had fought so hard to overcome her deep sense of violation, this validation was a strange world indeed.

Impulsively, he leaned into her with a very gentle kiss. Later they would learn that the interaction with the family, and the kiss, had been captured by a local videographer. In a matter of hours, it would be captioned and find its way to the web as yet one more part of the meme that was echoing through popular culture.

Still, the most amazing moment came when the eighty or so marchers turned the corner to face thousands of largely silent people. Their raucous camaraderie and attitude quickly began to dampen. Very likely they expected combativeness or assault, only to experience countless eyes gazing upon them.

On multiple occasions, one of the marchers would try to start a cheer or shout out a jeering comment. To the credit of the Team Leaders and the Mission volunteers, any time someone in the crowds began to respond or to heckle, they quickly and gently intervened. The result was that for the next thirty minutes of the march, and for hours afterward, a degree of quietude prevailed.

As the marchers passed, many of those lining the street followed them silently. The numbers grew as the blocks passed. In the end, the marchers, with police clearing the way ahead, were enveloped by layer upon layer of largely quiet watchers.

Later when he would speak with his closest confidantes, Pitcairn would hear a range of remarkable feedback. Some broadcasters were stunned into silence. Others offered color commentary to fill the unexpectedly open space. For days to come, commentators would stretch themselves to describe what they had seen and experienced. Conclusions would be hard to draw, yet there was wide agreement that some kind of inflection point had been transited.

The aftermath was hardly anticlimactic. For many who had gathered, there was a buzz which Pitcairn imagined was a kind of psycho-spiritual contact high. He couldn't help wondering what, if anything, would last.

Extricating themselves was complicated at first. Many people were seeking them out, including several reporters. They had agreed to not talk with the journalists so as not to risk turning the event into a matter of celebrity. "Principles, not personalities," Maria Elena had suggested to him, stealing one of the more-profound principles of the Twelve Steps of Recovery. There was no doubt that egos could easily run amok to the detriment of the fledgling movement.

Within minutes, Cecelia had arrived with a small phalanx of volunteers to lead them away from the masses around them. "We were prepared just in case there was violence," she said, looking heavenward. "Thankfully, we can use our people now to get you out of here."

After a short debriefing with a few members of the Mission, and a great deal of expressed gratitude, Cecelia and Ray Lee planned for the follow-up, with much more foundation to be laid. Then they arranged for a driver to take Pitcairn and Maria Elena to their hotel.

"Cito, I am wasted," she said. "I don't know if I can sleep, but I'm going to try." She turned, went into the suite's bedroom, and closed the door.

Pitcairn sat down with his journal and phone. As expected, the voice and text messages had once again mushroomed, but they didn't interest him at the moment. Instead, he settled onto the sofa, crossed his legs beneath him, and slipped into meditation.

Surprisingly, both of them were successful. Maria Elena slept, then took another long, hot bath. After a fruitful time in solitude, Pitcairn had begun to compose the thoughts that would become his first commentary on what was unfolding. It seemed that he had so many ideas and so much material that the number of pieces and their breadth would be extensive.

When he heard the bath water running, he stuck his head around the door and called her name. "Emmy, how about I order something to eat and have it delivered. I don't know about you, but I've had enough of humanity for now."

"Please," she replied. "And thank you." A pause followed. "And I love you, Cito."

A short while later, over unexpectedly good dumplings, noodles and garlic string beans from a nearby Chinese bistro, they watched a movie. It brought a semblance of normalcy that was much needed.

▸49◂

THE FOLLOWING MORNING, THEIR NEED FOR SOLITUDE WAS still great, and they ordered breakfast from room service. Pitcairn was deep in his attempts to shape the material he planned to write. Maria Elena doggedly worked through her electronic correspondence. When they finally left for their flight to Atlanta and then to Albuquerque, they both felt like some structure had been established for how to navigate as they moved forward into a whole new world unfolding rapidly before them. That much was clear from the many news accounts about the effects already rippling across America and beyond, news accounts Pitcairn intentionally pulled himself away from.

At the airport, they were aware of the many looks directed to them. Interestingly, perhaps because of the much-touted southern hospitality, no one encroached into their privacy either on their first flight or during the short layover. When they finally settled into the larger aircraft that would take them across the country and home, Maria Elena was happy to have a window seat because it would be easier for her to nap.

Pitcairn planned to continue reviewing and shaping the material in his journal. But instead, he noticed a dark-skinned, younger man across the aisle who was watching him. He looked at him and nodded, and the man stuck out his hand.

"Mr. Pitcairn, my pleasure," he said with an accent that Pitcairn could not place.

"Pitcairn is good enough. And you?"

"Idris. Idris Nehemiah."

"Middle Eastern?" Pitcairn asked.

"By birth, yes, but Canadian. My family immigrated when I was younger."

"Where you headed?"

"Visiting friends from medical school who live in Santa Fe. I'm in my final year at the Medical College of Georgia in Augusta, and on break to study for my medical comprehensives."

"Ah . . . and what's your specialty going to be?"

A look came to the young man's face. "Trauma care."

Pitcairn nodded, instantly aware of the connection that had triggered Idris's interest. He laughed. "I guess you know who we are?"

Idris smiled broadly. "Indeed. As I said, a pleasure."

He could sense that the young man wanted to say more. "And . . . ," he offered.

"And my second interest is compassion care," he replied, raising his eyebrows as if to punctuate the relevance.

"Got it. I guess that makes us kindred spirits."

"Yes, sir. It does."

"What did you think about Richmond, Idris?"

The young man looked away to think.

"I was watching it with a couple of friends from school. One of them is really into alternative medicine." He looked Pitcairn in the eye. "He called it a soul retrieval."

"Soul retrieval!" Pitcairn exclaimed as he recalled the experiences with Elise.

"Yeah, he's got this whole shamanic thing going on. And he said he felt like we were being re-embodied, souls called back from the realm of the lost. Souls retrieved."

Something rattled deep in Pitcairn's gut. It had the kind of resonance he had learned through experience to trust. A cascade of thoughts raced in his mind, and he was caught in a short reverie. Realizing that the silence was probably getting awkward, he asked, "Would you be willing to write down your name and email address for me, Idris? You just gave me a puzzle piece. I want to give you credit when I write about it."

"Okay, but you'll also want to credit my friend, Buddy."

"Buddy?"

Idris burst out in merriment. "Oh yeah. Actually, Nathan Forrester. Born and bred deep down south. Descended from Confederates and slave owners. A heretic in his family. And an agitator."

He paused. "Yeah. Buddy. And he loved what he saw happening in Richmond."

Pitcairn shook his head. "What a world. Idris the doctor, Buddy the southerner, and an alcoholic journalist came together on a plane. Sounds like the set-up for a comedy routine."

The younger man smiled and tilted his head in a slight skew that reflected the point. "And you might as well include Abby, since she spurred on some of the conversation: Abigail Van Hooten."

"Okay, man. Write it down." Pitcairn offered him his pen and turned to a blank page in his journal. "And if you want, feel free to write down any other thoughts that might come to you. No idea what I might do with them. You just never know."

As Idris wrote, Pitcairn's mind freewheeled. He sank deep into thought which was broken by sound of his name.

"Pitcairn?" Idris asked.

"Sorry. There's a whole lot of stuff flying around in my head right now."

"If I might ask, what puzzle piece did you find?"

Pitcairn thought before he spoke. "I think my first writing on all these matters will be titled "A Retrieving of Souls." It fits so well, Idris. You nailed it. Buddy nailed it. Of course, it would be a heretic southerner. Buddy." He laughed again.

Idris studied him carefully for a moment. "Pitcairn, I assume you and Maria Elena have seen all the reported plans for similar activities in communities all over the country?"

Pitcairn grew somber—deadly earnestness, Clint would have called it, a phrase from AA's Big Book. For a moment, he felt a deep pang of gratitude for his old sponsor and friend."

"Yeah, Idris. I tried to not get caught up in them." He shrugged. "It looks like there is something taking hold. Something really useful."

"We'll see," Idris replied. "Sure seems to be the case."

▸50◂

WHILE IT WOULD TAKE WEEKS OF WRITING TO CAPTURE ALL that he felt needed to be said, Pitcairn had to start somewhere. He remembered the encouragement he once got from an older woman in recovery who had since died.

"There's a first step for everything." While on the surface she was talking about the Twelve Steps of Recovery, the wisdom behind the statement was pointing toward the whole of life.

A Retrieving of Souls

Today, as I begin to write about all that has transpired, *Live Dangerously. Underestimate Her* activities are caroming around the United States and beyond. It is very reminiscent of the *Crucifix Protests* that followed a similar pattern a few years ago. There is, however, an important difference. This most recent upwelling is driven not by protest, and not by celebrity. Instead, it is thousands upon thousands of watchers, not voices, for they are silent, all of whom have reached a tipping point. Enduring violence, including racism and misogyny, is no longer an acceptable status quo.

It would be foolish to think of this as a fait accompli. The cultural enmity and violence that has emerged in recent years in the United States and around the world is a continuation of long-held tendencies in humanity. Though they have accelerated, they are not new. All cultural evolutions follow a very long arc.

Still, there's a first step for everything. The way is made with every step that follows.

Only a few weeks ago, a bomb blast shook Santa Fe. While completely unexpected, it was devastating to entire communities. It also killed a young man who was the son of close friends. I wrote about Lucas before. Regardless, his death continues to produce ripple effects.

I traveled along with my companion, Maria Elena Maldonado, to the southern Appalachian region seeking to understand the roots of the violence. We toppled into a mess that played out in a number of communities. Many of you watched that on national television. Quite a few of you have no doubt been being pummeled by all the commentators with their opinions. Also no doubt, most of you are probably ill informed about it, because the carnival barkers only want you to hear what will support their points of view and rile you up. Such is the state of our information flows in this current world.

I will write of many of those things, as will Maria Elena, since we have first-hand knowledge, and experiences that cannot be refuted. We have lived them, and will make good use of our understanding.

Regardless, through the assistance of a group of people who appeared like apparitions out of the ether and who become confidantes and friends, the inherent innocence work I have long engaged in has been deepened considerably.

At the risk of sounding like a heretic, while a lot of deeds have come to pass, some horrific and some beautiful, at the heart of all these matters is that inherent innocence. Everyone is doing the best they are able. They may be delusional, misinformed, or mentally ill, but everything is everyone's best for the given time, place, circumstances, and state of being in which they find themselves.

Just to be clear, that does not mean everyone gets a pass. We must act, but more importantly, we must understand.

That's the context for what I have learned about post-traumatic stress and post-traumatic growth. The same terrible occurrences that can destroy people and lives can produce inner transformations that change the entire trajectory of those people and their lives.

Yes! Let me affirm that statement. It is not a matter of what befalls us, what the ancient Greeks called fate, that defines us or our lives. It is what is done with what comes to us that creates destiny out of fate.

What we do with fate is very much dependent on the degree to which we have been nurtured in any number of important ways. In the case of the bomber, he was the product of toxic outcomes in his family system. For the record, that included a man who volunteered in our military and fought in Vietnam, an honorable man who was traumatized by that war and passed that trauma on to his son. The results are horrific.

However, that same man has a daughter who emerged from the same toxic environment as her half-brother. She is magnificent. While in her humility she would flinch at that characterization, she is as near to an opposite from her brother as you can imagine.

That is the branch in the proverbial woods. Somehow one path leads to devastating effects; the other produces beautiful and remarkable results.

Maria Elena was swept into much of this, as most of you would know from news accounts. Out of the mess came an even more-remarkable outcome, the recent event in Richmond, Virginia, and the emergence of the movement now known as *Live Dangerously. Underestimate Her*.

To what does all this amount?

Much will come forth in future writings. Necessarily, it will be more practical. But here I want to talk about the big picture, a very big picture that emerged as a result of interactions with some remarkable people.

Today, depth psychologists and others will tell you they believe that all of our collective human development is always on a spiral, either moving upward or downward. It is never static. And our evolution cannot go ever upward, or downward, instead we progress as a whole, while sometimes regressing. Yet over time, it all somehow becomes progress.

Some of the people in this body of knowledge and practice believe that just as the universe is ever-expanding with countless contractions, emergences, explosions, and the like, nothing will stop the progression of human advancement. Everything belongs. Everything somehow is embedded in the expansion and progression.

So it is that every trauma and every growth is part of the whole. We must have both. Yet much can be done to increase the growth and diminish some of the trauma. In fact, some of the trauma can be shaped toward growth.

That's where we all come in. We are active participants in the process. The process is us for all intents and purposes. Yet we must come to understand well enough that we can cooperate with as much awareness as we can muster.

Pitcairn stopped at that point. Truth be told, he was just not sure about the last few paragraphs. He would have to think further. And conversations with Tony, Elise, Lulu, Kari, and others would follow.

He felt quite amused. "Who am I to not be part of the unfolding?" he asked himself out loud. "Progress, not perfection," he said, citing a key AA understanding.

He would re-read his work later. It was a good first step.

Then he jotted down another note to come back to the idea of soul retrieval. He realized there was so much more to be said about our re-embodiment, individually and collectively.

▸EPILOGUE ◂

THE WEEK AFTER THEIR RETURN WAS FILLED WITH COMPLEX-ities: wonderful, heartbreaking, and everything in between. Maria Elena was released from her position with the mayor of Albuquerque because the political community considered her too notorious. However, she was immediately offered a senior adviser position with New Mexico's junior senator, Maxine Anderson, which allowed her to be a national spokesperson for the movement that was now associated with her message.

One of Pitcairn's long-time friends in recovery died of an overdose of fentanyl-laced heroin. It was a blast of reality, since he'd been clean and sober for a number of years. The fact that it happened while he was with a prostitute on Central Avenue made the death all the more disheartening, even as it reminded many people of the powerful nature of addiction. Clint used to say that some would have to die so that some could live sober. That idea clearly applied far beyond the realm of addiction.

Speaking and writing invitations were proliferating, so much so that they had hired a friend part-time to manage their schedules and planning. All the while, many of the connections they had established were flourishing. Pitcairn was especially delighted to have regular contact with Elise. The connection proved beyond doubt that not only could we not predict the affairs of any day, we also could not imagine the companions who would find us along the way.

On the Saturday after their return, an unusually powerful, late-season storm dumped nearly a foot of snow during the day and overnight across the high desert. Pitcairn woke early. The morning weather report told him the state would likely be shut down for a few days while the sun took care of melting the snow from roadways. Maria Elena had really wanted to return to the cavern where the events all began, and it occurred to him they could pull out their cross-country skis and have the West Mesa to themselves.

When he heard her stirring, he prepared oatmeal with apple butter and pistachios: fuel for the trek and for the cold. Then he made a few wraps with tortillas and a variety of fillings. Snacks for Lincoln and Lucy were added to two backpacks with other supplies for the cold and wet day.

When Maria Elena appeared in the kitchen, he asked, "Ready for an adventure?"

Her eyebrows raised. "Cito, it snowed last night."

"Yep, and we are going to the cavern." He could see she was in a quandary. "Cross-country skis, baby."

"Oh shit . . . I'm not sure I remember how."

"Emmy, you got this. Trust me."

"Okay, but if it goes badly, we are coming home and spending the day by the fire."

"Fair enough. Regardless, the Jeep will get us to the top of the escarpment. And off we'll go. The forecast is that we'll have remnant clouds for the trek up and sun for the ride down across the hills."

She looked skeptical but couldn't resist the invitation.

Soon they were angling across the West Mesa, the dark figures of cholla cactus stark against the blanket of white. Around them, the chamisa and other brush were cloaked in snow, the juniper and cedar trees splotchy where the wet stuff had found angles on which to stick.

The boxers romped or slogged, depending on the terrain. Overhead, the cloud cover was just beginning to thin and break, but its presence overnight had kept the temperature from plummeting. Pitcairn and Maria Elena had to stop twice to peel off layers as they warmed.

When they slipped down into the arroyo that would bring them to the cave, it was magical. The striations of sediment were overlaid with bands of snow, making it into a work of art.

Maria Elena had stopped to catch her breath, not only from exertion but also from the beauty that gave new meaning to the idea of breathtaking. At that moment, the first open sky emerged to the west. Ahead of them, the layer of white was untouched as it snaked uphill toward the distant volcano, dark red overlaid with snow beneath the pale, clear blue above the lip of the arroyo.

"My God! It's paradise, Cito!" she exclaimed.

At that moment, Lucy bolted up the arroyo, blasting through the snow and causing Pitcairn to laugh with delight. "There goes trouble in paradise, Emmy."

She laughed with him, though still awed by the landscape.

"Let's go, Cito. I can't wait to see things from the cave. And this," she swung her arms expansively forward in a gesture toward the arroyo, "This is like a passage through beauty. We are walking in beauty, just like the Navajo say in their blessing ceremony."

A short while later, they removed their skis and clomped up the last incline to the cavern. The dogs quickly entered the dark recess, enticed by mysterious scents and escape from the cold snow underfoot.

Pitcairn and Maria Elena spread their tarps just inside the mouth so they could take in the panorama that sprawled across the horizon. The snow-spackled Sandia Mountains were still shrouded in clouds at their peaks, though the clearing was moving quickly from west to east.

"Emmy, we may have scored big-time. Looks like we'll get to see the sun come fully up over the mountains. Damn!"

She settled into crossed legs as he unloaded items from their packs. The dogs curled up beside her to rest, and the sounds of his busyness slowly faded. Soon, he too settled onto the sloping, sandy floor.

Stillness crept over them as the sky continued to shift over a largely static landscape descending into the valley, then rising to mountains. There was little movement in the city, though smoke from fireplaces and heat from furnaces spiraled and etched their way into the scene.

Maria Elena, after an exhilarating run across the snow later down over the undulations of the mesa, would struggle to put words to the experience. Finally, she would call it a "vicarious meditation with God." Pitcairn would laugh, though he would not disagree, merely adding, "Life gives us moments, and for those moments, we live."

In the absence of activity, with the gentle rhythmic sounds of the dogs breathing steadily amid the snow muffling and softening the world, they lapsed into deep silence. For almost twenty minutes, as the skies cleared, they would be in a kind of suspended awareness.

Into that space came a feeling of connection for Pitcairn. It emerged slowly, creeping over him like warmth. Then for an instant, it was if the separation between him and Maria Elena softened. He imagined they were one, as a word rose through the still small voice: *"Preciosas."*

Preciosa. It was the first word from the still small voice that they had heard together, a profound moment amid the Crucifix Protests. A word Maria Elena had heard from an auntie who nurtured her amid the difficulties of childhood. An experience of love and safety. Then as now, it had a potent effect.

He heard the sharp intake of her breath bring him back to the world. As he turned, an aura shone around her. Her hands were cupped around her talisman as tears crept softly down her cheeks.

She whispered. "Did you hear it, Cito? Preciosas. Plural. You and me." She cocked her head. "Jesus, Cito, you look like a saint or something!"

"Preciosas." A laugh burst forth from deep within his belly. "And I ain't no fucking saint, Emmy."

* * *

Light of the sun cascades across the high desert, a world made pristine by a carpet of white. An infinity of refractions fills the atmosphere, each a single tiny reflection of the light illuminating all things. For eternity, light has revealed and transformed that upon which it falls.

* * *

Walking in Beauty:
Closing Prayer from the Diné
Blessing Way Ceremony

In beauty I walk.
With beauty before me I walk.
With beauty behind me I walk.
With beauty above me I walk.
With beauty around me I walk.
It has become beauty again.

Hózhóogo naasháa dooShitsijí' hózhóogo naasháa dooShikéédéé hózhóogo
naasháa dooShideigi hózhóogo naasháa dooT'áá altso shinaagóó hózhóogo
naasháa dooHózhó náhásdlíí'Hózhó náhásdlíí'Hózhó náhásdlíí'
Hózhó náhásdlíí'

Today I will walk out, today everything negative will leave.
I will be as I was before I will have a cool breeze over me.
I will have a light body.
I will be happy forever.
Nothing will hinder me.
I walk with beauty before me.
I walk with beauty behind me.
I walk with beauty below me.
I walk with beauty above me.
I walk with beauty around me.
My words will be beautiful.
In beauty all day long may I walk.
Through the returning seasons, may I walk.
On the trail marked with pollen, may I walk.
With dew about my feet, may I walk.
With beauty before me, may I walk.
With beauty behind me may I walk.
With beauty below me may I walk.
With beauty above me may I walk.
With beauty all around me may I walk.

In old age wandering a trail of beauty, lively, may I walk.
In old age wandering on a trail of beauty,
living again, may I walk.
My words will be beautiful.

▸ AFTERWORD ◂

AFTER READING *A KILLER'S GRACE* AND THE MANUSCRIPT FOR *The Dark Side of Grace,* a dear friend, Robert, asked me out for coffee and conversation. He wanted to know if I believed in evil.

After assuring him there was a lot yet to be revealed in my own psycho-spiritual development and adventures, I offered a few thoughts.

"I can only speak from my personal experience, and working with others on their own difficulties. It seems we all have "shadow selves" which are not necessarily bad or good but those parts of us that are denied, disowned, or misunderstood. Things we cannot or do not see. So too with others.

So far, none of these has proven to be "evil," though some have been destructive. In the end, when brought into the light of awareness, they resolve themselves.

Others have told me of "evil" encounters, but I cannot vouch for those. Regardless, nothing I have come to see has not ultimately resolved, usually in a curious or mysterious way.

Largely, I find it all quite positive in the end, even it is quite uncomfortable. Sometimes it can be pretty ugly in the interim. I'm reminded of the recovery wisdom that if we are not yet at peace, we are not yet finished."

Somewhere in researching the foundations of science, psychology, and spirituality for the ideas in *The Dark Side of Grace*, I stumbled across the proposition that our notion of "evil" has steered far afield from its roots. The Greek root "ev" is translated as "good," and the Latin word "il" means "for not." So "evil" was never originally thought to have a reality unto itself but was understood as good that was absent. That seems very much like darkness being the absence of light. No wonder I love Carl Jung's idea that our psycho-spiritual need is for light to illuminate us.

If you have further interest in these and similar explorations, free content is released regularly at SeeingTrue.com, the website where I continue to advance my own experiences as more continues to be revealed. More-focused recovery content, also free, can be found at ProgressiveRecovery.org. More broadly, you can track all of my wanderings and wonderings at RonaldChapman.com. And since a few people have already asked about what is to come, a third novel that furthers the story of Pitcairn and Maria Elena is already underway, which is currently titled *Grace Will Find a Way*. And there is another to follow that it seems, as well as a prequel about Etido's story that is already written, and tentatively titled *One Man's Life*.

There are countless credits to be offered to more people than I can recall to mention. Let's just say they have all been wisdom teachers to and for me. Further, that I could not have done it without them. Not this novel or other writings. Not recovery. Not understanding my own shadow self. Not the forgiveness and compassion that have come for others. Not the life I am so fortunate to be living. Certainly not whatever gratitude and humility have somehow found me . . . despite my tendencies toward excess.

Regardless, I need to recognize a few people. To Mari and Monique, I owe you a profound thanks for keeping me on track, which is not a small thing, nor a simple one. To Marty and Scott Gerber, thank you for faith in my work, and willingness to delve and shape with me. Then the great gift of feedback that came through the wise eyes of Ellen Elliott, my faithful friend Lee Gooden, and the fun and insightful Women of Words book group in Stone Mountain, Georgia: Gayle, Maggie, Rene, Ella, Deborah, Deloris, Laila, Valencia, Linda, and Sylvia. Susan Olson has been a great gift with exploration of my soul's journey home and the dreams that have fueled it.

Nothing is ever really an individual effort. Not if we are honest with ourselves.

Now a few thoughts about the Divine Feminine. I have been deeply awed by and privileged to know a powerhouse mix of young and youngish women who I believe are poised to transform our world. As an older white guy, I can admit I'm pretty sure the days of male leadership and culture are waning after a remarkable run with immense benefits produced. Yet just as poles sometimes must switch—and as Ram Dass so clearly saw, every path must end, for it cannot take us where we next need to go, whether it is really a Divine Feminine, or Woman Power which I would characterize as communitarian—there's a change coming.

To Pam, Lydia, Lezlie, Jenny, Angie, Becky, Kathleen, Kimberley, LaVerne, Michelle, Natalie, Brianne, Carmel, Diana, Rees, Joni, Janine, Maggie, Sharon, Deb, Amy, Netania, Amanda, and who knows how many I will not remember to recognize, bring it on. We need who you are and what you represent. I'm grateful for you. I can't wait to see what good will be brought forth through you. And for Roby, Art and Chris, and Sam, who have aided me in my own grounding. Thankfully, you have not denied your own feminine side, and I have grown immensely because of that.

Now a final note. The concept of post-traumatic growth, the flip side of post-traumatic stress, is, in the words of the pioneering psychologist, Dr. Rich Tedeschi, "The reconstruction of a core belief system that has been challenged or shattered by what's happening." It is not yet accepted by all mental-health professionals.

The Posttraumatic Growth Research Group in the Department of Psychological Science at the University of North Carolina, Charlotte, offers the following (https://ptgi.charlotte.edu/what-is-ptg/):

What is *posttraumatic growth*? It is positive change experienced as a result of the struggle with a major life crisis or a traumatic event. Although we coined the term *posttraumatic growth*, the idea that human beings can be changed by their encounters with life challenges, sometimes in radically positive ways, is not new. The theme is present in ancient spiritual and religious traditions, literature, and philosophy. What *is* reasonably new is the systematic study of this phenomenon by psychologists, social workers, counselors, and scholars in other traditions of clinical practice and scientific investigation.

What forms does posttraumatic growth take? Post-traumatic growth tends to occur in five general areas. Sometimes people who must face major life crises develop a sense that new opportunities have emerged from the struggle, opening up possibilities that were not present before. A second area is a change in relationships with others. Some people experience closer relationships with some specific people, and they can also experience an increased sense of connection to others who suffer. A third area of possible change is an increased sense of one's own strength—*"if I lived through that, I can face anything."* A fourth aspect of posttraumatic growth experienced by some people is a greater appreciation for life in general. The fifth area involves the spiritual or religious domain. Some individuals experience a deepening of their spiritual lives; however, this deepening can also involve a significant change in one's belief system.

Some Clarifications:

Most of us, when we face very difficult losses or great suffering, will have a variety of highly distressing psychological reactions. Just because individuals experience growth does not mean they will not suffer. Distress is typical when we face traumatic events.

We most definitely are not implying that traumatic events are good—they are not. But for many of us, life crises are inevitable, and we are not given the choice between suffering and growth on the one hand and no suffering and no change on the other.

Posttraumatic growth is not universal. It is not uncommon but neither does everybody who faces a traumatic event experience growth.

Our hope is that you never face a major loss or crisis, but most of us eventually do, and perhaps you may also experience an encounter with posttraumatic growth.

▸ABOUT THE AUTHOR◂

AS A WORKSHOP LEADER, FACILITATOR, AND MOTIVATIONAL speaker for 35 years, Ronald Chapman has shown countless people the means to work toward their own growth and transformation through his practice of *Seeing True* and his *Progressive Recovery* approach for 12-step recovery. He is the author of the novels *A Killer's Grace* and *My Name is Wonder: A Tale of Adventure;* the recovery guide *Progressive Recovery Through the Twelve Steps: Emotionally Sober for Life;* and the inspirational books *Seeing True: Ninety Contemplations in Ninety Days* and *What a Wonderful World: Seeing Through New Eyes.*